One More Shot

One More Shot

VICTORIA DENAULT

New York Boston

This book is a work of fiction. Names, characters, places, and incidents are the product of the author's imagination or are used fictitiously. Any resemblance to actual events, locales, or persons, living or dead, is coincidental.

Forever Yours
Hachette Book Group
1290 Avenue of the Americas
New York, NY 10104
hachettebookgroup.com
twitter.com/foreverromance

First published as an ebook and as a print on demand edition: June 2015

Forever Yours is an imprint of Grand Central Publishing.
The Forever Yours name and logo are trademarks of Hachette Book Group, Inc.

The publisher is not responsible for websites (or their content) that are not owned by the publisher.

The Hachette Speakers Bureau provides a wide range of authors for speaking events. To find out more, go to www.hachettespeakersbureau.com or call (866) 376-6591.

ISBN 978-1-4555-3560-6 (ebook edition)
ISBN 978-1-4555-6406-4 (print on demand edition)

For the girls who were my Rose and Callie
growing up: AML, LS, TL, JJ and AC

Acknowledgments

First and foremost, thank you to my brilliant agent, Kimberly Brower. From the moment we first spoke I thought I was in good hands, but now I know I'm in great hands. I'm forever grateful for your guidance and business savvy. A million thanks to my incredible editors, Dana Hamilton and Leah Hultenschmidt. You push me and my characters to be the best we can be, and your encouragement and support are invaluable. Thanks to the team at Hachette/Forever Yours. From cover design to marketing—it takes a village, and I'm very lucky to have you as mine. Jennifer K, thank you for always saying "Yes. But…" whenever I tried to convince myself I shouldn't be a writer. Crystal R, thank you for proving the Internet isn't just full of weirdos. You are a ray of sunshine, and your enthusiasm for my work, and books in general, makes my world a better place. Also on that note, thank you Sarah J, Sarah L and Phoebe for reading my drafts, even the not-so-great ones. To fellow writer Crissy, thank you for being my soul sister, for letting me ramble on about Jessie, Jordan, Callie, Rose, and all the other people who live in my head, and knowing it doesn't make me crazy. I'm also forever grateful to the UCLA Extension Writers' Program for all the knowledge and support their instructors, staff, and fellow students provided. Gus and Belle, thanks for snuggling me while I write and being patient when your walk schedule gets pushed by inspiration. Thanks, Mom and Dad, for buying me every book I ever wanted growing up. That love of reading turned into a love for writing. Last but never, ever least, thank you, Jack, for being the only romantic lead I will ever want or need.

Prologue

Jordan

Five years earlier

You're drunk. Again. I told you I'm not talking to you when you're drunk. Not about this."

She doesn't even look at me. She keeps her eyes on the tabletop she's wiping down with much more vigor than necessary. I sigh and run a hand through my hair. "Callie, I've had few beers. I'm not drunk."

"Five. You've had five beers. I know because I served them."

"Not drunk," I repeat, even though… Yeah, I may be a little drunk.

She looks up, but not at me. She looks at the group I walked into O'Malley's with—Luc, my ex-girlfriend Hannah, one of her friends and two girls Luc and I met at the lake today. "Really? If you're not drunk, then you're just plain stupid to come in here with your girlfriend and ask me for my sister's phone number."

"Okay, now you're the one who must be drunk," I bark back. "Hannah and I haven't been together since last year."

"Then why are you always with her?"

"She's dating one of the guys on the Royales now so she's decided we should be friends." I roll my eyes and then lean forward and put

my hand over hers so she stops the incessant table scrubbing. "Callie, please. Just give me her new number."

She pulls her hand away and straightens up, pushing her shoulders back and stepping around the table to stand toe-to-toe with me. She's maybe half an inch taller than Jessie, with the same petite build, but Callie has this way of carrying herself when she's pissed off that makes her seem more intimidating than an MFA wrestler.

"No."

She turns on her heel and storms off. I follow her because I can't let this go. I haven't been able to let it go since I got back to Silver Bay last month. And Callie's right—when I'm sober I can convince myself I'm okay with the way things are. I use the anger in my heart to justify the choices I've made. It worked without a hiccup while I was living in Quebec, playing in my first NHL season. But since I've been back in Silver Bay for the summer, it's been harder. I don't know if it's because there are so many memories here or because I see her sisters around town or what. But lately, after a few drinks…the anger starts to feel like longing. Longing for her.

Callie walks over to the servers' station in the corner and starts to tap an order into the screen. I walk over and cover it with my hand. She swats it away and swears under her breath.

"Do it again and I will punch you." I know that's not an idle threat.

"If you don't give me her number, I'll tell the police to raid this place and you'll get caught working here underage. Poor old Billy will get fined and you might even go to jail."

She looks up and levels me with an icy stare. "You're here underage too, jackass. And the NHL would just love for you to get busted for underage drinking."

Fuck. She's right. So much for that plan. I go back to my original idea—begging.

"Please. I just want to know how she's doing," When once again my pleas are met with a cold, impassive stare, I grab a pen off the servers' station and grab Callie's hand. She tries to pull away but my grip is firm. I flip her hand over and scrawl my number neatly on the skin of her wrist. "If you won't give me her number, then please just give her mine. Because maybe she wants to know how I'm doing too."

"She knows exactly how you're doing." Callie tugs her wrist out of my hand. "She's got the Internet in Arizona, you know."

"What the fuck does that mean?"

"There are hockey websites that report more than just stats," she explains bitterly.

I feel defensive suddenly—and embarrassed. "She left me, Callie. What was I supposed to do?"

"Not fuck half of Canada," she snaps.

"You? You're going to judge my sexual history? Really?"

A flicker of pain ripples over her face, replacing the anger for just a moment and I feel like a sack of shit. Did I really just imply Callie's a slut? What the fuck is wrong with me? "Callie. I'm sorry. I didn't mean it that way. I just—"

"She's seeing someone else."

"She's what?" The music is pretty loud in here. And there are a ton of people chattering all around us. I must have misunderstood what Callie just said because it sounded like she said…

"Jessie is seeing someone," Callie repeats slowly and clearly.

Callie turns and marches back to the tables she's serving. I stand there for what feels like forever, just staring after her. My chest starts to feel tight, like my rib cage has shrunk, and my limbs feel cold, like my blood has stopped circulating. Jessie is seeing someone. Not casually dating again, not hooking up, not thinking about me. She's seeing someone else. She doesn't give a fuck if I'm thinking about her or missing her or regretting anything. She's gone. It's over.

"Hey!" Luc wanders over, one arm over each of the girls from the lake. "Emily and Lisa want to show us the hot tub at their place."

I walk over numbly and join them. "I don't have my suit."

"Then I guess you'll have to go without one." The sultry brunette smiles at me and winks. "Don't worry. I won't wear one either so you'll feel more comfortable."

Her hand loops around my back. "I like the way you think, Lori."

"It's Lisa," she corrects, like it matters.

"Sorry, honey. I'll make it up to you," I reply suggestively as we all head toward the exit. I catch Callie staring at me as I go and I turn away. Fuck her and fuck her sister. I'm done with giving a shit.

Chapter 1

Jordan

Despite my better judgment, my eyes flutter open. I'm not at home. I think I knew that before I opened my eyes, but I'm not sure exactly where I am. I'm…on a bed. A big bed. Probably a king. But not *my* king. I would have nicer sheets.

I squint against the light, not that there is much of it, but it's still more than I would like to have hit my pupils after what feels like only fifteen minutes' sleep. There's a desk in the corner and a flat screen on the wall and dark blue and white striped curtains. There is also a naked woman lying facedown beside me.

I shift onto my side, ignoring the mild throbbing in my foot and, as the sheets turn and twist around me, I realize that I'm naked too. I look down at her. All I can see is pale skin—like never-been-on-a-beach pale—and dyed blond hair. I'm thinking it's enough to take care of my morning wood.

I run a hand down her bare back, over her ass and down the back of her thigh. She stretches and makes a little moaning sound as my hand makes it to the back of her knee.

"Round three?" she giggles into the pillow.

Three? I guess I was a busy boy last night. A drunk, busy boy. She rolls toward me.

"Such big blue eyes..." She leans closer and kisses me, her hands wandering under the sheets. "Such big everything."

The night is slowly coming back to me. We won a home game. I sat and watched from the team box high above the ice, ridiculously frustrated. Afterward, I joined my teammates at a bar to celebrate. I wanted to drink away my frustration at not being able to play thanks to my stupid ankle.

Hours later, my teammate Alexandre invited a bunch of people back to his place. That's when I had decided to screw my frustration away with one of the girls who tagged along because obviously drinking alone wasn't going to improve my mood. It never does but I've yet to stop trying. Fucking random girls has never helped my problems either, but I keep doing it. I've never been one to learn from my mistakes, at least not quickly.

Her name was...Jenny? Julie? Jackie? It began with a fucking J, I know that because I avoid girls whose names begin with J. Normally that's a deal breaker for me, especially when I'm drunk. But desperate times called for desperate measures, and I was so over being injured and unable to play hockey—the only thing I've ever done for a living—that I was desperate for a distraction. This J girl was it.

"You're a freaking animal," she coos, her hand moving from my ass to my hard-on. "I had no idea hockey players had so much stamina."

I just grunt, gently turn her toward the mattress and move myself over her back. I nudge her legs open, kneel between them and then pull her backward by her hips so she's on all fours.

I grab a condom off the bedside table where there is a pile of them in a bowl. I realize I'm still at Alexandre's apartment because he's the only one ballsy enough to leave condoms around his house in candy dishes.

I tear the condom wrapper with my teeth and start to put it on when my cell phone starts ringing. My head begins to pound in rhythm with the shrill ring. Great. I stop what I'm doing and extract it from the back pocket of my jeans, which for some unknown reason are draped over the lamp beside the bed.

I see my parents' number on the call display and roll my eyes as my dick deflates.

"I have to take this," I tell Julie-Jenny-Jackie.

She groans in dismay and I ignore her.

"Hi, Mom. It's a little early to call," I say into the phone as I yawn.

"Jordan, it's one in the afternoon," she lets me know tersely.

I blink. Shit. "Sorry, it was a late night."

"Should you be having late nights when you're still injured?" she asks pointedly.

I try not to be annoyed and remind myself she's just doing her job. Moms are supposed to ride their sons' asses.

"We won and went out to celebrate," I defend myself. "It's fine. I'm fine. The ankle is getting better every day."

"Okay, then…" I can still hear the judgment in her voice, but we both ignore it.

"When do you leave for New York?" I ask, changing the subject. My parents were supposed to be going to Brooklyn this weekend to visit my older brother, Devin, his wife, Ashleigh, and their two-year-old son, Conner.

The girl beside me gets out of bed and gathers her clothes. "I have to go. Work," she whispers, and disappears into the bathroom.

"Well, we were supposed to go tomorrow but we had to push back our flight to Monday. Honey..." She pauses and there's something in her tone that makes my stomach clench uncomfortably. "Lily Caplan died."

I feel a wave of relief to hear that my parents aren't sick, but as the news settles in it instantly feels like a bomb has exploded in my chest. My heart skips a beat and my mouth goes dry. "Mrs. Caplan?"

The name conjures up images in my head of three beautiful, spirited but sad teenage girls, not the silver-haired shrew of a woman it belongs to.

"Yes. I guess it happened a couple days ago. I just found out this morning," she says, and her tone is soothing. I know she knows this news makes me feel off-balance—like a hormonal, impetuous teenager, because that's what I was the last time the Caplans were in my life. She also knows that because of my turbulent past with one Caplan in particular, this news hits me harder than the rest of my family. "It was sudden but not completely unexpected. She had those heart problems."

"I know..." I swallow and ignore the dyed blonde with the J name as she leans in and kisses my cheek before heading for the bedroom door.

"Call me," she whispers a little too loudly. I nod quickly at the blonde and she frowns as she leaves the room.

"Are they back?" I bark out the question gruffly because I don't want to be asking it. I don't want to care. I don't want to know...only I do want to know. Badly.

"Rose arrived last night. Callie got here this morning," my mother volunteers easily. "Jessie is supposed to be arriving this afternoon."

She's back. She said she would never go home again. Everyone swore she was gone forever. But Jessie is back. The vault in the recesses of my brain, the one where I crammed all the memories of her, suddenly bursts open, and my breath catches in my throat and I cough.

"The funeral is Saturday. We're going, of course, but I thought it would be nice if you could come as well," my mom goes on. "You boys were all so close to them, and Devin and Luc can't make it because they're playing. But since you're not playing right now..."

"Isn't Cole going to go?" I ask quickly, almost nervously. I fucking hate that I feel this out of sorts all of a sudden.

"Yes, but Cole wasn't best friends with her," she says simply. My mom has never been one to get too involved in our romantic lives. She doesn't want to be that kind of overbearing woman. But clearly she feels strongly about this. "You should be here, Jordan."

"I'll see what I can do," I mutter. "Thanks for telling me, Mom."

"Do you want me to say anything to... them? From you specifically?" she asks quietly in a voice full of unspoken words.

"No." My mother sighs her discontent so I clear my throat, roll my eyes and add, "Fine. Tell them I'm thinking of them and everything."

"I will. I love you, Jordy," she says in a voice that clearly says she approves of my message.

"Love you too," I say, and hang up.

As I throw on my underwear, slide my injured foot into my aircast and dig around the room for the rest of my clothes, Alexandre appears in the doorway. He's in nothing but Seattle Winterhawks track pants and he's holding two coffee mugs. His dark blue eyes are twinkling and his dark brown hair is askew.

"You sure know how to make a girl scream," he says with his heavy French Canadian accent and a wry smile. He hands me one of the mugs. "I'm surprised you didn't set off car alarms last night."

I smile, but it's short-lived, and take a sip of the coffee before putting it down to pull my shirt over my head. "I have to go to the rink. I need to talk to Coach."

"Why? Did she rebreak your ankle or break some new part of your body?" He laughs.

I make a face at his crappy joke and shake my head. "A friend of the family died."

"Je suis désolé, mon ami," he offers condolences in his native French.

"Yeah," I reply because I don't have time to explain to Alex that after the way Lily Caplan treated her grandkids, she wasn't exactly my favorite person.

I grab the mug again and take a few more sips as I walk out into Alex's main living area, which has floor-to-ceiling, south-facing windows and reclaimed barn board floors. A sultry-looking brunette in nothing but Alex's plaid dress shirt from last night stands behind the kitchen island cooking eggs on the stovetop.

"Hey." I give her an awkward wave.

"Jackie says to tell you to stop by Hooters any time and she'll get you free wings," the brunette tells me.

"Tell Jackie thanks," I say, and try not to roll my eyes. Even after all these years as a NHL player, I'm still always shocked when the same girls who throw themselves at you the first night they meet you just because you're a professional athlete expect a shot at girlfriend status. Of course, in their defense, I'm not turning them down.

"Why do you need to talk to Coach?" Alex wants to know.

"I need to go back home," I explain, and try to tame my wild bedhead with my hands. "For the funeral. Just a couple of days."

Alex shrugs and then gives me a hug. "Okay. Take care, eh?"

I nod and smile. "Thanks for the guest room."

"Sure." Alex smirks. "But next time remind me to buy earplugs for my neighbors."

Outside I'm greeted with a crisp, sunny fall afternoon. It's not raining, which in Seattle is always a plus. When I was traded to the Seattle Winterhawks last season, I wasn't all that thrilled about living so far from home. At least when I played in Quebec City, it was only an eight-hour drive from my hometown in Maine. But Seattle is fun, my team has been great and the fans here are a small but passionate bunch. I'm happy now professionally. At least I was until I broke my left ankle. Hockey is the only thing I've ever wanted to do with my life. It's the only thing I've ever been *great* at and the one thing I have never screwed up. This is the first injury in my professional career. It's a big one, and I couldn't be handling it worse if I tried.

As I drive to the rink I call my brother, Devin.

"Hey, Jordan," he says easily, answering on the second ring. "What's up?"

"Lily Caplan died."

"I know." Devin sounds stunned for a minute. "Mom told Ashleigh."

"She wants me to go home for the funeral," I respond as I

pull my SUV off the I-5 and down the familiar downtown Seattle streets to the hockey arena.

"Makes sense," he says.

"How does it make sense?" I demand. I was calling him for support—so he could help me brainstorm excuses for not showing up. "Mrs. Caplan hated me. She hated all of us. She thought we were—and I quote—'derelict hockey punks.'"

"She's dead," Devin reminds me snarkily as I slow at a stop sign and lean my head against the leather headrest. "This isn't about her. It's about supporting your best friend."

"Ex–best friend," I retort. "We haven't talked in years."

"And whose fault is that?" Devin mutters almost under his breath—almost inaudibly—but I hear it and it pisses me off.

"She left town, remember? Why does everyone blame that on me?"

I wave my players' pass at the security guard at the gate to player parking. He's obviously a little surprised to see me on a day off, but he raises the gate without question. "I should be concentrating on getting my leg healed. My family should be supporting that."

"Oh, I'm sorry," Devin counters, and the sarcasm rings loud and clear through the Bluetooth. "Is your leg going to stop healing just because it's in Maine instead of Seattle?"

"Go fuck yourself."

"Love you too, bro." He laughs, enjoying this way too much if you ask me. But when the laughter dies he grows serious. "Look, Jordy. I would be there if I could and so would Luc. The Caplan girls are family. We've all given you and Jessie enough time to figure out how to be grown-ups, yet you can't seem to do it. So I'm telling you be a grown-up and go and support her."

"Fine. I'll go if the coach lets me."

"He'll let you."

"Shut up."

"Shutting up," Devin promises, and then the line goes dead. I sigh loudly, get out of the car and slam the door. Hopefully Devin is wrong and Coach Sweetzer has some reason he needs me here. Because as painful and frustrating as it was to be here dealing with my injury and not being able to play hockey, seeing Jessie Caplan again would be worse—*much* worse.

Chapter 2

Jessie

I walk through the Silver Bay Jetport, which looks more like something a child made with Legos than an actual airport. It's a tiny, bleak, gray concrete block of a building with oblong single-pane windows and acid-green plastic chairs in the waiting areas. As I adjust my bag on the escalator step beside my feet, I look up and my eyes instantly land on my sisters. All the tension that has been building in my shoulders throughout the journey suddenly dissipates. No matter what happens now, having them with me makes it easier. It's been that way my whole life, and even after a few years living in different states, it still rings true. Every time I see them, life just feels better.

They're standing together at the bottom of the escalator, and they look exactly like I expect them to—beautiful and sad. Callie, who is a mere thirteen months younger than me, is wrapped in an oversized wool sweater with an Aztec pattern on it, tattered skinny jeans and tan Ugg boots. Her long hair is covering most of her face as she stares down at the iPhone in her hands. Rose, a mere twelve months and twenty-four days younger than Callie, is wearing black leggings, knee-high leather riding boots and a gray peacoat. Her long, pin-straight hair is pulled back in a low ponytail. Her dark eyes are staring back at me with empathy.

Grandma Lily used to say we were varying shades of the same person, inside and out. It was completely true, but I was shocked that she'd noticed. Callie, Rose and I share the same noses, lips and chins, but Rose is darkest in coloring and deepest in personality. She's intuitive, shy and philosophical with almost-black hair and almost–coal colored eyes. Callie's looks are the middle ground between Rose and me with chestnut brown hair and coffee-colored eyes. But she's not in the middle when it comes to disposition. Callie is loud, assertive and wild. Although I have the most vibrant coloring—auburn hair, fairly bright green eyes with only the slightest specks of the brown my sisters got, my personality is squarely in the middle of them. I'm not as sensitive as Rose and not as wild as Callie. I tend to be thoughtful like Rose but have a temper that, when pushed, matches Callie's. And, unfortunately, I share Callie's attraction to the wrong type of men, but unlike Callie, I have Rose's deep-seated longing for true love. The two traits don't mix.

I beeline to them and we hug—one giant family hug—for a long moment. When I pull away, Rosie's eyes are brimming with tears and Callie's mocha-colored ones are as hard as nails. I would expect nothing less.

"Come on," Callie insists, taking my suitcase from me. "It looks like it might snow, and I refuse to drive in that shit."

Rosie and I both roll our eyes and follow the angry middle child as she storms through the tiny airport. I keep my eyes down and try not to make eye contact with anyone. Silver Bay, Maine, is a small place, and everyone here used to know exactly who we were. Chances are they still do. I'm in absolutely no mood to deal with small talk with anyone from my past—a past I have worked hard to stay as far away from as possible.

We pile into the massive Ford F-150 Callie leads us to. I glance at Rosie with a smirk because the truck is a bit over the top, and she smiles back with a shrug.

"Has it been that long since you've driven in winter conditions that you think you needed to rent this beast?" I joke to Callie.

Callie turns and gives me a strange stare, her eyes hiding something. "At least we'll be able to leave the house in this puppy no matter what ridiculous weather this useless town throws at us."

"Remember how we used to have to beg Dev or Jordy for lifts when there was even one flake of snow on the ground?" Rose has a fondness in her voice and a nostalgic smile on her full pink lips. "Our stupid Honda hatchback would only slide sideways in the winter."

I swallow and take a deep breath but say nothing. I've been here maybe a minute and a half and there's already a Garrison boy reference. I shouldn't be shocked it happened so soon. The Garrison brothers, and their honorary brother, Luc, were a huge part of my life. They were part of every good memory I had of this town. The problem was, that one bad memory of them…of *him*…eclipsed the good.

The rest of the ride is silent as I stare out the window and take in the familiar sights. I feel my chest tighten when I can't keep the memories from clouding my brain. We pass our old elementary school, the one Lily put us in when we first moved in with her after our mom died when I was eight. I can't help but remember how Jordan used to split his lunches with me in fifth grade when he realized that Lily wasn't supplying me with one.

We pass the high school. I remember a hot summer night, sitting on that football field with two six-packs we'd stolen from Mr. and Mrs. Garrison. Lying on the fifty-yard line, drinking and watching the sky for shooting stars as we laughed at stupid jokes; just our small tight group of "besties," as I liked to call them. It was me, Jordy, Luc, Callie, Devin, Leah, Cole and Rose.

As we barrel down the road, I'm reminded that Callie drives like a crazy person. I still wonder how she got her license. I think she bribed the guy at the DMV. Silver Bay Arena blurs by my window, and I remember kissing Chance Echolls for the first time on the rink inside at sixteen—and wishing it was Jordan. I smile sadly at the memories. God, I was so young and so completely naive. It feels like it was a hundred years ago, but it was only six. And every year of those six Jordan Garrison has done something—or someone—that proves how naive I was for believing he was the perfect boy for me. Hockey blogs, sports papers, even celebrity gossip sites have enjoyed keeping track of his sexcapades, making it impossible for me to ignore.

"Lotta memories," Rose whispers thoughtfully as she rubs my arm.

I nod but say nothing. I know the worst memories are yet to come. I don't know how the hell I'm going to spend a second in that house and not completely melt down. Everything about it holds bad memories now. It's literally a box of rejection, fear, heartache and loneliness held together by peeling white clapboard and a cracked stone foundation. I know how dramatic that sounds, but being that our grandmother never wanted us to live with her, the house was never a warm or comforting refuge for me. And kissing my best friend, giving my virginity to him there and then later having him rip my heart out did nothing to endear me to the hundred-year-old farmhouse.

Before I know it, we're pulling up the long dirt drive and Callie careens to a stop. We're beside the decrepit barn that we only ever used as a tomb for old toys and broken lawn furniture. She throws the Ford into park and we all pile out. I yank my suitcase out of the back and Rose helpfully pushes the tailgate back up.

Callie heads straight for the porch and stands on it, the key dangling from her hand, her eyes narrowed on me. "I can make a reservation at the motel if it's, you know...more comfortable."

I shake my head. "No, it's fine." I can't afford a motel room since my internship barely pays minimum wage. Besides, I have a perfectly fine, free house to stay in, no matter the memories it conjures up.

I walk up the porch, Rosie trudging along behind me. Callie opens the door and makes room for me to pass. I step into the kitchen and blink. It hasn't changed a stitch. The white Formica countertops, the scuffed dark wood cabinets, the yellow sunflower accessories Lily loved so much. God, I still hate them. I let go of my bag and run a hand along the countertop—the one next to the sink, across from the table. The one where I kissed him for the first time.

Callie grabs my hand and guides it off the counter, dragging me to the kitchen table. "Okay, enough of that."

She knows I'm thinking about him, and I'm grateful she isn't about to let me wallow. Callie has always tried to save me from myself. I love her dearly for it. She pushes me down into a chair as she walks over to the fridge and grabs three beers. She hands one to me and one to Rose before twisting the cap off her own.

"So, now what?" I ask and sip the cool frothy Corona.

"Well, tomorrow we have appointments at the funeral home and with Lily's lawyer," Callie explains. "Until then, we drink."

"That's it? That's the big plan?" I smile, and she smiles back.

"Yes. That and..." Callie nods vigorously as she tilts back in her chair like a misbehaving eighth grader. She grabs a bottle of Patrón off the buffet hutch behind her. "We drink so much that you pass out. I'm having enough trouble adjusting to the time zone, I don't need your sobbing keeping me up."

My jaw drops open and I stare at her in shock.

"Drink," Callie commands, and clinks her bottle with mine.

I think it's probably about an hour or an hour and a half later. We're on our third beers and we've done two shots of Patrón; Rose has told us all about her senior year so far at University of Vermont. Callie's made us giggle with crazy stories of life in LA, and I'm smiling—*really* smiling. I know I'm a big part of the reason that they're as well adjusted as they are, and I'm proud of that. But even more so, I'm simply relieved. They deserve everything they want in life, and it seems like they're getting it.

"Do you think..." Rose starts, her tone low and soft. She bites her lip and circles the rim of her beer bottle with her index finger before continuing. "Do you think she wished we'd been here? Been with her when she...died?"

She's talking about Grandma Lily, of course. The reason for this reunion. Callie clears her throat, probably just to stop the depressing silence that's filling the room.

"It was sudden, Rose. Her heart just stopped in the middle of the grocery store. I don't think she had time to wish for anything." Callie sips her beer and leans back against the old red and yellow plaid couch. "She's never asked us to visit since we left town. Hell, she doesn't…*didn't* even call on birthdays. She died alone because she wanted to be alone."

"But she let me come back every summer. She never charged me rent or anything," Rose says timidly.

Rose's dark eyes get watery as she shifts on the musty carpet we're sitting on. I have never been able to see my sisters upset. It feels like something is clawing at my heart, tearing away tiny little chunks. And after the life we've had, there's not too my chunks left to tear.

"Maybe we should say some nice things about her," I suggest because I know it's what Rose wants. Rose romanticizes everything. She needs to believe there is good in everything. I admire that in her and I'm grateful for it. I would see the world a lot more bleakly if she weren't around. "Lily took us in. Even though she thought of us as a burden, she still took on that burden. She could have left us in foster care. Separated. But she didn't."

Rose nods at that and gives me a weak but thankful smile. We both turn to Callie, waiting for her to share a positive memory of our grandmother.

"She never hit us," Callie says, rolling her eyes. "All her punches were emotional so at least she didn't mess with our pretty faces."

Now it's my turn to roll my eyes. Rose shakes her head but smiles despite herself.

Then suddenly there's a knock on the front door and it swings open. We all turn toward the intrusion. A serene, smiling face peeks around the door and I see arms holding a huge pan covered with tin foil.

"Donna!" Callie calls out happily, and scurries to get up off the floor.

"Hi, girls," Donna Garrison responds. "Sorry to interrupt."

She walks into the kitchen and we follow her. She looks exactly like I remember. Of course, unlike her sons, I had seen her in the last six years. Twice in the last six years she and her husband, Wyatt, have taken golf vacations to Arizona and stopped by to visit me at school. It was awkward both times. It's not her making it uncomfortable, it's me. I can't let go of the humiliation because she knows what happened between me and her son. And I've always felt like I can't hate him and still love her. But I do still love her, and that's why I'm awkward.

She still has the same shoulder-length honey hair, although now it's a little gray on the sides. And the same smiling sky-blue eyes that look exactly like his. Something pinches inside my chest, but I ignore it. She places the casserole pan on the stovetop and immediately starts digging in the big canvas bag on her shoulder.

"I brought you some perogies and other essentials," she tells us, placing milk, coffee grounds, bread, butter and homemade jam on the kitchen table.

Callie reaches out and hugs her. "You always take such good care of us. Thank you."

Donna closes her eyes and hugs my sister tightly. "My pleasure. As always."

When she lets go of Callie, she automatically reaches for Rose, who willingly embraces her. And then Rose steps away and Donna is standing in front of me. She puts her hands on my shoulders and pulls me to her.

"Welcome back, Jessie, honey," she whispers in my ear. "It's so good to see you. I just wish it wasn't for these reasons."

I nod. It's all I can do. If I try to talk, I will cry. Why is this still so hard? After all these years, I still can't stop associating her with my loss of him. I hate myself for it.

"Wyatt says you can keep the truck as long as you need," Donna announces, and I shoot Callie a withering stare. I should have known she was driving Wyatt Garrison's truck. "And if you need help with anything, just call. You know we're here for you."

We all smile and nod.

"The boys said to tell you—all of you—how sorry they are you're going through this. I know they wish they could be here," Donna tells us simply.

As she turns to the door, she grabs my hand and gives it a squeeze. Her pale blue eyes level on me, and it's like she two-handed me in the abdomen with a hockey stick when as she says, "Jordan told me to tell you he's thinking of you."

I nod again, barely containing the urge to scream.

"Thanks again, Donna." Rose hugs her again. "You're the best. Hopefully we can all have dinner with you and Wyatt before we leave."

"I'd love that, honey." Donna smiles and heads out the door.

Rose closes the door behind the woman I'd always wished was my mother and stares at me nervously. I turn and find Callie's concerned stare on me too.

"I need another shot. Now," I announce in a shaky voice as I reach for the Patrón. I drink from the bottle.

"He has no right sending messages through his mother," Callie says, seething, as she hands me another beer. I promptly open it and chug. "What a cowardly thing to do."

"He's had *years* to say something, and he waits all this time and then can't even say it himself?" Rose muses with an angry shake of her head that causes her dark hair to tumble around her shoulders in waves. "God, why does he have to be such a dick?"

I sink into the nearest chair and continue to chug the beer. Rosie scurries to get me another.

"I hope he skates headfirst into the boards," Callie rants, and cracks a new beer of her own.

"He's not playing right now," I mumble. "He's injured."

Callie slams her beer on the table so hard I'm surprised the bottle doesn't break. "Why do you know that?"

"Because it's all over the damn news," I explain defensively, and feel my cheeks getting red. "I live in freaking Seattle, remember?"

"Yeah, unfortunately, I do," Callie retorts as she twists a lock of her light brown hair around her finger. "I still don't know how the hell you two ended up in the same city."

"Sea-Tac Sports Therapy offered me the best internship," I remind her, and it's a fact. I'd done my undergraduate degree in kinesiology at the University of Arizona and continued into a two-year graduate program in physical therapy. The final stage involved an internship at a rehab facility or hospital. The only paid one I was offered was in Seattle. Two weeks after I moved there, Jordan Garrison was traded from the Quebec City Royales to the Seattle Winterhawks. Life liked to shit on me like that.

"What's got him sidelined?" Callie asks with an evil grin. "Chlamydia? Gonorrhea? Syphilis?"

I smirk at her dark humor. "Broken ankle."

"Good. I'm glad he's injured," Rosie says hotly, but it's forced. The girl doesn't have a vindictive bone in her body. "I hope he doesn't play for the whole season."

"Can we just change the subject?" I beg, running my fingers through my long hair and tugging absently on a tangle.

"Fine," Callie relents, and sags in her chair as if the fight has physically left her. "Rose, let's make a voodoo doll with his face on it after she passes out."

"Ha-ha." I roll my eyes at her as Rosie chuckles.

It's past midnight. We had all said good night and gone upstairs to our teenage bedrooms over an hour ago, but the room spun every time I tried to lie down. And so here I am in the dark, in the kitchen, staring at the goddamn countertop where it all began.

I wonder if he really told Donna he was thinking about me. I wonder, if he really said it, if he meant it. Is he just thinking about me because my cold, emotionally vacant grandmother died? Is that the first time he's thought of me in a while? Years? Probably. God, I wish I could say this was the first time I had thought of him. Or of this countertop.

I run my hand over it again and feel that familiar sharp pain in my chest. I'm too drunk to fight it, so I let the memory take over.

Chapter 3

Jessie

Six years ago

So, have you lost it yet?"

I stare at Callie, horrified.

"First of all, shut up!" I hiss, and glance around to see if anyone heard her.

Luckily the party is a total rager. The music is loud, everyone is talking animatedly among themselves. Some drunk girls from my class are dancing on the Echolls' dining room table, attracting the attention of most, and a boisterous game of quarters is going on in the kitchen. Thankfully, no one is paying attention to my sister's blunt inquiry about my virginity.

"Second of all," I continue, plopping down beside her on the couch. I lean toward her ear so I can be as quiet as possible. "You just saw me in the kitchen ten minutes ago. Of course we haven't...yet."

Callie shrugs and sips the vodka-infused pink lemonade in her red plastic cup. "Ten minutes is a long time for an eighteen-year-old boy. Trust me. I know."

I have nothing to say to that. She does *know. Callie lost her vir-*

ginity four months ago to a guy who works at the Trinity Community College bookstore. She and our friend Amber liked to hang out there and pretend they were students.

Callie was very different from me. Where I had thought and rethought and over-thought every aspect of what I wanted my first time to be like, Callie had made the decision on a whim. She didn't care if she ever saw the guy again. In fact, she didn't want to see the guy again. Steve, the guy, had tried to see her again, calling the house a couple of times. but she always made me say she was out.

"He was nice and cute and it was sweet," she had told me. "I don't want to ruin that by getting to know him too well. Besides, he's an education major at a community college. He's going to end up teaching at our high school or something, and I am not staying in this craptastic town for the rest of my life."

So, whereas my sister gave it up and moved on, I had been dating Chance Echolls for almost a year—ten months and eleven days to be precise—and had just recently decided it was time to take that ultimate step. It was a long time to wait, at least in Callie's opinion. I'd thought Chance was cute ever since I first saw him, when I was nine, but if he had felt the same about me, he hadn't shown it until ten months ago when he'd shown up at the local hockey arena where I was working at the concession booth and asked me on a date.

Callie said, if she were me, she would have done it with Chance on that very first date. But I needed more. Chance was special. He was different. And he wanted me. This shocked the entire town, I'm sure. On top of being a hockey phenom, which wasn't uncommon in our small town, actually, because every boy played hockey, Chance was also the youngest son of the mayor and his prestigious lawyer wife. Unlike the handful of other local boys who were good enough hockey players to realistically entertain the idea of making a career out of it, the Echolls boys would not skip college and throw themselves into the NHL draft right out of high school. Scholarship or not, people like the Echollses went to college. Chance spent just about every weekend of this year, our senior year, visiting schools across the country. Michigan State, Bowling Green, Boston College, Vermont—every school in the US that had a first-rate hockey team. He would go to college wherever he wanted. His life was, and always would be, very different from mine.

My sisters and I were from a family that was also renowned in Silver Bay, but for very different reasons. My dad had grown up in Silver Bay. The city's best hockey player and biggest troublemaker. No one was surprised when he was drafted first round, first pick by the Sacramento Storm. He left his high school girlfriend behind, and when he came home that summer, after scoring the winning goal in the Stanley Cup final, he met his firstborn—me. People who know my parents say my father had always loved my mother and that when he married her that summer, it was out of love, not duty. I guess my sisters could be seen as proof of that. Either that or he just kept repeating his mistakes.

My father's fabulous NHL career ended prematurely when he celebrated too hard after a win and drove his car through a guardrail and into a ravine. He didn't die, but he broke his leg in four places, and his career was over. Silver Bay's golden boy was now its biggest disappointment. He continued to drink, never really held down a job and blew through any of the savings we'd had. Eventually my mom left him. I remember Rose cried about it, but Callie and I didn't. We were old enough, even at six and seven, to realize that we'd all be happier without him. We started over in a one-bedroom apartment in San

Diego. Mom worked as a waitress. No health benefits, so she ignored the cramps and pain…until I found her collapsed on the bathroom floor.

Three months later, the cervical cancer took my mom's life. I felt like my heart was shattered, and for the first time in my young life, I knew what real fear was. We were alone. We had no one to protect us, no one to love us. The State of California was unable to find our father but did find our paternal grandmother, Lily. She showed up, got us out of foster care and flew us back to Silver Bay, Maine. Yeah, people in this town knew exactly where I had come from, and probably figured they knew where I would end up: nowhere. Especially not with Chance Echolls. So I took it slow. I wanted to make sure it was real and solid, so I didn't add "tramp" to the list of adjectives people in this town could use to describe me.

"So, it's almost midnight," Callie says, looking at her watch. "Are you going to make this happen or what?"

"I can't find him," I say, not afraid to show my frustration. "I thought he said he was going out to the driveway to play ball hockey with some of the guys, but he's not there."

"I saw him go upstairs a while ago," Callie tells me, pointing to the staircase. "Maybe he's in line for the bathroom."

I take a deep breath and she smiles, giving me a shove. "Remember, no one is saying you have to do this. Not tonight and definitely not with him."

I raise a warning eyebrow at her. "Don't start."

She sips her beer and shrugs her shoulders. "Look, I'm just saying, if he's worth it, he'll wait."

"You've been telling me to go faster for months and now you're saying slow down?!" I give her a hard stare, but she just shrugs. "Well,

think what you want, but I can't think of another person I would rather be with."

"What about Jordy?"

"What?!" I say this so loud our friend Leah and Jordan's younger brother, Cole, stop playing tonsil hockey on the couch across from us stop and look over.

Callie politely waits for them to go back to making out before she responds.

"I'm just saying, you and Jordan are really close," she laments, refusing to look me at me. She doesn't want to see the complete disdain in my eyes. "You guys really care about each other."

"He's with Hannah," I remind her flatly.

"Hannah is a waste of viable organs," Callie replies bluntly.

I can't argue with that so I just shrug. I've come to accept Jordan's relationship with Hannah even if she hasn't accepted my friendship with him. It was a big bone of contention between us for the first few months they were together. Jordy and I even stopped talking for almost a week. But I couldn't take how it felt to be without him in my life. It was too painful. And he must have felt the same way because he showed up in the middle of the night one night and we talked it out. He promised to try not to let Hannah keep us from being friends, and I promised to stop bitching about her. It was incredibly hard though, especially lately. The two of them were in this dramatic, ridiculous on-again, off-again phase right now. Well, Jordan called it a phase. I thought it was just Hannah being her true, high-maintenance, melodramatic self.

To be honest, not that I would ever admit it, I had developed a crush on Jordan years ago. I'd known him since I was eight but suddenly, around fourteen, I began to wonder what it would be like to kiss him. By sixteen, my wonder was turning into a full-on crush. I thought about him all the time, and the way I acted around him began to change. I giggled more and I made up reasons to call him and even took the long route to my math class just so I could walk by his locker. And it felt like the way he acted around me was changing too. He stopped teasing me the way he used to about my skinny legs and sometimes I would catch him looking at me in English class instead of sleeping or doodling in his notebook, like he usually did.

But then my grandmother retired and announced she was leaving my sisters and me alone while she stayed at her trailer home in Florida, and I had to grow up, fast. My life became about taking care of my sisters and keeping our secret from the school so no one called the state and put us in foster care. I confided in Jordan, because he was my best friend, and he helped us keep the secret, which made me feel even more strongly about him. He helped my sisters and me any and every way we needed it—fixing the water heater when it broke, shoveling our driveway after snowstorms, even staying over on the couch when the power was out and we were scared to death. And I knew I couldn't risk altering that friendship so I purposely ignored my feelings. There were other, less risky boys to crush on, like Chance Echolls. And when Jordan began seeing Hannah, it stung because I realized the crush was probably one-sided anyway.

"I'm going to find Chance," I tell my sister, and she nods, looking resigned.

I stand up and she grabs my hand, giving it a squeeze. "Love you, dumbass."

"Love you too, jackass."

I start climbing the stairs and see Jordan bounding down toward me. He smiles brightly, creating that adorable dimple on his cheek.

"The line for the bathroom is brutal," he warns.

"Oh, well," I say, not bothering to fill him in on my real mission. "Going to play ball hockey?"

He nods. "See ya later!"

When I get to the top of the stairs, the butterflies in my stomach start fluttering wildly. I have no hesitation about this... well, nothing I can't talk myself out of, anyway. Chance is so sweet and so hot and he cares about me. When I told him I wasn't ready—when he first tried to "go there" a few months ago—he didn't even blink. He promised to wait with me so we could have our first time together.

It was hard dating him and hiding our secret. I was constantly lying to him about little things so he wouldn't know that my grandmother didn't live at home with us anymore. I wanted to tell him the truth, but I knew that the fewer people who knew, the better off we were. I'd been eighteen for five weeks now, but Lily was still Callie and Rose's legal guardian so we didn't feel comfortable telling more than just the Garrison family about our situation. And we didn't willingly tell Donna and Wyatt Garrison, they'd become suspicious because Jordan was spending so much time at our place and kept borrowing tools and asking his mom to have us over for dinner. Donna figured it out, but she vowed not to tell anyone as long as we let her check on us regularly and we promised to come to her if we needed anything. Jordan's mom had been my mother's best friend in high school so she had a soft spot for us and treated us like we were her own.

Despite Callie's complaining, when I was thinking about applying for guardianship of my sisters and staying in Silver Bay until Rose was eighteen. Callie wanted to keep the secret going and keep living off the meager checks Grandma Lily sent so that I could go away to college. She swore she and Rose would be fine. Even Mr. and Mrs. Garrison thought I should apply to colleges other than the local community college, so I had. But I only applied to schools with full scholarships in sports therapy, which made getting in an even bigger long shot.

No matter what happened with my future, Chance would go away—but we'd stay together. He told me that. He'd promised me. I believed him. If he was willing to stay with me, I had to give him something that made it worth it, didn't I?

There's a line for the bathroom, but Chance isn't in it. So, I wait and twist my hands nervously. I smooth the tiny pale pink cotton sundress I'm wearing. I'm normally not a pink girl—or a dress girl—but Chance said he likes girly girls so I've been trying to make an effort to dress more feminine.

I had noticed a lot of the girls at the Silver Bay Bucks hockey games wore high heels and low-cut shirts and lots of makeup. I wanted to show him I could be that way too—minus the makeup. Anything more than mascara and lip gloss made my face itch. And I had opted for flip-flops tonight because Callie, Rose and I had walked here from our house about a mile away.

The bathroom door opens and I smile expectantly, but it's Luc Richard, not Chance Echolls. I blink, surprised, and wonder where he could be. If he'd been playing ball hockey, maybe he had worked up a sweat. Maybe he'd gone to his room to change.

That would be perfect since I figured that's where we would end up tonight, anyway. We could go back to my place, since I had already lied and said Grandma Lily was in Boston, but with Chance's parents gone to Montreal, we didn't have to.

I walk down the hall to his room. His door is closed so I knock.

"Busy!" he calls out gruffly.

"Chance?" I call tentatively, and put my hand on the door handle. "It's just me."

The knob twists in my hand and I push the door open and slip in. The room is dark. I stupidly wonder if his lightbulb burned out. Why else would he be in here in the dark? I reach for the switch and that's when I hear the swearing.

A girl *swearing.*

And someone is moving haphazardly through the room.

I flip the switch and the room floods with light.

Chance is standing beside his desk, he's got underwear on, barely covering his ass, and one foot in the leg of his jeans. In his bed, wrapped in his navy blue comforter, is Amber Maloney—one of my closest friends.

She's peering at me with wide, terrified brown eyes. The sundress she wore tonight is in a heap next to the bed, and there's an empty silver condom wrapper on top of it.

I turn to Chance, my eyes flooding with tears.

"Jessica..."

That's all he says—my name. Because what the hell else can he say? There is no way to lie his way out of this.

I fling the door open and run down the hall, almost knocking over Jordan's girlfriend, Hannah, in line for the bathroom. She swears at me, perturbed, but I keep moving. When I realize Chance isn't even trying to chase me, my heart breaks completely in half.

I hear Callie call my name as I land at the bottom of the stairs and run through the living room. I can hear her footsteps behind me, but I don't stop. I head through the kitchen past Luc and Rose, who are sitting at the table playing cards. Out of the corner of my tear-blurred vision I see Rose jump up and reach for me, but I keep running out the side door.

My flip-flops smack wildly on the driveway as I dodge teenage boys, hockey sticks and a net, and continue for the road. Jordan calls my name and I almost stop. I want to tell him what happened. I want to cry on his shoulder like I have about every other completely devastating event in my life, but I can't. Not here. Not with everyone around to mock me.

So I keep running. I run the entire way back to my house and then collapse on the porch, sweating, my lungs burning and tears streaking down my face. I lie there on my back in the middle of the porch floor and choke back sobs as I struggle for breath.

I push the heels of my hands into my eyes and will myself to stop crying.

I have survived worse than Chance Echolls cheating on me. I know this, rationally, I do. But right now… it feels worse than anything I've ever felt in my life. I just wanted this… this one thing… to go right. My father left. My mom died. My grandmother was nothing but a bank account to me. I just wanted this… Chance… to love me, even though my feelings for him weren't as strong as my feelings for Jordan. But I loved the idea that someone so perfect could love me. If Chance Echolls wanted me, then maybe I was better than my crappy life made me look. But clearly, that wasn't the case. I couldn't have Jordan, and Chance never thought I was special. The tears are pure self-pity and I know it, but that just makes me cry harder.

I'm sobbing so heavily that I don't even hear heavy footsteps moments later as they make their way up my dirt driveway.

"Holy shit, you can run," he pants. I scramble to my feet.

I hastily dig the house key out from under the doormat and rush to unlock the door so I can disappear inside and lock him out. Lock the world out. But my shaky hands aren't quick enough, and he climbs the porch and grabs the key from me before I can get it in the lock.

"Go away, Jordan," I beg, and rest my head against the lead glass windowpane in the door, refusing to turn and face him. "Go back to the party and your girlfriend."

"No way," he replies, and wraps his arms around my shoulders, hugging me from behind. "Besides, we're doing the off-again thing. She's pissed about God knows what."

I wiggle wildly trying to shrug him off. "I want to be alone!"

"Too bad," he tells me firmly. "I'm bigger so I win."

He's been using that argument since we were eleven.

I choke on a sob. "Please."

I let him turn me around and put one of those big mitts he calls hands under my chin. He forces my head upward. I close my eyes, too embarrassed to look at him.

"You have to tell me what happened," he informs me softly. "You always tell me everything eventually, so just tell me."

"Chance and I are… done." I open my eyes and sniff then shudder.

He pulls me to him so my face is mushed up against his chest. I inhale deeply and my nostrils fill with his scent—Dove soap and Old Spice sport deodorant. It makes me feel slightly better. I wait for him to ask more questions. Why? What happened? Are you sure? But he doesn't.

"Do you want to know what happened?" I finally croak.

"Nope," he says simply, and runs a hand along the back of my head, smoothing my hair. "I don't care. I just care that you're all right."

"I'm not," I sputter, and another sob shakes me again.

"You'll be fine," he insists almost too casually. "You'll be better than fine. You'll be awesome."

"How can you say that?" I demand, pulling away from him.

"Jessie, I have been your best friend since you were eight," he reminds me softly. "You always get through things. You're always awesome. This asshole isn't going to change that."

"But…I thought he wanted me," I whisper brokenly.

He makes a bit of a face at that, like he swallowed something that tastes bad, but he doesn't argue. Instead he asks, "Why do you think he doesn't suddenly?"

"He…" I swallow and shake my head. A whole new flood of tears threaten to flow down my cheeks. "He was with Amber."

I grab the key from Jordan's hand and shove it into the lock, throwing the door open and charging into the kitchen. He follows behind me, shutting the door and leaning against it.

"What do you mean, he was with Amber?" Jordan repeats, confused, his blond eyebrows pinching together. "Amber, our friend?"

"Yeah, the girl I thought was one of my best friends." I throw the key in the general direction of the fridge.

"So, what? Like, he was talking to her and you got all delusional and thought—"

"He was NAKED and she was NAKED. In his BED," I scream, and the tears start spilling again. "I can't believe…He said he was…He would wait…"

"Whoa!" Jordan pushes off the door and grabs me by the wrist and pulls me in for another hug, but I push against his chest and pull my arm free from his grasp. I walk to the other side of the room.

"Can you just go?" I beg again. "I don't want to talk about it."

He hesitates then nods and turns to the door. "Okay. I'll go back to the party and beat the living shit out of him."

He pulls the door open and I rush to him and grab the back of his shirt. Luckily he stops walking. He could very well drag me all the way back there without much exertion, considering he's a six-two pillar of pure muscle and I'm a weak little human.

"Jordy, you can't!"

"I have to. Someone has to. The asshole can't get away with that," he rants angrily, thumping a fist on the wall beside the doorframe. "You don't deserve that."

He reaches behind his back and grabs my hand, pulling it loose from his shirt. Then he turns and looks down at me, the anger in his sky blue eyes morphing into concern.

"Oh, fuck..." He swallows and suddenly looks shy. "Did you...And him...Did you have...sex already?"

"No." I shake my head and pull away from him, turning and staring down at the counter. I'm too embarrassed to meet his gaze.

I had mentioned it to Jordan. Well, he had asked me if Chance and I had. I had told him not yet, but soon. I wasn't comfortable getting into too many details like that with him. I asked him if he and Hannah had and he said yes. I remember that made me feel angry. And sad.

"Good," Jordan replies quietly with a loud sigh of relief. "'Cause then I would really have to kill him. Like, for real. And then I wouldn't get drafted because the NHL doesn't draft kids in prison."

"He promised he would wait...he said he wanted it to be with me..." I start to cry again.

Jordan walks over and forcibly turns me to face him. I dip my chin and snap my eyes shut, refusing to look at him. He bends at the waist, trying to get low enough to look at my face. When that is too awkward, he places his hands firmly on my hips. He lifts me up and plops me down on the counter so I'm higher—closer to his height by a little bit anyway—and then he sticks his hand under my chin again and lifts my face.

My eyes flutter open. I don't think I have ever seen him look so serious.

"It's better this way," he explains quietly. "Better you found out before than after."

"I just…I just thought we had something. Like really…And I…" I burst into tears again. "What is wrong with me?! Why doesn't anyone want me?"

I cover my face with my hands and feel his ridiculously long, warm limbs wrap around my back. His chest is pressed against my face again.

"Jessie, come on, please," he begs softly, his breath tickling my ear. "Get a grip for me. Okay? I need you to get a grip."

I look up at him and choke back another sob.

"Chance is not worth this," he insists. "There is nothing wrong with you! He's got something wrong with him for doing this to you."

I will myself to stop crying and believe what he's saying. I'm desperate for any words that make this better. And he's giving them to me. I have to believe him. He's Jordan. My best friend. He's right about everything. He's the best.

"And Chance did want you," Jordan goes on, his eyes wide and sincere. "He probably still does. Half this goddamn town does. It makes me fucking crazy."

I blink.

He heaves a heavy breath and looks at the ceiling for a moment.

"Do you know how the guys talk about you in the locker room? I have to hear it every freaking day. And he does it too. Chance tells me how hot you are—what he can't wait to do to you—because he knows how it makes me feel."

He reaches up and cups my face. His thumbs sweep over my tear-stained cheeks, trying to wipe them dry.

"You're beautiful," he says in a voice barely over a whisper. "You're strong and smart and funny and so fucking beautiful..."

My tears have halted completely and I'm having trouble breathing, but not from strangled sobs this time. Is this really happening? Is he just being nice, or are my forbidden feelings mutual?

"There is nothing wrong with you," he repeats, his head dipping down so close to mine our noses almost touch. "You're perfect. Chance may not know it but I know it. I've known it my whole life."

"Jordan..."

"I love you," he blurts out in a soft, barely audible voice filled with aching honesty. "He doesn't. But I do."

And then he lets go of my face and steps back.

I feel an overwhelming sense of panic that he might leave. Just go out the door and never come back. That somehow now I'm losing him too. I grab his arm and almost topple off the counter. I feel dizzy. I feel panicked. I feel... I feel like I would rather die than not kiss him right now.

Chapter 4

Jessie

I pull on his arm and he moves closer, but his face is cast downward at the yellow linoleum under his size thirteen feet. I keep pulling him closer until he is inches from my knees. Less than inches, millimeters.

"What did you say?"

"Never mind."

"Jordy…"

He shakes his head and tries to take a step away from me, but I still have him by his giant wrist. I keep him firmly in place. Finally, he looks up at me. He looks so vulnerable and terrified. His cheeks are pink, his eyes wide and glassy, his full bottom lip jutting out just a little more than normal. For the first time in our lives, I'm scared he might cry.

I reach out with my free hand and cup the back of his neck. And then I do it, without the slightest hesitation or apprehension—I kiss my best friend.

And he kisses me back.

There's no faltering. No reservation when our lips touch. There's only a feeling—like a lightning bolt—that blasts through my body. I feel… bulletproof. Sitting on my grandma's crappy countertop, when just moments before I was consumed by betrayal and abandonment, I feel bulletproof.

Kissing Jordan is a myriad of intoxicating contradictions. He's gentle but dominant. His lips are firm against mine but his tongue is soft as it meets mine. This is better than any kiss I've ever had or imagined having.

He grabs my head, his hands tangle in my hair, and without thinking, I part my legs and tug on his shirt, guiding his torso between my thighs. The hem of my summer dress slides up and Jordan drops his hands to my lower back and pulls me toward the edge of the counter. My center, protected by nothing but the silky black Victoria's Secret bikini underwear I ordered online for a night with Chance, is now firmly pressed up against the front of his green cotton cargo shorts.

I can feel it—thick, long and solid—pressing against me from under the front of his shorts. My breath catches in my throat.

Jordan pulls his mouth back from mine a fraction of an inch and his eyes flutter open at the same time mine do. He is so beautiful. I always knew that somewhere in the recesses of my heart and mind, but finally admitting it to myself gives me a feeling like being on a roller coaster.

"I want it to be you," I tell him, shocking myself as much as him. It doesn't surprise me that I mean what I say—I mean it with everything in me. What surprises me is the fact that I feel no embarrassment telling him.

"Jessie, you don't have…"

"I want you," I repeat firmly, and barely brush my lips against his. "Unless… you don't."

"I do," he argues quickly, and kisses me, his tongue grazing my bottom lip as he pulls back. "I want it with you. I've wanted it forever."

But then it hits me, like burst of cold air wrapping itself around me. "But…Hannah."

"I told you, it's off-again tonight," he whispers. "And there's no more on-again. I only want you."

And then we're kissing again, and it's hot and needy and I start to wrap my fingers under the hem of his Silver Bay Bucks T-shirt. My fingertips graze his bare abs and he shudders. I pull the shirt up as high as I can, so it's gathered under his armpits. He takes over, pulling it over his head, and I find myself kissing his bare chest and abdomen. I know in my heart I never would have been this brave with Chance. I don't know if it's my emotional state or just the fact that it's Jordan, but whatever the reason, I'm bold.

He lets out a small sigh and leans down to kiss the side of my jaw and then my neck. Jordan's hands land on my knees and start sliding up my thighs. His fingertips touch the fabric of my panties and I shiver with nervous anticipation, but he pulls back.

I look up, blinking in confusion. He smiles softly and takes my hand, pulling me off the counter.

"Not here," he says shyly. "Upstairs."

Wordlessly I let him lead me to the living room and up the staircase. My bedroom is the first door at the top. It's the tiniest room in the three-bedroom house, but I don't have to share like Callie and Rose do. It's painted bubblegum pink. Lily painted it that color in preparation for my arrival just as she'd painted Callie and Rose's room an overwhelming sunshine yellow. Even back then, at eight, I disliked pink but, unlike Callie, who had repainted her room a forest green two years ago, I left mine that color. It's the only proof I have that Grandma Lily ever attempted to care.

Jordan knows exactly which room is mine and walks right into it. He's been in it a million times before, but somehow this time feels different, forbidden.

I take a step toward him and reach out to place my hand on his bare chest. I let it slide down to his abdomen and over the downy trail of blond hair below his belly button. My heart skips a beat. His hands reach around my back, and as he kisses my lips again, he also starts to lower the zipper on my sundress. My heart skips again.

A revelation blossoms in the back of my head: I'm not shy. I'm not embarrassed. I don't feel any of the weird awkwardness I had anticipated when I thought about doing this with Chance. Instead I feel comfortable, almost giddy, and I feel loved. The butterflies in my stomach are excitement, not nerves. Because it's Jordan. Because it's right.

And then I'm standing in front of him in nothing but my Victoria's Secret bra and matching panties that cost me almost a whole week's pay from my part-time job. He's staring down at me. His cornflower blue eyes are darker than I've ever seen them. I reach up and wrap my arms around his neck, letting him lower me onto the bed, then lower himself on top of me.

Our kissing gains intensity, and I can't get enough of his lips on mine or his tongue in my mouth. His hips are pushing down into me; I instinctively wrap my legs around his waist and tilt my pelvis into his thrusts. I don't know if it's the right thing to do, but it feels right and he doesn't object.

I'm eighteen years old. I've been dating a hockey player. I've dry humped before. But it's never made me feel this…out of control.

I reach down, undo the button and zipper on his shorts then hook my thumbs in the waistband and start hitching them down over his muscular butt. He balances on one arm, kisses the curve of my breast above my bra and uses his free hand to pull my underwear down my legs.

And then he's naked. Well, except for his ankles, which still have his shorts wrapped around them. And I'm naked, except for my bra. He's lying on top of me gently and I can feel him—that one part of him I have never felt before—warm and solid, against my thigh.

He runs a hand through my hair and brushes his lips to my cheek.

"I don't have anything..." he confesses softly, his voice cracking with angst.

"It's okay," I whisper back. "I'm on the pill."

"What?" he says, obviously shocked. He shouldn't be. He knows I plan everything.

I had no intention of telling Chance about the birth control I started taking the month after we started dating. It was supposed to be my secret backup plan in case the condom failed, like they said it could in health class. But... I've never lied to Jordan in my life, and I'm not starting now.

"But... are you sure?" he wants to know. "I've never... not without..."

"We don't have to," I respond quickly, suddenly afraid that I've said the wrong thing. "We can stop if you... want to wait... until we have that too. But if you don't want to stop... that's okay too."

He stares at me for a long minute and then he shakes his head. "I don't want to stop."

"Then don't," I reply, and kiss him, parting his lips with my tongue.

And then we're dry humping again but without clothes, and this is definitely a first for me. His hard-on is grinding into my thigh—so high up my thigh—and so close but not close enough. As he kisses my neck, collarbone and chest, his hand drifts lower and lower. And lower. He slides a finger into me and I buck my hips instinctively.

He's gentle, so gentle, and I appreciate it, but I want more. I want him—all of him. I reach down and wrap my left hand around him, pulling gently.

"Fuck," he hisses into my neck, and slides another finger into me. I groan and writhe and stroke him more firmly this time. And then his fingers are gone and he shifts his hips, making me lose my grasp on him. With his hands on either side of my head, he rests his hips against mine and looks down between us.

I follow his gaze and there we are—our bodies grazing each other in a way they never have before. I reach down and touch his tip, carefully placing it where it needs to be. He moves his hips forward—slowly.

I feel my body stretch and willingly shape itself around him. There's a quick sharp sensation of discomfort, which is gone before I can do anything more than furrow my brow. He's looking intently, cautiously, at my face now, and I meet his eyes. They're like the ocean at night.

"Is it okay?" he asks hesitantly.

I nod and smile.

He smiles back and continues to slowly, gently move farther inside me until he's completely engulfed. He pauses for a heartbeat and kisses my lips softly before he pulls out a little bit and pushes back in.

It feels good.

I wrap my arms around him and pull his lips to mine. He kisses back hungrily. I move my hips a little bit, tilting my pelvis as he thrusts gently. It makes him groan and nip at my neck with his teeth and lips. It makes me feel tingly…and warm. He's on an elbow now, his forearm against the side of my face, and his hand is tangled in my long hair splayed on the pillow. His other hand is on my hip and his whole body is covering mine. It feels so good; better than anything has felt in my entire life. I get this overwhelming sensation of warmth and I can't feel my toes. I start having trouble breathing, and so does he. We're not kissing now. His lips are open against my neck and mine are open near his ear; we're just panting onto each other's skin.

And then I can't keep my eyes open. I quiver and feel myself tighten around him—I seriously can't feel my limbs as a wave of pure, euphoria washes through me. Jordan swears and shakes and swears again. And then he can't hold himself up anymore and he drops onto my chest. I wonder if he also can't feel his limbs. My core is still trembling around him. I really hope that's normal.

"Oh, God," he whispers into the pillow beside my face. "Fuck. I've never felt…that was…Fuck, it feels…"

"What? What's wrong?"

"Nothing," he insists, and tilts his head so his lips are against my cheek. "God, nothing. It's not wrong at all. It's great."

Slowly he starts to move, pulling his body off mine, sliding out of me. He lies down next to me and I roll to face him. His eyes are suddenly timid again.

"Are you…I mean was that…fine?"

"It was amazing," I confirm, blushing. I smile self-consciously. "It was way better than Callie said it would be."

He laughs at that and I laugh too. But then I hear the distinctive creek of the front door.

"Jessie?" Rose's voice echoes from the kitchen all the way upstairs.

"Shit!" I jump up, taking the comforter with me, and run to slam the bedroom door shut.

Jordan grabs his shorts and pulls them on. His T-shirt is still downstairs. Fuck. He throws my dress at me.

"Oh God, I can't let her see us," I whisper. I hear her call my name again, and this time it's closer. She must be in the living room or at the bottom of the stairs.

"I know," Jordan agrees, and quickly kisses my forehead, which makes my stomach flip. "I'll go."

He turns and opens one of my bedroom windows, the one next to the drainpipe. He's climbed up and down it before, like when we were fighting about Hannah a few months ago and I wouldn't let him in the front door.

I hear Rose's feet on the stairs and I struggle back into my dress, pulling on my underwear just as Jordan's long legs disappear over the window ledge. He glances at me.

"I'll see you tomorrow."

"Okay."

"Jessie, I love you," he says, and then there is a knock on my door. Rosie rattles the handle.

I open my mouth to tell him I love him too, but he's already gone. Rosie opens my door, and the whole thing suddenly feels like a dream.

Chapter 5

Jordan

Thanks for picking me up," I tell my dad as he hugs me.

He nods and takes my bag off my shoulder as I hobble out the airport doors with him. He glances at my booted foot.

"How's it coming along?" he wants to know.

I shrug. "The infection in the incision is almost gone. And the bone is pretty much set. Now it's just finishing the antibiotics and some conditioning and physical therapy." I try not to look as frustrated and pissed off as I am.

Last season, I broke my ankle blocking a shot during playoffs. It should have healed before the summer ended. As luck would have it, one of the bones set wrong and I had to have surgery to fix it. Then the surgical incision got infected. All this made me miss the start of the hockey season, so I was ready to snap.

"When do they think you'll be back in the game?" he asks as he tosses my bag into the back of his old pickup truck.

I raise an eyebrow. Devin and I pitched in and bought him a brand-new Ford F-150 last Christmas. Where the hell is it?

"They're thinking mid-October. Where is the new truck?" I ask as I hop into the cab beside him.

"We lent it to the girls," he informs me quietly. "Your mom didn't want them to have to pay for a rental, and I didn't want them to have this one. It's old and the tires aren't as good."

I smile. I can't help it. My parents were never rich. Growing up we were barely middle class, but our lives were never hard. They provided us with the best in hockey equipment, even when my dad's blueberry farm struggled and money was low. They kept us in line—not with threats or violence, but with chores, rules and good old-fashioned groundings. Our house was tiny, drafty and crammed two boys in every bedroom, but they always made room for anyone who needed some help—whether it was a stray cat, my best friend, Luc, or the orphaned daughters of my mom's high school best friend. I'm lucky. I know that.

"That was very nice of you guys," I tell him, and then chew on my bottom lip.

"It's so great to see them all again, even in these unfortunate circumstances." He smiles lightly. "Callie is still a firecracker. Your mom and I picked her up at the airport. She hasn't changed a bit."

"Where is she living now?" I can't help but wonder as the familiar scenery of my youth drifts by outside.

"Venice Beach. California. She's a wardrobe designer assistant person or something like that. She works on commercials and music videos and stuff."

I nod. I could totally see Callie doing that. She always used to love to style her sisters and pick out clothes for us guys. Sometimes her selections were too weird to wear, but there was no denying she loved doing it. And she always said she would live somewhere with no snow. Good for her.

My dad turns up the long, winding road where our house is located, along with the humble family blueberry farm that kept us in hockey equipment.

"And Rose?" I prompt.

He smiles even bigger, hazel eyes twinkling a little. I think Rose was always his favorite. "Little Rosie isn't so little. She's almost finished her bachelor's degree and she's applying to master's programs. She works part-time tutoring kids. She's...you know... Rosie. She's a gem."

"They're all here now?" I ask, but I know he knows what I'm *not* asking.

"Yep. All of them. They were at the funeral home this morning arranging everything and now they're meeting your mom for an early dinner." He explains this swiftly and as matter-of-factly as he can. "Funeral is ten tomorrow morning."

She's here. My stomach twists with dread at the confirmation. I really don't want to see her again. It's going to do nothing but bring back all the anger and rejection I felt back then. My dad keeps his gaze level on the driveway and adjusts the brim of his baseball hat as he eases the truck to a stop. "Does she know you're coming?" he asks quietly, putting the truck in park.

"Not unless Mom told her." I take my Seattle Winterhawks cap off and scratch the back of my head.

"Your mom is definitely not doing that," he announces with a wry shake of his head as he opens his door. "She knows better than to stick her nose in that dog's breakfast."

I can't help but laugh at that. "If that was true, she wouldn't have guilted me into coming here."

He shoots me a serious look across the hood of the truck. "Your mom simply suggested you support an old friend. If you felt guilty about that...well, that's on you. Besides, I think she may be regretting that decision. When your mom mentioned you said hello, Jessie looked like she might throw up."

Wow. Harsh.

"So now I'm just making things worse by being here? Fantastic." As we make our way to the unassuming Craftsman I grew up in, I wonder if I can find a flight back to Seattle tonight.

He looks skeptical as he opens the front door and a wave of happiness hits me despite everything that's going on. Devin and I have told our parents we'll support them if they want to give up the farm and retire early. We offered to buy them a more modern home closer to town, but they refused, and every time I come home I'm secretly glad. This house is a sanctuary filled with my happy childhood memories. It's hard not to feel good when I'm inside it.

I hobble by him and take my bag out of his hand. "I'm going to hop on the Internet and see if there's a flight to Logan later today. If I can get to Boston, I can find a flight to Seattle."

He drops his keys in the lopsided ceramic bowl on the hall table that I made in the 4H Club when I was eight and then crosses his arms over his chest. "Jordan Jonathan Garrison. I don't know what the heck happened between you two. I never knew and I don't want to know now, but her grandmother died. That's got to be painful, especially with the messed-up relationship they had with the old woman. You spent your entire youth looking out for Jessie and she did the same for you. This is your last chance to honor that friendship. I think you should."

"I don't want to stir anything," I argue, and try to look innocent.

"Stir anything in her or in yourself?" my dad shoots back with an arched eyebrow. I don't answer him. He takes off the Brooklyn Barons baseball cap I figure my brother must have given him, rubs his nearly bald head, and walks up the stairs and disappears around the corner into the kitchen.

As I carry my bag down the hall my dad calls out, "Last chance!"

"I get it!" I reply tersely, and head into my old bedroom, dropping my bag on my old bed. I can't believe they haven't changed this place yet. I glance around. Two walls are a bright indigo blue and two are a dark hunter green—this is because I shared my room with my younger brother, Cole, and we couldn't agree on a color. He got two green walls and I got two blue. I remember Jessie helped me paint the room. I also remember she tried to convince me to paint it orange because that was her favorite color. I almost agreed because I loved to see her happy.

I shake off the memory and limp back out of my room. "Dad! I'm going to go to town, grab a beer and see Cole, okay?"

"Sure thing. Be safe."

Twenty minutes later, my younger brother Cole is grinning at me from across the bar as he pours me a pint of Sam Adams. He pours one for himself and we clink glasses.

"Aren't you working?" I ask as I take a sip.

"I'm not working, I'm managing," he corrects me with an evil grin on his freckled face. "And fuck it. How often do I get a visit from you after August?"

I smile. Cole is awesome. Always has been. Sure, Dev and I used to bust his balls all the time—that's what older brothers do—but he's probably the best person out of the three of us. Two years younger than me, four and a half younger than Dev, Cole followed in our hockey footsteps. Looking back, I think he did it because it was expected, not because he had the same drive Devin and I do.

Cole was a natural just like us, but unlike us, he decided not to go straight into the NHL draft after high school. He wanted to go to college. I couldn't imagine wasting three or four years with more school when I could be just playing hockey. Neither could Devin. But Cole wanted it. He got into the University of Maine on a full scholarship and played hockey for them while earning a business admin degree.

In his junior year, he took a brutal hit in the middle of a playoff game. He went headfirst into the boards and snapped two vertebrae in his back. After almost six month of rehab, he was all right, but his hockey career was over. He would never play in the NHL. I think Devin and I took it harder than he did. We wanted him there with us. He worked just as hard as we did—harder, because he was getting a college degree on top of everything—and it didn't seem fair that his dream was taken away. But Cole never became bitter or angry, he simply adapted.

He moved back to Silver Bay after college, started working at the local pub and coaching the high school hockey team. He moved back in with Mom and Dad. He seemed happy. Devin and I thought he was crazy, but he had a plan. Billy, the old guy who owned the pub called O'Malley's where Cole worked, was ready to retire. Living with Mom and Dad, Cole had managed to save a ton of money, and he got a loan from the bank to buy the place. Cole renamed the pub Last Call.

O'Malley's had been a dive. In a year, Cole had turned Last Call into a rocking attraction for tourists and locals alike. He was even working on plans to add a dining room and full kitchen to the back.

"So, I don't know if you heard, but Callie, Jessie and Rosie's grandmother died," Cole informs me.

"Why do you think I'm here?" I give him a look like he's a moron.

He scratches his head full of ginger hair and tries to look confused, but the smirk on his face says he knows he's being a smartass. "Why would you come home for that? You hate each other."

"Hate is a strong word, Cole," I mutter, and take another sip of beer. A big sip.

"Yeah, I know," Cole muses with a nod and a smile. "And their anti-Jordan feelings are strong. Callie uses cuss words to describe you that even make me blush."

"Good to know she's expanding her vocabulary," I snark, and roll my eyes.

"Didn't Callie punch you?"

My smile fades at that less-than-perfect memory. "Sort of."

Cole laughs and slaps the bar. "I remember now—at the bonfire, down by the lake. She freakin' got you good in the gut! Man, she was pissed. And Rosie was so drunk she puked in the fire. Good times." He grins at the memories.

I shake my head because my little brother is a moron. "Look, Mom thought I should be here, so I'm here. And when I tried to back out earlier today, Dad laid into me. So I'm going to the damn funeral."

Cole swallows a big gulp of beer and then opens his mouth like he is going to say something, but he freezes and his jaw just hangs open. Then he points behind me. "Speak of the devils! They're here!"

My heart starts to hammer so suddenly it startles me. Everything moves in slow motion as I place my beer on the bar in front of me, spinning around on my bar stool as a familiar voice rings over the crowd.

"Little Cole Garrison! Look at you, all grown up!" Callie is bouncing toward us, Rosie skipping along behind her.

They both freeze at the sight of me. I try to smile but it probably looks more like a grimace. It feels like one.

"What the hell are you doing here?" Callie hisses vehemently, her big brown eyes glaring at me.

I raise my hands like she's pointing a gun at my chest and stand up. "My mom told me what happened. I came for the funeral. She wanted me to support you guys."

Callie blinks, stunned, but it only lasts a second. Then she storms through the space between us and comes right at me. For a split second I worry she's going to hit me again, but her arms remain firmly crossed over her chest. Her face is so flushed with anger that even the freckles on the bridge of her nose look pink.

"We don't want your support. *She* doesn't want it."

She pushes past me and reaches across the bar to hug Cole. He smiles easily and returns the hug. I watch Rose as she stands a careful distance from me, behind her sister. I glance past her, searching, my heart still hammering.

"She's not here," Rose says flatly. "I mean, she's *here* in the Bay, but she isn't here in the bar."

"Oh." My heart slows and my chest fills with a new feeling. I thought it would be relief but it is, without a doubt, disappointment. I am disappointed she's not here. Why the fuck am I disappointed she's not here?

Rose is still staring at me with her wide, dark eyes. "Do you want to know how she is?"

"He doesn't get to know that," Callie snaps, interrupting my conversation with the littlest, most rational Caplan sister. Callie grabs the beer Cole poured her and smiles at him. "We'll be sitting over there. Come join us when you're done with the Evil Garrison."

"Evil? Really?!" I call after her, but she ignores me and keeps walking over to one of the girls she graduated with who's standing over by the pool tables.

Rose reaches over and hugs Cole, taking the beer he pours her, but she doesn't run off to follow her sister right away. Instead, her tiny hand raises the beer to her lips and her almost-black eyes bore into me over the foam as she sips it. I drop back down onto my stool.

"How are you?" I offer, knowing full well I could be setting myself up for another tirade.

"I'm good, you know, considering," she replies quietly.

I nod. "Sorry about your…about Lily."

"You know we weren't all that close," Rose says quietly, licking her full lips that look so much like Jessie's. "But thank you."

I nod and give her a small smile. Rose has always been the softhearted one. The fact that she's not walking away makes me cautiously optimistic.

"So you don't hate my guts anymore?" I ask tentatively, hopefully.

She swallows another sip and her pretty lips almost turn up in a smile. Almost.

"I never hated you, Jordy. I was hurt," she confesses in a cheerless voice. "Hurt for her."

I nod solemnly. "I know. But, Rose, Jessie took off before I could explain. She abandoned me. I didn't abandon her."

She raises her dark, narrow eyebrows showing her doubt, but before she can respond Callie screams her name.

"Rose Caplan, get over here NOW!"

Rose turns from me and beelines to her sister. Cole gives me a compassionate smile and slides a fresh beer my way.

"Guess no one is really over that whole stealing Jessie's virginity thing, huh?"

I give him a hard stare. "Clearly. And I didn't steal it. It was mutual and...never mind."

An hour later I decide I better go home. I'm tired. I have to take another round of antibiotics for my stupid ankle. I hug my brother good-bye and hobble past Callie and Rose as quickly as possible, keeping my head down and my eyes averted. I really don't need another cheap shot thrown my way. Luckily, Callie does nothing but glare as I pass.

Walking down the sidewalk toward where the truck is parked, I hear the door open behind me. I glance over my shoulder and see Rose slip under the railing that divides the entryway from the sidewalk. She marches up to me.

"I'm glad you came back for the funeral, Jordy. I want you to know it means a lot to me."

"Thanks, Rosie." I give her a small hug. Her admission starts to add even more cracks in the hard armor that's been encasing my heart for six years.

When I let her go, she levels me with an intense, serious stare. "You will never see her again after tomorrow."

"What?"

"We're going to sell the house. Jessie is never going to come back to Silver Bay after that. I don't think any of us will." Rose speaks quietly, her eyes as dark as the sky above us. "So, you know, if you have anything to say to her…If you feel like you owe her even the slightest apology for how it all blew up, this would be the time to say it."

"I'm not the only one who screwed up," I remind her because I've been reminding myself of that every day for six years. It's that reminder that keeps me from feeling sorry for myself.

"Then I guess you're here to say good-bye." Rose turns and runs back into the bar.

I get back in my dad's truck grappling with the new, unexpected feelings that have started to brew inside me. Up until the second Cole said they were at the bar, I was completely dreading having to be in the same room with Jessie again. But when I realized she wasn't there, I was genuinely, and completely unexpectedly, disappointed. Suddenly I wanted to see her again. Maybe it was just because I wanted to get it over with but then Rose's words—*you will never see her again after tomorrow*—felt like a threat.

God, how the hell did we get here? As I drive home the memories of the clusterfuck that was my only true attempt at a real relationship fill my head.

Chapter 6

Jordan

Six years earlier

I knock on the door, totally freaking out inside. I keep telling myself that admitting I'm in love with her doesn't have to change how we are with each other, but the jackhammer that has replaced my heart seems to disagree.

Rose answers and lets me in. She tells me Jessie is on her way home from work and I'm welcome to wait. I sit in the living room and watch Survivor *with Rose, who is obsessed with the show and swears as soon as she's old enough, she'll apply to be a contestant.*

I can barely pay attention to who is being voted off the island because I'm obsessing over what to say to Jessie when I see her. It's been almost twenty-four hours since we had sex, and I haven't said anything to her. I haven't seen her or talked to her. This isn't how I wanted it to be. I wanted to wake up this morning, drive over to Hannah's and tell her we were totally done, then drive straight to Jessie's house.

But my mother had woken me up before the sun rose, reminding me that we had to be in Boston all day. I was meeting with a series of sports agents. My parents had set it up weeks ago. My whole world was about to change, and everyone from coaches to trainers to family friends told my parents to get me an agent before *the NHL draft. I'd agreed to the meetings not knowing the timing would be the worst thing ever. I'd spent the whole day and half the evening in Boston. I'd wanted to text her but my dad wanted me focused, so he took my phone away for the day.*

I decided to sign with a guy from a smaller, New England–based sports agency. My parents seemed pleased and I was just relieved it was over. As much as I wanted to be a professional hockey player, as the dream got closer and closer to becoming a reality, I started to panic. There were so many decisions, so many new people trying to push their way into my life and so many uncertainties. I'd been feeling that panic for a couple of months now, and now my personal life was adding anxiety to the mix.

By the time my dad gave me my phone back, it was dead. And of course Luc, Devin or Cole had removed the charger from the car, probably to use in one of their own vehicles, so it was a long, communication-free drive back to Maine.

As soon as we got home I hijacked the car, drove over to Hannah's and made it clear that our off-again phase was permanent. To say she didn't take it well would be an understatement of epic proportions. She started to cry—the kind of uncontrollable, snot-filled, ugly-cry I'd never seen before. It freaked me right the hell out.

"Hannah... come on..." I had begged and tried to rub her shoulder, but she shrugged me off. "We'll still be friends."

"I don't want to be friends, Jordan!" she cried, her voice heavy with pain. "I thought were going to be together forever."

"Han, we were constantly breaking up."

"And making up! We always make up. And we talked about a future!"

"You talked about a future," I corrected her.

"You didn't stop me!" she wailed, more tears trickling down her cheeks.

"I didn't think things would change like this."

"What? What changed?" She lifted her face to look up at me, and she looked so panicked suddenly it shocked me. "I can fix it. I'll change back to whatever you liked before. Just tell me."

"It's not you," I say. "It's me. I... want something else."

"You just need some time."

"I don't need time," I muttered.

"Don't do this!" Hannah burst into tears again, and her sister Kristi came running in and told me to leave.

I came directly here to see Jessie. I was leaving the next morning with my parents to go to Minnesota for the NHL draft and I wouldn't be back for a week. I had to see Jessie first. I had to make sure she... we were okay. Or more important, I had to ensure there was a "we."

I hear tires rolling up the driveway and glance out the window. Instead of Jessie's crappy old red Honda hatchback parking by the barn, I see Chance Echolls' SUV parking next to my truck.

"What the hell..." I whisper as I watch them get out of the truck. There's a bouquet of Gerber daisies in her hand.

Rose is watching too. She shrugs and simply says, "Maybe they got back together."

I want to vomit. I storm out onto the porch as they walk up. Chance is in the middle of saying something to Jessie when I haul off and punch him.

"Jordan!" Jessie screams, and jumps in front of me, pushing her

flowers into my chest to stop me from reaching down and hitting him again.

"What the hell, Garrison?!" Chance yells.

He gets back on his feet rubbing his jaw and runs his tongue over his bloody lip. He turns to Jessie with accusatory eyes. "You told him what happened between us, didn't you? Why the hell do you tell him everything?"

"I was upset," Jessie yells defensively.

"Get the fuck out of here, Jordan! This has nothing to do with you," Chance barks at me, his blue eyes flared in anger and his dark hair still askew from his fall.

I stare down at Jessie, completely ignoring him. I grab the flowers and shake them. Petals fall to the dirt. "What's this? He gives you flowers and everything is okay?"

Angrily she says, "My stupid car won't start. He was at the rink and he offered me a ride. I called you, but you didn't answer."

I swallow hard and throw the flowers across the driveway. She doesn't seem to care.

"So, you forgave him?" I ask with a thick lump forming in my throat. "You're what, dating him again?"

"What the hell do you care, Garrison? You're dating Hannah," Chance pipes in. I swallow down the urge to deck him again.

"Not anymore," I manage through my anger.

"You broke up with Hannah? Why?" he yells at me. "Is it because Jessie broke up with me? You want my girlfriend! I knew it, you asshole!"

"Asshole?" I turned on him, towering over his five-nine frame. I use my height advantage the way I do on the ice—to intimidate. "You knew I liked her because I fucking told you I did a fucking year ago and you went after her, anyway. You're the fucking asshole!"

He pushes me. Hard. Chance was never a fighter, not on the ice or off. And neither was I, most of the time. But having feelings for Jessie seems to make both us of do crazy things because I shove him and he shoves me back and the next thing I know, we're on the ground throwing punches. And then Rose and Jessie are screaming and pulling us apart with more strength than I realized they had.

Jessie hooks me under my arms, grabs my shirt and drags me across the dirt for almost a foot before I hear the neck of my shirt tear. Rose jumps on Chance's back and wraps her arms and legs around his torso, pinning his arms to his sides.

I pick myself up off the ground, and once again Jessie jumps in between us, facing me as Rose clambers off Chance's back. She sandwiches herself in between us, facing Chance.

"Oh my God, your nose is bleeding!" Rose squeals at Chance, and starts to drag him back into their house.

I feel like I'm drowning in a sea of frustration, embarrassment and anger. I just get into my car and drive away. Jessie calls after me, but I ignore her. I'm so angry and so...I don't even know how to describe it. I've never felt like this. I want to hate her and I want to love her. I'm an effing disaster.

When I get home, my parents are in the basement den watching TV. They call out a greeting but don't come up, which is good. I can feel my face swelling near my eye and I don't want them to see it yet. I need a cover story first.

I head straight to my bedroom. Cole and Luc are sitting on Cole's bed, video game controllers in their hands. Luckily the sound from the Legend of Zelda *coming out of our TV drowns out their voices when they see my face.*

"What the hell, Jordy!" Cole yelps and drops his controller.

Luc's brown eyes get wide and he swears in French.

"Shh! I don't want to deal with Mom and Dad right now," I say, and head toward the laundry hamper, looking for a dirty towel I can use.

"You were in a fight?" Cole asks skeptically. "Were you playing pickup hockey or something?"

I shake my head as I pull a towel out of the bottom of the hamper and raise it to my face, gingerly rubbing off the little bit of blood I can feel crusted to my lip. Luc walks over and grabs the towel from my hand.

"This thing is disgusting," he scolds me. "You're going to get an infection."

He opens the bedroom door and heads out of the room. I drop back onto my bed and put my hands over my face, trying to calm the screwed-up feelings raging through me.

"Who did you fight?"

"Chance Echolls."

"Shut up!" Cole's hazel eyes grow wide and he grins. "He's a little shit. I hope he looks worse than you."

"I think he does."

"Good." Cole grins as Luc walks back into the room with a clean, damp facecloth and another towel wrapped around some ice from our kitchen freezer. "He fought Chance."

Luc's eyes land on me, but he's not nearly as excited about the news as Cole was. "Over Jessie?"

I take the wet facecloth from him and walk over to the full-length mirror behind the closed bedroom door. "Sort of. Yeah."

"Did he start it? Did he find out about you two?" Luc asks as I carefully clean my face.

"You two?" Cole pipes in, completely confused. "As in you and Jessie? As in...like a couple thing?"

"I started the fight. I went over to see Jessie. She was at work. And when she got home, he was with her."

"You didn't talk to her all day? She was a virgin, man," Luc reminds me. "You can't do that and then bail on her."

"She was a virgin? Who, Jessie? And she's not a virgin now?!" Cole interjects, and jumps up from the bed. He puts his hands out, palms up flat begging us to stop. "Wait! Wait! Wait! Who banged her? You or Chance? It was Chance, right?"

"I didn't bail on her, Luc." I shoot an angry look to my best friend. "I was at her house to tell her that. But he was there and he got her flowers. And I freaking lost it."

"No, seriously, who slept with Jessie?!" Cole asks again, his voice rising with frustration.

"Shut up," I snap, and turn back to Luc. "It's all messed up now."

Cole grabs my shoulders. "Jordan, either you answer my questions or I go downstairs and tell Mom about your screwed-up face. And then you *can answer her questions."*

"Cole, don't be a dick," Luc scolds him, giving him a shove so he stumbles back and lands on his bed. Luc turns back to me. "Call her. Talk this out..."

Suddenly there's a tap on the bedroom window. All three of our heads spin toward it. Luc is the closest so he pulls back the green curtains. "She's here," he whispers, and I step forward and see the top of Jessie's head visible in the darkened backyard. "Fuck, she must really like you."

"Speaking of fuck..." Cole starts.

"Shut up," Luc and I command in unison.

Luc unlocks and opens the window. I step forward and lean my whole frame, from my waist up, out the window. "Come here."

She reaches up, grabs my hands and lets me lift her through the window. When her feet reach the window ledge, she puts her arms on my shoulders and I put my hands on her waist and place her softly on the floor in front of me.

The feeling of her waist under my hands and her arms around my neck makes me instantly hot. I take a step back to quell the feelings, but she reaches out and touches the cut on the corner of my mouth.

"Cole, let's go to my room," Luc suggests quietly.

"Hey, Jessie…I was just curious…Did you have sex with my brother?" Cole blurts out, his hazel eyes focuses on Jessie.

Jessie looks stunned. I turn to face my brother, reach out and cuff the side of his head.

"Ow!" he cries. Luc grabs him and yanks him out of the room, closing the door behind them.

Alone, two feet from each other, I stare at her. She looks like she's been crying, and it makes my chest ache. "Are you back together with Chance?"

"Does it matter?" she asks quietly, glancing up to catch my eye.

"Yeah, it matters! I…I want to be with you." I explain. "I broke up with Hannah."

She still isn't looking at me, her head tilted down and her eyes on the floor between us. I can't see her expression. I drop down, sitting on the end of my bed, hoping to put myself in her sight line. I catch a glimpse of her face and she looks sad. So sad. "I texted you today. Three times. You never responded. And when my car wouldn't start, I called you but it went straight to voicemail. I assumed you were blowing me off."

"My phone died. Remember, I was in Boston with my parents meeting agents," I explain.

She blinks as guilt flashes over her pretty face. "I forgot. I'm sorry. How did it go?"

"Fine," I reply curtly. "Jessie, are you with him again?"

"He showed up at the rink with flowers, trying to apologize. I would have ignored him completely if my stupid car had started," she replies, and our eyes finally meet.

Jessie's eyes are the color of moss when she looks at me: dark and serious. I reach out and take her hands in mine. God, I love the feeling of touching her, even when it's something small like this. I can't get over how different it feels from touching her just last week, before we had sex. Before, the heat it caused felt exciting but awkward. Now it feels exciting and unnerving in a new way—a way I like.

"You're going to go high in the draft next week." Jessie tells me something the media and my parents have told me a hundred times this year. "Like in the top five. And the first five teams to draw players are Brooklyn, Ann Arbor, Quebec City, Sacramento and Jacksonville."

"So?" I say, lacing my fingers through hers.

"So, I applied to Florida State, University of Arizona and Nebraska State. They're the only places that offer a full scholarship in kinesiology and sports therapy."

I already know this because I helped her fill out the applications. Being a physical therapist has been Jessie's dream as long as I can remember.

"None of those schools is anywhere near where you'll probably end up next year," Jessie whispers like this hurts to admit. "We're never going to see each other."

I tug on her hands to make her look me in the eye again. "I'm going to be making a lot of money, Jessie. More than I'll need. I can pay for you to go to school wherever I am."

"Jordan, no."

"Yes! I'm going to be freaked out in a new place with no family. I want you with me."

"I can't take your money." She shakes her head and her gorgeous hair tumbles into her face.

I reach up and grab her hips and pull her toward me. When her knees hit the edge of the mattress I keep pulling—pulling her down. She knows what I'm doing and without hesitation she puts a knee on either side of me and lets me guide her into my lap.

My body is roaring with hormones but all I really want to do is hug her, so I do. She wraps her arms tightly around my neck, burying her face in my shoulder.

"I can't use your money, Jordy," she whispers. "I want to be with you, but I can't do that. I won't be that girl. I've watched girls in this town use hockey players to get a free ride my whole life, and I don't want to be that."

I look up at her. "So, you don't want to be with me?"

Her green eyes are gloomy as she rests her forehead against mine. "I want to be with you more than I've ever wanted anything in my life."

"Then who cares how it happens, Jessie?" I ask, and then I do the only thing I really want to do, which is kiss her.

She kisses me back without hesitation. I feel her body relax, and I use my hands at the small of her back to pull her even closer. Her hands go into my hair at the back of my head and she pushes down just a little bit, making the space between her legs rub against my erection. I lean back, taking her with me.

Her lips are so freaking soft and her tongue moves with mine so easily. And now her warm, small body is flat on top of mine, except her legs, which are still bent on either side of my hips, and I put my hands on her ass to push her into me again. She lets out this crazy hot little sigh and I worry I might come in my pants.

Desperate to touch her skin, my hands find their way under her sweatshirt. She rocks again on my lap and moves her hands down my sides and under my shirt. I wrap a hand around her back and flip her so she's on her side beside me on her bed, and I break the kiss to press my lips to that spot just under her earlobe—the spot she liked my lips on last time. As soon as I suck the tender flesh into my mouth, she reaches for the front of my jeans.

"Jordy..." she sighs, popping my button as I do the same to her.

My fingers find their way quicker than hers and before I know it, I'm slipping through her slick folds and pushing a finger into her. She arches her back a little and whispers my name again as her fingers push into my underwear and find the tip of my cock. The gentle contact and the feel of her wetness brings a heat to my balls and stars to my eyes. How can she make me want to come so quickly? It's insane. It's scary.

"We can't. Not now," she says, but her she moves her hand deeper into my underwear and presses me into her palm as she curls her fingers over me.

"I know," I agree, and push another finger into her warm, wet pussy. She squeezes me in return.

My thumb rubs over the area above her opening and she bucks into my hand and gasps so I do it again. With every push of her hips her hand, wrapped around my cock, pulls and pushes, creating an incredible friction. We start to develop a rhythm, and in a few minutes I know I'm going to lose it. And I think she is too because she's wetter and her skin is hotter and she's panting against my neck.

"Jordy…oh god, I'm…"

"Yes. God. Yes. Do it. Please," I beg, and my orgasm starts to crawl through my body, gaining momentum as it rumbles toward its exit. And for the first time in my life I try to fight it, wanting her to have one first.

"I'm…" She presses her open mouth to mine instead of finishing the sentence, and with her tongue in my mouth we both climax.

Her body goes limp on the bed beside me, her mouth falling away from me and resting on her arm. Her other hand stays in my jeans still loosely holding me. I slip my hand out of her underwear and she shudders a little. I wrap it around her back, pull her closer and rest my palm on her perfect ass.

"Jordan, I…"

There's a loud knock on my door and before we can even move, the door swings open.

"Jordy, are you done packing beca—" My mother freezes, her mouth hanging open midsentence.

Jessie and I are frozen. My mother's eyes sweep over Jessie's back, pausing at my hand on the ass of her jeans, and then they sweep up to find my guilty, terrified face. She blinks and steps back out of the room, closing the door behind her.

Jessie, suddenly unfrozen, scurries off the bed, back over toward the window. Worried she's going to climb right back out and break her neck, I grab her by the shoulders. Her hands cover her face.

"Oh God, Jordy, now your mom thinks I'm a whore!"

I laugh, and it comes out higher and louder than my normal laugh because of the fear and adrenaline running through my veins. I try to hug her again but she squirms away, realizes her pants are undone and rushes to do them up.

"She didn't see anything but my hand on your ass, don't worry," I assure her, but I'm worried she may have also seen Jessie's hand in the front of my jeans.

Jessie covers her face with her hands again.

"My mom loves you like a daughter," I quietly assure her. "If anyone is on her shit list for this, it's me."

"I'm so embarrassed," she whispers as there is another knock at the door.

"I'm coming in!" Luc's voice booms, and the door slowly creaks open. His head pokes in, eyes closed and then he opens one eye.

"Just come in, for crying out loud," I grumble.

Luc grins as he steps inside. He looks like he can barely contain his laughter. He opens his mouth to speak, closes it and smiles again, then clears his throat awkwardly and finally talks.

"Donna asked me to drive Jessie home," he explains.

"I'm so embarrassed," she groans again.

"It's fine," Luc assures her like I did. "She's not pissed, I swear. She's just shocked."

Jessie uncovers her face and looks at him hopefully. He nods and reaches out to take her hand, leading her toward the door. "Trust me, I know the difference. She caught Kelsey Stoll in my room last year and she did more than just blush and stutter. She freaking yelled. No stuttering. No blushing. Just rage."

I remember that incident and can't help but smile as he leads Jessie out of the room.

She turns in the doorway and runs back, rocking up on her tiptoes to give me a solid kiss on the mouth. "Good luck in the draft."

I watch her tiny body disappear from sight and then sit on my bed and wait for my mother to appear. I'm not the first kid to get caught in a compromising position in this house. Last summer my father walked in on Devin in the basement den with some girl from the community college straddling his lap in nothing but jeans and a bra.

Even though they grounded him—no TV or video games and no nights out other than hockey practice for two weeks—I think my dad was pretty impressed that he'd scored a college chick. I know I was. And like Luc told Jessie, right before Thanksgiving, my mom caught Kelsey, a girl who went to the Catholic school, sneaking out of Luc's room at three in the morning. He wasn't allowed to borrow the car for two weeks, and no video games.

So, my mom was used to punishing us for this kind of thing, and I had a good idea of what was coming, but still this feels like it might be more severe because it was Jessie. My mom will probably feel the need to protect her honor or something.

There's a knock at the door, and I can see her shadow in the crack, since Jessie and Luc never closed it, but she doesn't come in.

"Oh, so now you wait for me to say enter?" I call out, slightly amused despite the gravity of the situation. "Enter!"

She steps inside, closes the door and leans against, it crossing her arms over her chest. She opens her mouth to speak, but falters when her blue eyes so similar to mine take in my battered face.

"Who hit you?" she demands, and steps closer, reaching out and gingerly touching the scab forming by my lip.

"Chance Echolls. Because I hit him first."

She folds her arms again. "Over Jessie?"

"Yes. Over Jessie."

"Jordan..." She says my name, but nothing else.

"Mom, we're... we want to be together," I say, and I know it sounds so lame, but I hope she doesn't dismiss this—or me—as just being a teenager thing. This feels like the least teenagery thing I've ever said to her.

She doesn't dismiss me at all. She smiles. It's small and she's fighting it, but she smiles. "Okay."

"That's it?"

She kind of shrugs and lets the smile take a little more shape on her face. "Jessie is a wonderful young woman. She's smart, she's kind and she cares about you very much. I'm happy you realize how much you care about her too."

I feel my shoulders relax. I didn't realize I was tensing them so much. But then my mother sighs and her smile disappears.

"I thought this might happen—the two of you—but I didn't think it would happen so soon. I thought maybe in a few years after she finished college, and when you were more mature and ready for a real relationship."

"I'm ready now," I declare.

She doesn't even try to hide the fact that she doesn't believe me. I feel a ripple of frustration run through me. "I'm about to go off to live in a different city, away from you and Dad, and start a career—not a job. A career."

"Does Hannah know about this?" my mother asks. "Because she's been calling the house phone all night. She said you weren't answering your cell and she needed to talk to you."

"I ended it with Hannah. She didn't take it well," I admit.

"Jordan, she thought you were committed to her," my mother reminds me. "You must have broken her heart."

I feel more frustration. "What was I supposed to do? Stay with her even though I like Jessie?"

"Of course not. I just feel bad for the poor girl." My mother walks toward the bedroom door. "I'm going to get you some ice. The draft is televised, you know. Probably best if you don't look so rough."

She leaves and as I wait for her return, I think about my conversation with Jessie. Basically I just invited her to move away with me. And she looked like she was ready to do it. I'm both terrified and excited by that. I know I love her, but everything is suddenly moving so fast. The look on my mother's face—like she thinks this is a mistake—isn't helping my sudden anxiety either. When she comes back with a bag of frozen peas for my face, I tell her again how much I love Jessie.

"Breaking up with Hannah was the adult thing to do, Mom," I say firmly, and turn to look her in the eye so she knows I'm serious. "I wasn't as serious about Hannah as I am about Jessie."

She pauses, looking at me like a slow kid who has trouble tying his shoelaces or something. I start to feel frustrated again but she gives my shoulder a squeeze, as if to calm me down.

"Something tells me there was a time when I could have caught you and Hannah in the same compromising position I caught you and Jessie in." Her expression is stern and before I can lie and say no, she continues. "I have accepted that my sons are not waiting for marriage. That's the way life works nowadays, but I will not look the other way if I think you're not respecting these girls. Or if I think you're only interested in them for…one thing. Do you understand, Jordan?"

I swallow back any flippant comment I might consider making and just nod. "It's not just about…that. I swear."

She stares at me for a minute and I fight the urge to look away. This is so freaking uncomfortable, but I know that the adult thing to do is to not squirm or look away. If this is what it takes to make her think that I am an adult, then I can do it. I think it works because she nods at me and gives me a small smile.

"So, what's my punishment?" I ask as I lie back on my bed, holding the peas to my face.

She shakes her head and a strand of her light hair falls out of the low ponytail she's sporting. "No punishment."

"What?"

"Are you in love with Jessie?" she asks simply.

I nod without hesitation.

"I won't punish you for love, but you will never do that again in this house. Understand? And wherever that does happen, you better be using protection."

"Oh my God. Mom!" I shift the peas so they cover more of my face as my cheeks start turning pink.

"This may be an adult relationship with Jessie, but neither of you is mature enough for a child," she says frankly and seriously. "So, promise me. Protection."

"God, Mom!"

"Promise me, Jordan."

"Yes. Of course! Man. Fine. I promise! Now stop talking about it."

I hear her laugh as she walks out of the room.

Chapter 7

Jessie

I stare at myself in the full-length mirror behind my old bedroom door. I'm fairly certain I look okay for a funeral. I decided on a pair of charcoal gray pants and a pretty, crocheted cardigan in the same color. Under it, I opted for a pale pink tank with lacey straps and edges. Grandma Lily loved pink. And although we had our issues when she was alive, she would have liked the pink, so I decided to give her this one last thing.

I have the faintest trace of dark circles under my eyes, but luckily makeup has made them all but invisible. I barely slept last night. I couldn't stop reliving the memories of our night together in this room. Finally, after hours, I resorted to an old trick I've relied on to pull my brain away from romantic memories and back to reality. I grabbed my phone, pulled up Google Images and punched in Jordan Garrison. The screen filled with his face, which you think would be even more painful, but it wasn't. Ninety percent of the photos weren't of him on the ice or in his uniform looking like a sexy, strong, rich and professional athlete. Most of the photos were of Jordan Garrison, the professional manwhore. Cell phone pictures of him people have given or sold to hockey blogs. Jordan in nightclubs, after games, grinding random skanks on dance floors, sticking his tongue down girls' throats on VIP room couches, walking in and out of hotels on road trips with different blondes, brunettes and redheads. There's paparazzi shots of him celebrating after he won the Stanley Cup with the Royales three years ago. He's helping some girl with big boobs and a low-cut shirt drink out of the Cup, beer slopping everywhere. My favorites are the shots of him licking off the beer that dribbled onto her cleavage. Those hurt the most because we used to talk about what he'd do if he won the Stanley Cup—every hockey players' dream—and his answer had been the same since he was twelve. *"I want to drink champagne out of the Cup with my family—and you. Promise you'll be there to celebrate with me, Jessie."* So yeah, that picture always managed to pull me back to reality and allow me to turn my brain off and sleep rather than wallow in unrequited love for a boy who simply didn't exist anymore.

I head downstairs to where Callie and Rose are waiting for me in the kitchen. Callie is in a plain, short but acceptable black cotton shirtdress with the sleeves rolled up, no nylons, black cowboy boots and a black-cropped leather jacket. Rose is in simple black pants and a dark green blouse with a thick black belt cinching her petite waist. I feel plain compared to them, which shouldn't matter—it's a damn funeral. My sisters, even on a somber day, shine. This feeling is nothing new. I grew up feeling that they outshined me. In a way, I was glad for it. It meant I'd done my job, the job no one else in our lives did, and protected them, keeping that brilliant glow from being tarnished.

As I pour a cup of coffee and stir sugar and milk into it, I realize Rose is intently watching my every move. I give her a suspicious glance.

"What?"

"What? What?" she asks, her coal-colored eyes wide with fake innocence.

"How was Last Call?" I ask because I didn't hear them come home.

"It was good," Rose begins, but she's suddenly looking everywhere but at me. "Cole says hi. He's going to be there today."

"That's nice of him," I reply, watching her fidget with her belt. "Who else from the old gang was there?"

"I hung out with Mandie most of the night," Callie blurts out rather aggressively, like she's trying to make sure Rose doesn't answer before her. "She's got a kid now, did you know that? No husband, just a kid. Some dude from Lewiston knocked her up."

"Oh." I sip my coffee. Rose is still fidgeting. "Rose, is something wrong?"

Callie turns to our younger sister. Her thick chestnut hair acts as a shield, so I can't see what she mouths to Rose.

"I just...I want to get to the church and get this over with," she confesses, and I see an anxious look in her eyes, like she used to get before recitals when she played the flute in high school.

"We should get going," Callie agrees, and I nod.

It's a ten-minute drive to the church, and the cab of the truck is filled with a weird, thick silence that I don't think is completely due to our dead grandmother. But I can't figure out what in the world is wrong.

When we pull into the church parking lot, I notice Donna and

Wyatt's other truck—the one they didn't lend us—is already there along with a few others.

Callie parks and I notice the door to the Garrison truck is open. I can see a foot dangling out. It's not wearing a shoe but a boot, like an air cast type of boot…And for a quick, insane second, I think: How did Wyatt break his foot? But as I think that, I see Wyatt standing by the church doors next to Donna, looking dapper in a dark blue suit. I stop breathing and my mouth goes dry.

"Who…? Who is that?"

And then the truck is an explosion of voices.

"He came down for the funeral."

"I told him you didn't want him here."

"He was at the bar last night looking for you."

"He's an asshole!"

"He *was* an asshole."

"He still is, Rose!"

My sisters' words assault my brain and I blink, gripping the door handle so tightly I think I might break my fingers. Despite their words and what I know in my heart, I start begging the universe that it's Cole or Devin or please, dear God, Luc getting out of that truck.

But then he's standing there—in full view—slamming the door shut with one hand and doing up his sport coat with the other. He's got a black wool beanie on his head, blond hair escaping in random wisps in every direction. He moves to turn toward the church, but his light blue eyes land on the truck we're sitting in—the truck he probably bought his parents. Those eyes find me through the windshield.

He looks so overwhelmingly the same, and yet he's completely unfamiliar at the same time. It's what I imagine having amnesia feels like—he looks so much like someone I should know and love, but I have no idea who he is anymore. The only thing that I do know, with complete certainty, is that he is still so gorgeous, looking at him makes it hard for me to breathe. Bastard.

"Jessie, please say something," Rose begs.

"I'm going to ask him to leave." Callie opens the driver's-side door.

I reach out and grab her hand. "Don't."

Both Rose and Callie stare at me.

"It's fine. I'm fine." I promise them this in a voice that doesn't even attempt to cover up the fact that I am anything but fine. "If he wants to be here, that's fine. It changes nothing. Let's just…let's just…go inside."

I open the passenger door and step out. I adjust my purse on my arm and toss on my sunglasses, then walk in a straight, swift line directly into the church. I don't stop for him or anyone. My heart is hammering so loudly in my chest it's blocking out all other sound.

The service is brief and simple. There are only about thirty people in attendance. Lily was only in Silver Bay for a few months a year, so she didn't have a lot of close friends here anymore. None of us speaks, we just let the pastor do his thing—talking about life and death and loss and heaven.

My eyes well up so quickly and unexpectedly, I'm startled. Lily Grace Caplan is gone. She hasn't been a significant part of our lives in years. I'm not sure she ever was, to be honest. And we haven't legally required a guardian in years either but somehow, as I stare at the coffin, I feel a dark, lonely cloud cover me. It's the same dark, lonely cloud the enveloped me when my mother died—because we're alone. Again.

The pastor finishes, everyone stands and I wipe away my eyes before anyone notices. I almost wished we'd had hymns and eulogies, or even communion. Anything that would make the service last longer. Now that it's all over, he will talk to me. I know it and I wish more than anything it won't happen. But, at the same time, a part of me really wants it to happen.

What the fuck is wrong with me?

Callie and Rose grab each of my hands as people wander over to our pew at the front to offer condolences and hugs. Eventually, Donna and Wyatt come into view. Donna hugs all of us, as does Wyatt, and then she smiles. "Devin and Ashleigh send their love. And Luc said to give you all big hugs. Their hockey schedules didn't allow for them to come back, but they all wish they were here."

"Luc called me this morning," Rose adds, and smiles. "He's been calling me a lot since he found out."

I smile at that news. It's good to know our childhood friends are still here for us, even if it can only be in spirit.

"Where's Jordan?" Callie asks, barely keeping the venom from her voice.

"He stepped outside after the service," Donna says. It seems she can barely keep the disappointment from her voice. "To get some air."

Of course he went outside instead of facing me. Coward.

Everyone makes their way out. My sisters and I need to get back to our house to host the meager, but obligatory, wake. Outside, what started as an overcast morning has turned into a sunny afternoon. I squint into the daylight and step out into the parking lot.

My eyes find him instinctively. Old habits never die. Jordan is sitting in the front seat of his parents' truck, directly in the middle, like a little kid would. He catches my eye when I step outside and straightens up a little. I stare back at him but don't show any reaction. I offer no smile or frown. I basically try to look like I'm looking right through him; like I'm not noticing the sadness in his pretty blue eyes or the way his full bottom lip is sticking out more than it should.

Callie hooks her arm through mine and guides me to the other truck. "I can punch him again if you'd like."

I smile. "Thanks for the offer. I'll keep it in mind."

Back at the house, the scene is subdued, as expected. Only about fifteen people show up, most of whom are our good friends rather than Lily's. People like Callie's high school friend Mandie; Cole and his girlfriend, Leah; and Rose's high school best friend, Kate, and her brother, Bruce.

Donna and Wyatt show up and join the crowd in the living room. Everyone is munching on the sandwiches, fruit and veggie platters we've laid out. Jordan doesn't seem to be with them.

Fucking coward.

"I'm going to go start the coffee and get out the dessert tray," I tell Callie, and then get up from where I was perched on the arm of Rosie's chair.

"Jessie, honey, can you also grab the Bundt cake I left in my truck?" Donna calls out to me. "It should be on the seat."

I nod and smile graciously. Leaving the living room, I head into the kitchen, flip on the coffeemaker and head out onto the porch, making my way to the driveway.

Jordan is leaning against his parents' old truck. He's just standing there in his stupid knitted hat with his stupid broken foot and his dumb sad eyes. He came all this way and he can't do anything more than stand there like he's Krazy-Glued to a Ford? Suddenly I hate him more than I ever have before.

Without a word, I storm over to the passenger-side door—the opposite side from where he is—and open it. I see the cake and pull it carefully off the seat. When I turn around he's standing directly in front of me, blocking the way back into the house.

I stare up at him as a flood of emotions roars through my body like a tsunami. I want to cry, punch him, scream and even laugh at the universe's one-two punch to my gut. The sun is behind him, making the tips of his flippy blond hair glow. He needs a haircut. He looks like a Muppet.

"Hey."

Hey? His big opening line after taking my virginity, breaking my heart and disappearing from my life for more than half a decade is "Hey?"

I think this, but I don't say a single word.

He clears his throat. "I'm sorry about Lily."

"Thank you." I sidestep him but he moves with me.

"Let me carry that for you," he offers, extending his long arms and big hands toward the cake.

"I have a dead grandmother, not broken arms," I snap, pulling the cake closer to my body as I glare at him. "I can carry a stupid cake."

He takes it out of my hands anyway. Asshole. I roll my eyes and storm back to the house. He hobbles behind me. Unfortunately, one of his strides is like two and a half of mine so although I am moving faster than him, he's still right behind me when we get to the porch.

"Jessie," he says as I reach for the door. "Can I talk to you for a second?"

I close my eyes, sigh and then turn to face him, crossing my arms over my chest as if to hide the scars on my heart…or protect it from new ones.

"I just wanted to say—" He moistens his lips and waits until I look up and meet his eye. "I wanted to tell you I'm sorry for what happened. You know, when we were younger."

He's sorry it happened. Jordan Garrison is sorry he took my virginity. Bitchin'. Now my day is complete.

"I'm sorry you're sorry," I reply coolly.

"What?" His blond eyebrows pinch together.

Rudely, I ask "Are you done talking?" and reach for the door again. "I have a roomful of people who care about me and my sisters inside. I haven't seen them in years and will most likely never see them again. So, if you'll excuse me…"

I swing the screen door open and slip inside, not waiting for him and the damn cake to follow. Cole and Leah and my sisters are in the kitchen. Callie is pouring coffee into mugs. She looks up and scowls as Jordan sticks his booted foot in the door to keep it from closing in his face. He enters the kitchen behind me.

"I thought you left," Callie says flatly. "Doesn't Seattle need you back?"

"I'm not ready to play yet," he mumbles, motioning toward the boot on his foot as he places the cake on the kitchen table.

"Yeah, well, if you stick around here you might have a few more broken bones by the time you head back," Callie mutters this coldly, and I place a soothing hand on her shoulder, giving it a squeeze.

Her brown eyes are angry but she shuts up. I fling open a drawer and turn to hand Jordan a knife. "Make yourself useful and cut the cake."

"Remember when you two were best friends?" Cole blurts out with a big, dopey smile across his freckled face. If looks could kill, Jordan and I would be arrested for murder, and they'd be scraping Cole Garrison off the walls of this kitchen for weeks.

"Cole, baby. Shut up," Leah says softly, in the same friendly voice she's always had. She was one of my best friends in high school and has been dating Cole since our senior year.

Donna waltzes in with a pile of dirty plates.

"Oh good, you found the cake!" she exclaims, either not noticing the tension in the room or purposely ignoring it. "Cole, don't just stand there. Help me with the dishes."

Jordan turns his attention to the cake he's cutting. Callie leaves the room with a tray full of coffee mugs, and Rose and Leah busy themselves getting plates for the cake.

"I'm not feeling very well," I announce quietly, and all the commotion in the kitchen stills again. "I'm sorry, but I need to go upstairs and lie down."

"Okay. If you have to. Callie and I can handle everything," Rose says hesitantly as she gives me a light hug.

I hug Leah, Cole and Donna and then turn and head into the living room and up the stairs. I throw myself down on my bed and will back the tears. He doesn't deserve them. He doesn't. I just want to sleep. Sleep until this whole stupid wake is over. Sleep until he's gone.

And then I want to leave this town and never ever come back.

Chapter 8

Jordan

It's almost five in the evening. The fall sun is sinking from the sky and the room is in shadows. The people have all gone home, including my parents. About a half hour ago Cole convinced Rose and Callie to go to the bar with him. It wasn't easy. Callie would much rather have stayed here and stabbed me with a fork, but somehow Cole convinced her to just leave me alone here to wait for Jessie.

It's weird being alone in their house. Well, alone with Jessie, who is still upstairs in her room. I haven't been inside this house since before I was drafted. Everything looks exactly the same but it feels different. It feels uninviting and uncomfortable, so I grab a beer from the fridge to take the edge off.

I thought I would be halfway back to Seattle by now. My plan was to head straight to the airport as soon as my parents were ready to leave the wake and jump on the first plane to Boston. I already knew I couldn't get back to Seattle before tomorrow, but I figured I would grab a hotel in Boston, drink a few at a local bar, find a girl who knew hockey, knew who I was and was impressed enough to spread her legs, and then fuck this uncomfortable visit out of my head forever. But then I'd turned around in that church parking lot and my eyes locked with hers and all the anger, betrayal and frustration that's consumed me was replaced by one thought: God, she's beautiful.

It's the first thing I used to think of every time I saw her every day of my teenage life, but I was shocked to find out that it was stronger than ever. She'd stared back at me with a look of confusion and shock, and as she got out of the car and walked closer, I could also see a glimmer of curiosity. She was searching my face for something the same way I knew I was searching hers...

She looked exactly the same as she did in high school. Same moss-green eyes, same lithe build, same pouty mouth, freckleless skin and long wavy auburn hair. It threw me for a loop because, although I didn't expect her to look incredibly different, I didn't expect her to look *exactly* the same—or for her looks to make me feel the same as I did in high school. But they did.

I'd kept my eyes fixed on her through the funeral service. It was impossible to pull them away, and the more I watched her the stronger the realization became—she didn't just look like the same as the girl I fell in love with, she *was* the same. She still twisted her delicate fingers when she was anxious. She still tucked her hair behind her left ear as a nervous habit. I knew before she did it that she would cup the back of Rose's head and smooth her hair in a gesture of comfort. And I knew she would hold Callie's hand and not let go even as Callie tried to pull away. She was always more concerned about her sisters' feelings than her own. I watched as she absently caught a tear with the back of her hand before it fell and I knew, without a doubt, her tears weren't over losing the relationship she'd had with her grandmother but over the loss of the possibility of ever having one. I knew this because I knew her. This Jessie was still my Jessie, inside and out.

I had told myself the girl who left me and ran off to Arizona wasn't the same girl who I thought I wanted to spend my life with, but after seeing her again, I was beginning to think I might be wrong. So I needed to talk to her—and do it much more meaningfully than that awkward encounter in the driveway.

I'm halfway through my beer when I hear her small feet on the stairs. For someone only five feet six inches and probably about one hundred and ten pounds, she walks like an elephant. Always has. The familiar heavy thumping almost makes me smile.

When she comes into the kitchen I notice she's changed into a pair of faded and torn hip-hugging jeans and a light blue, V-neck T-shirt with a tiny logo on the right breast that I can't read in the dim light. Her long hair is pulled back in a ponytail and what little makeup she had on for the funeral is gone. She's still the most beautiful girl I've ever seen. Everything about her, even when she was staring at me like she was willing me to drop dead earlier this afternoon, lights something deep inside me like it did when we were kids.

When she realizes I'm sitting there, on the counter, she jumps.

"I thought everyone left." Jessie gasps.

"They did. I stuck around."

Her surprise morphs to irritation as soon as she calms down. "Why?"

"Wanted to make sure you were okay," I say honestly.

"You're about six years too late with that," she responds sharply, and walks over to the fridge.

She pulls a beer out of the fridge, turns to face me again, twisting the top off with more force that necessary. As she takes a long sip, her eyes travel from my head to the countertop I am sitting on and then back to my head.

"We have chairs," she states, gently kicking one away from the kitchen table toward me.

"I'm partial to the counter." I shrug, and for a millisecond she freezes as she realizes I'm talking about exactly what she thinks I'm talking about.

She sips her beer again, so I sip mine. My eyes don't leave hers and hers don't leave mine. I'd give her an entire year's salary if it would get her to tell me what she's thinking.

"You should go, Jordan," she says coldly.

"When are you going?" I counter with my own question. "You know, leaving the Bay?"

She glares at me in silence for a long moment. Even when she's this hostile, she's the most beautiful woman I've ever seen.

"We have to meet the lawyer and deal with her will and then decide what to do with the house." She sighs, and I can see for the first time a little bit of sadness in her face. I know it's mostly sadness at losing her last living, known relative, but I hope some of that is for me too. Not that I want to make her sad, but…knowing she still has feelings other than anger for me would be a blessing. "I don't know how long all of it will take. I'm hoping less than a week."

"And where are you going after that?"

"Home," she replies, and her perfect, plump lips flatten into a hard line.

"And where is home? Are you still in Arizona?"

She lets out a frustrated gust of air and rolls her eyes. "Look, Jordan, you're an asshole. All the small talk in the world is not going to change that."

"I *was* an asshole," I agree freely. I pull off my hat and run a hand through my hair, knowing it's probably all over the damn place. I should have gotten a haircut before I came here. "I want to not be an asshole anymore. That's why I'm here. I regret what I did. I have since the moment it happened."

"Yeah, you said that," Jessie snaps, tugging her long hair out of the ponytail it had been in. "Well, if it makes you feel any better, I regret it too."

I smile with relief. "You regret leaving me."

"No," she snaps quickly with a look on her face like I'm insane. "I don't regret that part. That's the smartest thing I ever did."

She finishes her beer and walks closer to toss the bottle in the recycling bin by the door. I can finally read her T-shirt: Sea-Tac Sports Therapy.

I cock my head and my eyebrows pull together. "Sea-Tac?"

She glances down at the logo on her shirt and back up at me, her hand rising and covering the words as she turns away. Sea-Tac? That's what they call the Seattle-Tacoma area. Why is she wearing a shirt from a sports therapy place in my…

"Would you just go already?" Jessie demands, her eyes narrowed on me in anger. "You said your piece. You're sorry Lily's dead. You regret sleeping with me. Thanks for coming all this way to tell me that. Now go."

"Wait! What?" I try not to let my mouth hang open with my shock at her crazy rant. "Are you insane? Why do you think I regret sleeping with you?!"

"You said you regret what happened!" She bellows.

"I didn't mean I regret slee—" A knock at the door stops me mid-yell.

She storms toward it and flings it open. I have the distinct feeling she's thrilled there's an interruption. She'd probably let a serial killer in if it meant I would go away. I see a shadow walk in and sweep her into a hug.

"What the hell..." she whispers, and wiggles out of the embrace.

"I came as soon as I found out."

I lean over the sink and reach out to flip the light switch at the other end of the counter. The room fills with light and I can see the guest clearly. And he sees me.

"What the hell are you doing here, Echolls?" I ask gruffly.

I've run into Chance Echolls through the years because, although he didn't make the NHL like I did, he got a broadcasting degree and works for NBC covering games. But I had no idea Jessie had stayed in touch with him, and the revelation makes me nauseous.

"Jessie and I became friends again a few years ago," Chance says, an irritated edge to his voice. "I thought I would come support her. That's what friends do, right?"

Jessie steps away from Chance and shakes her head, a bitter smile on her lips. "If I didn't know better I would think this is some kind of practical joke."

I kind of have to agree with her there.

"I know I missed the funeral. I couldn't get here any sooner,"

Chance explains, adjusting the brim on his hat. "I had to cover a game last night. And I have to head to New York tomorrow night to cover a game between Brooklyn and Phoenix, but I wanted to come and see you in person. See if you're okay."

She shakes her head. "I'm fine. You shouldn't have come."

"You know, you could have told me you were dating him," Chance says quietly, and glances at me. "No need to keep secrets."

"You think I'm with him?" Jessie says it like Chance just suggested she was dating a prison inmate or something. "Why the hell would you think I would be dating *him*?!"

Chance looks confused and his icy eyes dart to me again. "Well, I mean, he's been after you since we were together and I kind of assumed, when you said you were moving to Seattle, he would try something."

If a two-headed alien marched into the room and bitch-slapped me across the face, I would have been less shocked than I am by what Chance Echolls just said.

"Seattle?" I repeat, and turn to stare at her. And suddenly I know why she's wearing a Sea-Tac Sports Therapy shirt. It's a facility in Seattle not far from our arena. And she has a kinesiology degree. She must be working there. "How long have we lived in the same city, Jessie?!"

"You didn't know, Garrison?" Chance smiles and I ball my fists at my sides to keep from punching him. "Jessica didn't tell you? Wow. She really does hates you."

Jessie and I stare at each other. She says nothing to combat Echolls' assumption. Why would she? She does hate me. I jump off the counter and a sharp short pain shoots up my leg. I wince but ignore it and storm past Chance, swinging the door open and turning to face her one last time.

"I'll talk to you later."

I'm reeling as I jump in my truck and pull out of her driveway.

She lives in Seattle. Who else knew that? Did my parents know? Did Luc? Cole? Devin?

Yeah, I know made a complete mess of everything when I was a kid, but so did she. So why did my family always seem to rush to protect her? Everyone seemed to think that I owed it to Jessie to come here, but they didn't owe it to me to tell me we were living in the same damn city?

Screw them all.

Chapter 9

Jessie

Six years earlier

I listen to Leah Talbot and Phoebe Horvath's conversation and smile to myself as I carefully pour hot water over the powdered hot chocolate mixture in the four Styrofoam cups in front of me.

"He hasn't asked me out on an official date. Not yet anyway," Phoebe is saying.

"He will. Cole told me he's interested," Leah says, and even with my back turned, I can hear Phoebe sigh in relief.

I turn and place two of the steaming cups on the counter in front of them.

"Thanks!" Leah grins, taking the steaming cup from the counter and brushing her platinum bangs from her face with her mitten-covered other hand.

I turn to gingerly lift the next two cups of hot chocolate off the back counter—the cups the girls purchased for Cole and Luc, who are on the ice with the peewee hockey team right now, teaching them drills. When I turn back around, both my sisters are standing with Leah and Phoebe.

They're both grinning like maniacs.

"What?" I ask as I carefully place the hot chocolates on the counter.

"You have mail," Callie says in a high-pitched, excited voice I have never heard her use before.

"What?"

Rosie jumps up and down excitedly, her big dark eyes suddenly brimming with tears. "It's big! And it says congratulations on the front!"

Callie pulls a large white envelope from her crazy tie-dyed crocheted purse and places it on the counter next to the hot chocolates. I look down at it. Just like Rosie squealed, it has the word Congratulations! in red ink diagonally just above my address. The return address is the University of Arizona.

"I got in," I murmur, and start to smile.

"YOU GOT IN!" Callie yells, then reaches across the counter to yank me into a hug. One of the hot chocolates starts to teeter. Leah reaches out and grabs it before it can do more than leave a wet brown drop on the counter.

"Congrats, Jessie!" Leah smiles brightly.

"Jess, that's awesome!" Phoebe says with a giant smile that might be fake. I happen to know Phoebe didn't apply anywhere because her family can't afford for her to go to college, and she doesn't have the grades for a scholarship.

"Your first choice!" Callie goes on, squeezing me so hard it hurts. I push her off me gently and pick up the envelope.

I meet her happy gaze and Rose's overjoyed one with a calm eye. "I got in, but it doesn't mean I got the scholarship."

I tear open the envelope and pull out the letter. I skim the words so quickly my brain can't absorb all of it, but I catch the important words: accepted; Kinesiology & Sports Therapy—Full Scholarship. There's also information about campus jobs and summer sessions if I want to start classes early.

"So?" Callie yanks the papers from my hand. She reads it and screams.

Rose bursts into happy tears the way I would have expected her to. This is a dream come true—a dream that was such a long shot I didn't dare dream it. I should be ecstatic, and I would have been… before Jordan.

"Everyone calm down," I insist, but I'm smiling. It might not be my dream now, but it was my dream very recently, and I achieved it. I let myself revel in that feeling of pride and accomplishment.

"This is so awesome! You're getting out of this craptastic town and you don't need a fucking hockey player to do it!" Callie claps, and then her grin falters for a second. "I mean you have one, but you don't need him."

Phoebe gives Callie a cool stare and then turns her brown eyes to me with a warmer, more inquisitive look. "A hockey player? I thought you and Chance broke up."

"We did." I nod and then freeze. I haven't told anyone except my sisters about Jordan and me. And before I can even decide if I should tell anyone, Rose does it for me.

"She's with Jordy now. Finally," Rosie says dreamily like she's talking about some star-crossed couple on the latest teen angst TV show.

"Jessie, you should be more excited!" Callie tells me sternly, waving the Arizona papers at me. "If you're worried about leaving Rose and me, don't be. I'll be fine. I'll make sure she's fine."

"She means I *will make sure* she's *fine," Rosie interjects, grinning. Callie ignores her, those big brown eyes still piercing into me.*

"Arizona is your dream school," Callie reminds me.

"It was only because it has a good program and a great scholarship..." I shrug and take the package and place it under the counter on top of my jacket. "But I...I'm thinking I might wait and start in the winter semester. At a different school."

"Why the hell would you do that? What other school?" Callie demands, anchoring her tiny hands on her curvy hips.

"Jordan?" Phoebe repeats, and then I see something weird cross her face. "Jordan Garrison?"

I nod and glance at her pretty if overpainted face. She looks confused. I move my eyes to Leah. Her ever-present smile suddenly disappears. The lack of it makes her usually wide, bright eyes look panicked instead of happy.

"Jordan Garrison. Cole's brother Jordan?" Leah says.

Callie ignores the girls and stares at me imploringly. "What school are you going to go to if not Arizona? And you applied for fall everywhere. If you delay, you'll lose the scholarship."

I suddenly feel uneasy with Phoebe and Leah both staring at me. The uncomfortable looks on their faces makes me think they know something I don't—and that it isn't good.

"Jordan is dating Hannah," Phoebe says matter-of-factly.

"He broke up with Hannah," I say firmly but quietly, because I really don't want to talk about it.

"Umm...when? Because I just saw her yesterday and she didn't mention it," Phoebe says. I turn and stare at her and she goes on. "Considering she acted like she was going to marry him, you think she would be upset or something."

I've talked to Jordan twice since he left for Minnesota two days ago for the NHL draft. Both times he sounded tired and very nervous.

He said the draft, which is a weeklong event filled with hockey scrimmages, fitness tests, press events and agent lunches, was way more intense than he thought it would be. He was overwhelmed. He missed me. He admitted he was lonely and although he didn't admit it, I knew he was scared.

He couldn't wait until his parents, Devin, Luc and Cole flew out to join him for the actual draft. He wished I could fly out too, but there was no way I could afford a plane ticket. We talked more about the future. He'd all but convinced me to go with him to whatever city drafted him and let him pay for school. I hadn't told him I would do it for sure, but when I lay awake at night trying to think of life somewhere he wasn't, I didn't like it one bit.

Never once did he mention Hannah, and he told me to my face before he left that he broke up with her. Jordan has never lied to me, and I believe in my heart he isn't doing it now. Phoebe must just be confused, or Hannah isn't telling anyone yet.

"Well, he broke up with her," I say more firmly this time.

Phoebe and Leah exchange glances but both say nothing. Then suddenly Luc and Cole are there. Luc starts to say something but sees Rose's teary face and his cocky smile drops. He pulls her into a hug. "What's wrong? Are you okay? Did something happen?"

Callie laughs and rolls her eyes at his overprotectiveness. "She's fine!"

Luc puts his big hands on my sister's little shoulders and pulls her off his chest to look into her face again. He seems skeptical. "Rose?"

Her face flushes a delightful pink and she lowers her coal-colored eyes. "These are happy tears. Jessie got into Arizona!"

Luc sighs in relief and looks up at me, his cocky grin back in full force. "Way to go, smartypants. So next time I get injured, you can fix me up?"

"Please, you're unfixable," Rose interjects, batting her long dark eyelashes and giving him a playful shove. He laughs at her and messes up her hair.

Callie and I exchange glances. When did Rose learn to flirt?

"Congrats! But Arizona is pretty far away," Cole says as he leans across the counter to hug me. "And it's a Garrison-free zone. Why would you want to live in a Garrison-free zone?"

"I don't," I admit, and then grin.

"Jordan will be happy to hear that," Luc says with a smile and a wink.

"Jessie!" Callie looks genuinely upset.

I ignore her and hand the boys their hot chocolates before shooing them all away. "Can you all wait for me outside while I close up?"

"Yeah. No worries." Luc nods and wraps an arm around Phoebe. It makes Rose's bright eyes darken. "Let's go to Bill's Pizza and celebrate!"

I nod and watch them go. Callie stays behind for a second, giving me her classic Callie death stare, until Rosie grabs her arm and drags her away. As soon as they're all out of sight, I climb onto the counter, grab the latch and roll down the metal gate that closes up the front of the concession stand.

Inside, alone, I dig my phone out of my jacket. I know Jordan's probably busy and has his phone turned off but I decide to text him anyway.

"I got into AZ. Full scholarship. Go me!" I type and add, "I miss you."

I finish locking up and as I'm shrugging into my jacket, my phone buzzes.

"Proud of you! Check your email ASAP, ok?"

My heart flip-flops. Check my email? Is that good or bad? Is he going to tell me Phoebe is right? He went back to Hannah? Did he change his mind and he doesn't want me to go with him next year? I'm suddenly so worried I'm teetering on the edge of a panic attack. I'm just so used to everything going wrong in my life.

I jog through the darkened, empty arena and wave a good-bye to Mr. Milner, the janitor, before joining my friends in the parking lot. It's a dark, cool June night in Silver Bay. The threat of rain hangs low in dark ominous clouds that cover half of the crescent moon. The group is gathered around Luc's pickup and my old Honda Civic hatchback. Still fumbling with my phone, I toss Callie the keys.

"Practice?" I ask, and she looks stunned. She has her permit but I haven't let her drive much. Mostly because when she does, she scares the crap out of me.

"Really?"

"Well, no matter what, I won't be here next year. You're going to have to get your license," I tell her. Rose gets into the backseat and I slide into the passenger seat while Callie jumps behind the wheel. Leah and Phoebe wedge themselves in between Luc and Cole in the cab of the Luc's pickup.

"Remember, the tires suck and the brakes scream if you stop too hard," I warn her, pulling up my email on my phone.

"You have to go to Arizona, Jessie," Callie says as she makes her way toward the parking lot exit, faster that I would have liked. "This is your dream."

"I'm going to be a physical therapist," I promise her. "I'm just thinking about going to another school, which isn't a big deal. Arizona wasn't my dream. It was just a school with a free ride."

"Which you got! Which you need!" Callie cries. "And you can even start in the summer! You could be out of this craptastic town right away! Besides, where else would you go?"

"I don't know yet..." I see his email, open it and hold my breath. Please don't let me down, Jordy...

J,

My agent came here for the draft. I guess that's what agents do. Anyway, I told him about you. About us. I had him get this info for you. Attached is stuff on the best sports therapy programs at schools in Jacksonville, Quebec City, Ann Arbor, New York and Sacramento. I'll likely be in one of these places and so I'm hoping you will be too. Please say yes. I promise you won't regret it!

Love you, J.

"Callie!" Rosie screams, and I look up to see my sister cutting a sharp turn in front of oncoming traffic. Our tires screech and the other driver slams on the horn.

"He had the right of way!" I holler at her.

"Relax. We didn't hit him. I know what I'm doing." Callie glances at me and her eyes land on the phone in my hands. "What are you reading?"

"An email from Jordan." My smile is so big it hurts my face.

"I love that you two are together." Rosie sighs dramatically from the backseat.

"Stop flirting with Big Bird and tell me where you think you're going to go to school if not Arizona," Callie demands.

"Well, I'm going to go over the curriculum at schools in Quebec City, Sacramento, New York and maybe—"

"No." Callie cuts me off, her voice deep and grave. She slams on the brakes, causing Luc to slam on his brakes behind us, swerving to avoid rear-ending us.

"Oh my God, Callie, you suck at driving!" Rose wails. "You're going to kill me next year."

Callie ignores her, staring straight at me with a look of disappointment she's never directed at me before. "You're following him."

"I'm thinking about studying at a school near him," I explain slowly, like what I'm saying is incredibly different from what she's saying. Well, it is. In my heart, it truly is.

"You're going with Jordan?" Rosie presses, her voice excited. "Oh, Jessie, that's so romantic!"

I glance into the backseat and see the look of pure support and happiness on my littlest sister's face; it causes a surge of happiness in my own. I smile. Callie glares at me.

"Don't do this. Don't rely on a guy," Callie hisses. "Don't be that type of girl."

Luc honks behind us.

"Umm...I don't understand what's happening here, but I don't like it," Rose murmurs cautiously, inching forward so she can see our faces.

"I don't need Jordan to get out of Silver Bay," I remind Callie, pulling the acceptance package from my bag and shaking it in her face. "I got out all on my own. But I want to be with him. I've needed him for years and he's always been there for me. Now I want to be there for him. And he wants me to be."

"Be his girlfriend, Jessie, fine. But do the long-distance thing," Callie barks. "You don't need to rush into this. You're too young to be so attached to someone."

"Just because you don't want a serious relationship doesn't mean I'm wrong to want this," I argue back hotly.

"So what? You're just going to move in with him? Really?"

"Or live in a dorm...I mean, we haven't gotten that far." We really haven't. That's something to talk about.

Am I ready to live with him? Although he spends so much time at our place now anyway and he's spent whole weekends over and everything, but...

"You gave in. You gave up. You're letting him take care of you."

"Maybe it's about time someone did!" I shout, and then let myself out of the car, slamming the door behind me. I stomp down the gravel shoulder of the road. Leah calls to me from the window of Luc's truck, but I ignore her.

I start the long walk home by myself.

Three days later, I walk into the living room carrying a bowl full of chips, dodging the bodies sitting on my floor in front of the TV, and place the bowl on the coffee table. We've got a full house here tonight. I invited about twenty people over to watch the NHL draft. Some are Jordan's teammates from the Silver Bay Bucks, some are friends from school. I just didn't want to be alone with my sisters for this since things with Callie and me had gone from bad to worse. I wanted to be around people who were happy for Jordan and me, not angry.

I sit on the floor in front of the La-Z-Boy recliner Rose is in, even though there is a perfectly acceptable space on the couch between Callie and Leah.

Callie and I haven't spoken since she found out I wanted to move away with Jordan. Rose looks up at me, gives me a sweet smile and squeezes my arm. She hates when Callie and I fight, and although she's not publicly taking sides, I know she's on mine. Rose thinks Jordan and I being together is, in her own words, "the most perfect thing in the universe." For once, Rose's sappy, unwavering belief in love doesn't confuse and worry me, it comforts me. Now I see that she's been right all along. We, the orphan Caplan kids, are all capable of being loved. We deserve to be loved. There are perfect romances out there and any of us can have one. Jordan and I are perfect for each other. We've always been perfect for each other, and now that we realize it, why would Callie want me to walk away?

"Oh, look! There's Luc!" Phoebe squeals, and I turn to the TV. Luc, Devin, and Cole had flown to Minnesota last night to join Jordan.

There, filling the screen of our crappy thirteen-inch television, is a reporter's microphone and Luc's face.

"Luc, you're here to support your Silver Bay teammate and friend Jordan Garrison, correct?"

As Luc nods, his long brown hair, which he's been trying to grow out, skims his cheekbone. He looks shy even with traces of his cocky smirk tugging his mouth upward. Rose lets out a little sigh, and I'm fairly certain Phoebe echoes it.

"Yes. I've lived with his family since I was fourteen. Jordan is a brother to me and I wanted to be here for him."

"He's got quite the cheering squad tonight, with his family and girlfriend and you," the reporter replies. "Having been drafted last year by the Las Vegas Vipers, what advice did you give him about this process?"

"Girlfriend?" Rosie repeats, glancing at me.

I swallow and ignore the fear knotting in my chest.

"They must mean Hannah," Mike Bradbury says as he opens a can of 7-Up with a pop and a hiss.

"Jordan isn't dating Hannah anymore," Rose informs him defensively.

"Since when?" Mike looks confused.

"Since my sister gave up her v-card and her mind," Callie blurts out hotly.

"Callie!" Rosie snaps.

"What?!" Mike looks startled, his big brown eyes jumping from Callie to Rose and then to me.

"Ignore her. She's drunk," I tell him.

Mike just shrugs and turns back to watch Luc finish some witty story in his French Canadian accent. He's probably seen Callie drunk enough times to know it's a real possibility.

There's a commercial break and then they're back. The NHL hopefuls are a blur of bodies sitting in seats in a large auditorium with family flanking each of them. I scan the large crowd but I can't spot Jordan before they pan to the stage where the president of the league announces that they're beginning the draft.

I'm suddenly so nervous I feel sick. I know how important this is to Jordy. I know he's spent his whole childhood working toward this moment. He wants this more than anything in the world. I know he is scared and excited, and I wish more than anything that he's happy with whoever picks him. I know I'll be happy just being with him.

The first team to draft is the team Devin plays for, the Brooklyn Barons. Lots of sports reporters have gone wild fantasizing that they'd play on the same team—and I know it would be Donna's dream to see her boys play with each other and not against each other—but Jordan said Brooklyn needs a goalie. Their current one is almost forty, which is a few years past normal retirement for this profession. And just as Jordan speculated to me, they draft a goalie.

The next team up is Sacramento.

"You could live in California again," Rosie whispers to me, and smiles. "Then Callie would change her tune. You know how badly she wants to move back there!"

I try to smile at her but my nerves are too intense. We watch as Sacramento drafts a defenseman. Some kid from Ottawa, Canada, who is a giant, taller than Jordan's six-two.

The owner of the Quebec City Royales is introduced and gets up on stage.

"The Quebec City Royales are excited to draft..." He pauses and his eyes narrow in on something—someone—in the crowd. "...from the Silver Bay Bucks in Silver Bay, Maine..."

I don't actually hear Jordan's name called because the group of people assembled in my living room start to scream, clap, jump up and down and hug each other. Even Callie is clapping. I crane my neck to see around Rose, who has jumped up to high-five Leah.

The camera is now focused tight on Jordan as he stands up. He's smiling a big, beautiful smile. Most people would think it's just happiness, but I see the relief in his eyes too. He's glad it's over. Donna and Wyatt are on either side of him, and he hugs them both, first his mom then his dad. As he moves toward the aisle, he hugs Luc, Cole and Devin. Devin whispers something in Jordan's ear that makes him laugh, and then he moves another foot to the right.

As Jordan moves down the row I see Hannah's perfectly curled, ash blond hair and her wide-set blue eyes. She reaches up to hug him, pressing her heavily glossed lips to Jordan's. When she lets go he quickly continues down the aisle, and as he subtly wipes her lipstick from his lips, my heart splinters.

Chapter 10

Jordan

My flight home was at seven in the morning but I made my dad drive me to the airport at six. I wanted out of there. Being back in Silver Bay with Jessie had clearly caused me to become drunk on nostalgia because only when drunk do I make assumptions as stupid as thinking I still had a connection with her.

I have a connection in Boston so I wander Logan Airport for a bit before deciding to waste time over a Crown and Coke in the first-class lounge. I'm on my second one when a smoking-hot brunette sits down beside me and orders a pinot grigio. She smiles when she catches me staring but it's reserved, not flirty.

I'm not in the mood for a random hookup in the first-class lounge bathroom but I'm trying to talk myself into it. But before I can even begin to hit on her, a tall blond dude walks over and kisses her softly on the cheek before sliding into the seat next to her. I turn away and concentrate on swirling the ice in my glass.

I can't help but overhear their conversation though because they're right next to me and their voices are so chipper they're hard to ignore. They're on their way to Cabo. She's super excited because they haven't been there since their senior trip in high school. She bought a new bikini and everything.

I order another drink and she excuses herself to use the restroom. When the bartender brings me my fresh drink, he asks the dude with the hot woman if he can get him another too. He laughs nervously and says yes, he needs the liquid courage. He's going to ask her to marry him on this trip. The bartender congratulates him and I fight not to roll my eyes. Chump.

But then he explains their story. They went to high school together, and it was on their senior trip to Cabo that they started dating so that's why he's proposing to her there. Normally this kind of story makes me want to snicker, but I'm listening to every word.

If Jessie hadn't left me and moved to Arizona, I would have probably been proposing soon too. We'd have been together for six years. She'd have a degree from some school in Quebec and probably even been working at Sea-Tac now just like she is now. The revelation makes me feel hollow.

The hot girl comes back as their flight is announced. As they get up and leave the lounge, she rubs his back and he takes her hand in his. It all looks so simple...and so...good. For the first time in a long time, that kind of togetherness looks appealing.

I head straight to the arena as soon as my plane lands. Coach made me promise I would check in before the road trip. I get there just as the team is lacing up for practice, and, to my surprise, the trainer tells me to lace up too. I smile and feel a rush of adrenaline push through my veins. If they're letting me skate. they think I might be able to play. Unfortunately, the practice doesn't go as well as I hope—or anyone hopes. My conditioning is beyond bad. I'm winded and lagging behind everyone in drills. When I get off the ice after a mere twenty-five minutes, my ankle is already stiff and swelling.

Mick, the head trainer, sends me to the medical room and puts my foot in an ice bath. When he comes back to check on me, he gives me a tight smile. "Well, it looks like the swelling is going down."

"Good."

"Let me go talk to Coach." Mick leaves the therapy room, and through the glass wall I watch him walk into the office of my hockey team's head coach, Jon Sweetzer.

I see my teammate Igor Aristov watching me from the table next to mine where he has his own ice pack on his knee.

"Is bad?" he asks me, concern lacing his thick Russian accent.

I nod.

Alex comes over, fresh from a massage he just got to loosen the hamstring that's been bugging him. He looks down at the red angry scar on my ankle and back up at me. "Is it infected again?"

"I don't think so," I reply, and pray it's not. I can't fucking handle that again. "I think it's just sensitive. I haven't been in a skate for almost four months."

"Yeah, but you haven't exactly been taking it easy." Alex smirks at me and makes a juvenile humping motion with his hips.

"Lots girls?" Igor asks.

"Yeah, Iggy." Alex gives my shoulder a shove. "A few weeks ago when we were out, he basically banged a girl at the freaking bar."

"That is so not true," I defend myself. "It wasn't at the bar, it was in the restroom. And we didn't have sex. She just blew me."

"And I'm still getting letters of complaint from my neighbors about the last time he borrowed my guest room." Alex chuckles and Igor joins him, lifting his hand to give me a celebratory high-five that I ignore. Suddenly I feel kind of like that asshole I told Jessie I wasn't.

Chris Dixon, one of the older married veterans on the team, wanders over. "Are we celebrating Garrison's return?"

I shake my head. "Doesn't look good."

"We're discussing his sexual conquests." Alex laughs. "You remember what those are, don't you, old man?"

Dix, as we call him, flips Alex the bird. "Yeah. I had one or two of those before I found something more fulfilling."

Alex groans at that comment and walks off toward the showers. Igor hops off the table and follows him. Dix starts to leave too but I grab his arm.

"When did you get married?" I ask, and he looks shocked by the question. We're pretty close. When I got traded to Seattle, he and his wife, Maxine, let me live in the guest house over their garage for a few months while I got settled. It was much better than a hotel. They always had me over for dinner, and Maxine's cooking made up for not being able to bring home one-night stands. Still, I'd told myself that Dix was missing out being tied to a wife and a baby—two now—instead of partying and sleeping around like the rest of us.

"I was twenty-five. I didn't make the NHL right from the draft. Spent a couple years on the farm team in Portland. I met Maxine when I was playing there," he says, and smiles at the memory. "She was hot as hell and full of attitude. Didn't want to date a hockey player, but I wore her down."

"So you had your fun before you made the NHL?" I surmise.

He shakes his head. "No. I dated Maxi down in Portland, but when I made the Winterhawks, she didn't want to move to Seattle with me. We broke up."

"I didn't know that."

"You were probably still in diapers," he jokes, and I roll my eyes. Dix is only thirty-two. "I thought I was fine with it and went on to enjoy the perks of being a pro athlete in a hockey-loving town. But I realized it wasn't all that fun."

"How?" I know I'm being a total chick here, but I'm honestly curious.

"I went back to Portland for the summer and saw her again. She was just so..." He smiles. "How can I say this in a way you'll understand? The sex was amazing but so was not having sex with her. And I decided I'd rather have both with one person, even if it was long distance, than just amazing sex with a hundred people."

I must look stunned because he laughs at my expression and slaps my shoulder. "Believe it or not, Garrison, it's probably going to happen to you one day too."

As I think about how to answer that, the coach's office door opens and Mick makes his way over to me again. His face is grim and I realize that this is anything but a good sign. "Coach wants us in his office."

I sigh and hop off the table, nodding good-bye to Dix as I follow Mick.

Ten minutes later I'm staring in disbelief at my coach as he says, "I'm gonna have you stay here for the road trip."

I feel a sharp pang of disappointment. I must be really far away from returning. If I was even remotely close, he'd let me travel with the team. I didn't realize this was still so bad. Fuck!

"Don't panic," Mick says calmly, and smiles a little bit at me. "I know that this seems like a setback, but it's not. We're just adjusting our plan for you."

I take a drink from my water bottle and wait to hear him out.

"We're looking into local therapy facilities," Mick continues. "So you can continue treatment while we're on the road. It's time to get aggressive with the rehab. We can't have you waiting around while we're at away games."

As his words sink in, a vision of Jessie in her grandmother's kitchen after the funeral flashes through my mind. I clear my throat and speak the words before I can even really think the idea through. "I'd like to go to Sea-Tac Sports Therapy, if it's okay."

"Actually, that's one of the places we're considering." Coach looks to Mick.

Mick nods. "It's a great facility and they handle a lot of professional athletes so if that's your preference, I'll make the call and set it up."

"Great. Thanks." I nod and add. "And I'd like to have Jessie Caplan work on my treatment if possible. She's newer there, I think."

Mick looks confused so I shrug nonchalantly. "Old family friend who happens to work there."

Mick nods. "I can request it."

"Hang in there, Jordan," Coach says, standing up and walking around his desk to clap his hand on my shoulder. "We'll get you through this as quick as we can. We want you back just as badly as you want to come back."

I just nod and try to smile, but I know it looks tight and forced. I turn without another word and leave the office, heading straight to the showers. This is either a brilliant idea or the stupidest thing

I could do, forcing myself into Jessie's life by invading her work space. Either way, I know I have to do it because I know exactly what Dix described feeling for Maxine. It wasn't just the sex that had felt good with Jessie so many years ago, it was everything else too. So I needed to see her again. Maybe I was insane, but I needed to know if we could get there again.

Chapter 11

Jessie

My mentor, Tori, is on the verge of being late again for our weekly check-in. I smile as she runs into the director's office with thirty seconds to spare. I hand her the sugar-free vanilla latte I knew she wouldn't have time to pick up herself and she smiles gratefully. Carl, the director of therapy at Sea-Tac, sits down at his desk across from us.

He glances over at Tori and smiles, his gray eyes crinkling in the corners. "As usual, I have heard nothing but good things about the work you two are doing together."

"She's the best intern I've ever worked with," Tori tells him, smiling at me.

I feel proud and happy. It's good to be recognized for my efforts here, especially after feeling like such a failure in life lately. All that past drama coming back to life with Chance and Jordan showing up in Silver Bay did nothing for my sense of self-confidence. Even though it had been weeks since it happened, I couldn't shake the bad feelings it had stirred up.

"Because of the great work you've been doing together, I'm giving you a new patient." Carl's smile has changed from one of approval to one of excitement. "It's a special assignment and it's a big celebrity patient, but I trust you two to keep it together and do your best."

He flips through some file folders on his desk, looking for one in particular. I glance at Tori, who seems unimpressed.

"Probably a football player," she tells me confidently. "We get them in here all the time."

Carl finds the file he's looking for and passes the blue folder to Tori.

She flips it open and scans it, then sits straight up in her seat and reads it again. Her head snaps up, her blond ponytail swishing, and she stares at Carl with wide eyes.

"This is a joke, right? You're teasing me, aren't you?" she asks excitedly. I lean over but I can't read the file because she's now clutching it to her chest.

Carl says, "No, Tori. It's real. They're trying to fast track him back into the game and they need our help."

My heart has started hammering in my chest. Get him back in the game…it's an athlete. I know it's not a football player—Carl said so. Tori is a hockey fan. Tori is a Winterhawks fan.

"Oh no…" I whisper, but no one is paying attention to me.

"It's going to have to be your main case from this point forward." Carl runs a hand through his salt-and-pepper hair. "You'll have to go to the arena and oversee his on-ice practices too. Make sure he's not overdoing it. His trainers say he's not the best with restraint."

"This can't be happening," I whisper, and tilt my head back, covering my face with my hands.

Tori claps her hands excitedly, clearly not reading my reaction properly. "I know! It's so great! I feel like I'm dreaming."

"Tori, I know how much you love the Winterhawks, which is why I gave this to you, but you need to keep it professional," Carl advises. His bushy eyebrows knit in a paternal way, and then he glances at me. "And, Jessie, I can't emphasize enough how big a deal this is. He's one of their top players. Normally I would never assign an intern to someone like him, but you were requested specifically."

I look up and see Carl and Tori staring at me. She looks less thrilled at that news.

"We were friends in high school," I mutter. Carl nods and Tori smiles.

"Mr. Garrison will be here in half an hour or so," Carl tells us simply. "So be ready."

As Tori and I leave his office, it takes everything in me not to run all the way down the hall and out the front door, never to return. I can't believe this is happening to me. For over six long years I have managed to avoid him, and now, just when I had started to think I was over him, I can't keep him out of my life.

"Jordan freaking Garrison!" Tori whispers excitedly as she drops down in her chair, but as she turns to me her excitement seems to falter. "Did you…was he your boyfriend?!"

"I dated a guy named Chance in high school," I find myself babbling. "He works for NBC now as a sports reporter. And Jordan dated a girl named Hannah Huet."

"Hannah. Right. I remember seeing pictures of him with her when he was a rookie in Quebec," Tori mutters, and I feel my blood turn cold. Hannah went to Quebec to visit him? Why? Were they…

"Really?" I question. "Are you sure?"

She shrugs. "I was a huge fan when he started in the league. I saw this shot of him leaving a nightclub drunk after they finished first in the league and won the President's Trophy. There was a curly-haired blond chick with him and a few other players. Caption said it was his hometown girlfriend."

I feel sick. Tori doesn't seem to notice as she glances around the office at the all the NHL memorabilia on the walls. I remember the first time I walked in here. I almost died. Every square inch of wall space is covered with Winterhawks posters. Avery Westwood, Igor Asimov, Chris Dixon and there's even a signed jersey from their goalie, Mike Choochinsky, under glass.

I stare at it again now and give Tori a quizzical look. "Should we…declutter?"

Tori laughs. "Nah. I think it'll put him at ease if he knows I know about hockey and have a vested interest in getting him back on the ice."

"Okay, then." I shrug, sinking into the chair behind my tiny desk. I drop my head onto it as Tori sits behind her desk and starts reading the details of Jordan's file out loud.

Tori's phone buzzes twenty-five minutes later, making me jump. She squeals like a fan girl at a boy band concert, then takes a deep breath to calm herself before she answers. Kelli, our receptionist, tells her what we both already know—Mr. Garrison is here for his appointment.

Tori says she will be right out and hangs up, and then she does something odd. She pulls her hair out of its ponytail and lets it flow loosely down around her shoulders. She looks good. Probably way better than I do right now.

"Why don't you go meet him and I'll just wait here," I suggest with a forced smile.

"Sure."

I spend the next five minutes praying the ground will open up and swallow me. But it doesn't. And then the office door is opening again and the giant lug I have known for over fourteen years walks in. He's dressed like a bum—a pair of gray workout pants and a red V-neck T-shirt under a black Winterhawks hoodie—but somehow still looks like a Calvin Klein model. He stops and stares at me. I avert my eyes.

"Mr. Garrison, you know Jessie Caplan, I'm told," Tori announces sharply, pointing to me. I frown because her tone is cold and distant. The polar opposite of the fan girl who walked out of this room five minutes ago.

"Jessie." Jordan smiles and winks at me. Clearly, he thinks this is hilarious.

I stand up and give him a terse nod as he moves past me, farther into the room. Tori offers him a seat and I move to stand next to her as she sits behind her desk, opening his file again. Jordan readjusts his Winterhawks cap and finally pulls his eyes off me. He notices the room's décor. He smirks. "This is your office?"

I shake my head. "It's Tori's office. I'm squatting in it during my internship."

His sky-blue eyes move up the wall behind Tori's desk, taking in all the posters. His smirk now has a hue of arrogance, and holy hell, do I ever want to slap it off his face. "I can get you one of mine and sign it if you want."

Tori stares at him for a long uncomfortable moment. I try to figure out what she's thinking. "That's not necessary, thank you."

Jordan's smile disappears instantly. His eyes find mine but I look away. The twinkle that's been in those clear blue eyes since he walked in disappears.

"I've been looking over your file and the treatment and setbacks you've had so far..." Tori slips right into business mode. "We'll start today by running you through some basic exercises to test the strength and flexibility in the ankle so we know what to focus on going forward. Jessie, will take you down to the training room and get started."

Jordan nods wordlessly while I turn and glare at Tori. What does she mean, I should take him down there? By myself? Where the hell is she going to be?

Tori stands and motions for Jordan to do the same. He walks toward the door and I whisper hotly, "What are you doing?"

"I'm supposed to let you run solo on one case before your internship ends," she explains in a low voice. "This is that case."

Jordan is standing in the hall now, arms crossed over his wide, muscular chest, his sky blue eyes staring at us impatiently. Tori gives me a little push at the small of my back. "Now go."

Now it was going to be just me and him for the next half hour as I lead him through a series of exercises. The training room is big and airy, so I can stand a nice comfortable distance from him as he does the exercises. And there are two other therapists in here with their patients, which makes it feel safer too.

After a few mobility exercises, during which I realize he's lost some range of motion, I pull over a chair and tell him to do heel raises on his bad foot, using the chair for balance. He rolls his eyes and in typical Jordan fashion starts to do the lifts without holding onto the chair. He's showing off.

I simply watch and take notes, keeping my best unimpressed look on my face. On only the fifth raise, he wobbles and curses under his breath as he grabs the chair. I make a note on his chart and keep my eyes on the paper because I hate watching him struggle. And I hate that I care, but I do. I know being sidelined from hockey is the worst possible thing that could happen to him. It's not just a career for him, it's something that gives him self-worth.

After he's struggled through a couple more, I toss him an elastic stretch band. He frowns. "You told me to do twenty. I'm only at twelve."

"You're not ready for twenty."

"I used to do heel raises holding fifty-pound weights," he says defensively. "I can do twenty empty-handed."

"You can try but it won't impress me. I'm not one of your puck bunnies. All it will do is put a stress fracture in that barely healed ankle of yours," I snap back.

He looks so furious I'm surprised he's not turning red. As he grabs the stretch band, I try not to smile at my victory. "Sit on the floor, wrap the band around your foot, and pull on the band to provide a little resistance when you point your foot."

He nods gruffly and does the exercise. It seems to bother him less than the balancing one. As he's on his final rep, Tori shows up and glances over my notes. She seems impressed. "Good level of detail," she praises. "Now what do you suggest we do next?"

"Massage and some ice and heat therapy."

She nods and smiles at me, but she never once acknowledges Jordan, which is not only weird but unprofessional. "Jessie, will you handle that, please, while I go and write up some notes for Mr. Garrison?"

I nod.

"Please, Tammy, call me Jordan. Or Jordy," Jordan offers, and as he glances at me, I shake my head and wince to let him know he just screwed up by calling her Tammy.

Tori glares at him. "Tori. My name is Tori."

"Sorry. I'm not good with names. Sorry, Tori."

Tori takes my clipboard to add my notes to hers and heads in one direction while I lead Jordan in the other, down a long hallway lined with doors that lead to private treatment rooms.

I enter one of the rooms and he follows, closing the door behind us. The room feels small and claustrophobic, but I can't figure out if that's because of his giant frame taking up so much space or the giant cloud of tension that hangs above us. I pat the treatment table and he obligingly sits on it, throwing his long, muscled bare leg on the table while the uninjured one dangles.

I pull up my stool and sit by his calf. My breath catches as I flex my fingers and tentatively reach out. This is the first time I have touched Jordan in six years. I'm so angry because I can't control the sparks I feel as my fingers slide over his skin. He shifts a little bit and I glance up at him, expecting to see a scowl of pain. But I find his blue eyes soft and his full bottom lip jutting out a little like it does when he's sad or concerned.

"Does it hurt?" I ask, easing off the pressure I had been using to dig into the flesh and muscle just above his ankle.

He shakes his head, then swallows.

"So your boss isn't very nice," he remarks gruffly.

"She's usually incredibly nice," I say simply. "I honestly don't know what that's all about. She was excited to work on you before you showed up."

"I guess it doesn't matter."

My fingers slide to his ankle and I roll the joint in my hands. I forgot how big his damn feet are—how damn big he is period. His ankle is double the size of mine. As kids, when it seemed like everyone would grow a couple of inches over summer break, Jordy would grow a foot. At twelve, he was so gangly and awkward—unless he was on skates. On skates he was always graceful and in control. And then when he hit sixteen his body filled out—muscles everywhere. His body became sculpted and he wasn't awkward on or off the ice. And that night—the night we had sex—I'd realized his body was built for more than just hockey. He was built for sex. He'd known exactly how to touch me, where to hold me and how to move his hips.

"What?"

"Excuse me?" I blink, taken aback.

"You're smiling. What are you thinking about?"

I suddenly realize he's right and stop doing it. I bow my head as I feel a blush creeping up my cheeks.

"Nothing. Sorry." I clear my throat and press a little deeper into the flesh around his red, angry scar. "Does that hurt?"

"Nope," he says quickly, but when I give him a stare he adds "Not a lot."

I stand up, grab a heating pad and turn it on, then wrap it around his lower leg and ankle. Now there's nothing to do but wait—and stare at each other.

That dimple in his chin is still there…and still sexy as all hell. I don't know *what's* going on with his hair. It's longer than I've ever seen it. Not surfer long like Luc's, just…overgrown. Right now a big chunk is sticking out sideways near his ear and I want to smooth it down or tuck it under his cap, but obviously I resist. The uncomfortable silence grows until finally he breaks it.

"You can ask not to work on me," Jordan says as he stares at his leg.

"I can't do that because you requested me and they want to make the Winterhawks happy," I tell him bluntly, and cross my arms. Frankly, I'm a little pissed that he's suggesting it. "Why did you do that, Jordan? Why force me to work with you?"

He finally pulls his eyes up to meet mine. "I wanted to see you, Jessie. I don't like the way things went in Silver Bay."

"Which time? At the funeral or when you tried to two-time me with Hannah when we were kids?"

He leans forward. "Are you kidding me right now? I never two-timed you!"

"Then why was she in Quebec with you? Did she just show up there like she did at the draft?" I ask as I fight to keep my voice down. "Am I supposed to believe that again?"

"She stayed in touch and came to a few games—as a friend—and then started dating one of my teammates," Jordan snaps. "You know, after you ran away. Remember that, Jessie? The part where you ran away?"

"So you're blameless? Really?"

"That's not what I'm saying!"

The timer on my watch beeps before I can answer him. I go and grab an ice pack out of the mini freezer and carry it back to him. I unwrap the heating pad from his leg and carefully replace it with the ice bag. He winces.

"Sorry," I say instantly, like I would with any other patient.

"Don't worry about it. We all make mistakes, but only one of us is willing to forgive them, I guess," Jordan whispers so quietly that it takes me a minute to realize what he said.

I look at him and he glances up from under the brim of his baseball cap. His blue eyes are dark, searching mine for something. Probably for a sign that I get what he's saying; that I'm not just a hardass bitch who can't give him credit for trying. I blink, feeling my face soften.

And then the door opens and Tori marches in. I step back from the table—from Jordan—and fiddle with the timer on my watch. Tori curtly hands him a typed up list of stretches she wants him to do at home.

"Thanks, Tori," he says with a smile—the big kind that makes his dimple appear in his cheek—and for a second it looks like she might fall for his charm. Then my watch beeps, and the cold, hard look takes over her face again. I walk over to peel the ice bag off his leg.

"Okay," Tori says, and claps her hands dismissively. "We're done for today."

I'm so relieved it's over, I almost sigh out loud. I don't know how I am going to spend this much time so close to him day after day. God help me.

"Okay, so tonight I need you to do the stretches I have listed there," Tori explains, pointing to the paper she just handed him. "And Jessie will be at the rink tomorrow morning to watch you skate."

"I will?!"

Tori turns her attention to me. "You're the lead, remember?"

"Yes," I say, nodding professionally.

Jordan rolls down the leg of his training pants, gets off the table and shakes Tori's hand, thanking her. Then he turns and extends his hand to me.

"See you tomorrow," I say simply as our hands join briefly, but there's a flutter deep in my belly from the feel of his skin. It's an old instinct or habit, my body reminding me of how he used to make me feel. I ignore it completely.

"Sure. At the rink." Jordan smirks, his blue eyes twinkling. "Just don't head to the concession stand out of habit."

He leaves the room. Tori is staring at me in complete confusion.

"What was that about a concession stand?" she asks.

"Why did you dump him on me?" I ignore her question completely. "I thought you wanted to work on him. I thought it was a dream come true."

She shrugs and looks away as we head down the hall toward our office. "I confused him with a different player."

"You thought he was someone else?"

"Yeah. I, uh, always confuse Jordan Garrison with Gregory Grant. I like Grant, not Garrison," she mutters. I try not to judge her, but I would never confuse Jordan with the less skilled, much older, fourth-line forward. "Besides, I really do have to let you lead a case."

I just nod because I don't know what else to do. I think there's more to why Tori suddenly doesn't want to work with Jordan, but if there is she doesn't want to tell me. She changes the subject to our next patient, Mr. Howard, who is recovering from a broken hip, and how grumpy he tends to be.

As she rants, I let out a small sigh in relief that I survived the first session with Jordan. And then I wonder how I'm going to do this all over again tomorrow.

Chapter 12

Jordan

I feel like shit. And I'm in a foul mood.

I hate being home when the team is on the road. It's not something I've had to deal with before because I've never been injured as seriously as I am now. Until now I've only had a pull or a strain and never missed more than a game at a time so I always traveled with the team. This—being left behind—fills me with a horrible sense of isolation and loneliness. That coupled with the weird emotional tug-of-war between anger and attraction that seeing Jessie causes is making me nuts.

Last night I sat at home and watched the game by myself. We'd won in OT. It was an exciting game, but that made it even more frustrating to not be a part of it. I did the stretches Tori and Jessie had assigned me, but that just made me think of Jessie. And that just made me more frustrated.

After four beers and Thai takeout for dinner, I lay awake and went over and over every moment of my time with her that day. Everything had been tense and awkward, not to mention frustrating. I was regretting the whole thing—but then she had to go and touch me.

She was very professional about it. My head knew that, but my heart...all my heart knew was that Jessie—*my* Jessie, the girl who had owned me for my entire life—was touching me again.

So, I'd tossed and turned all night because every time I closed my eyes, I had dreams about her. Or maybe flashbacks was a better way to describe it. When I first dozed off around midnight, I dreamed about the first time I ever saw Jessie.

My third-grade teacher, Mrs. Howlett, was at the front of the class waiting impatiently for us all to get seated. I pulled off my new winter coat—which was Devin's old one—and hung it at the back of the class. As I sat in my seat I glanced toward the front of the class again and that's when I saw her for the first time. Her hair was longer than any girl in class—all the way down her back, right to her bum. It was this color I'd never seen before: brown but with a glow to it. I remember thinking it would be like if you took strands of my brother Cole's orange hair and mixed it in with strands of my friend Luc's brown hair. She had a white satin headband in it. Mrs. Howlett clapped once and cleared her throat. "Everyone, we have a new student who just moved here from California. This is Jessica Caplan."

Without looking up from the linoleum floor, the little girl from California announced, "I prefer Jessie, please."

Mrs. Howlett nodded swiftly like she didn't really care what this Jessie kid preferred and told her to take a seat next to me because that seat had been vacant since my best friend, Luc Richard, had moved to Quebec with his mom. I did not want a girl sitting next to me. At that point in life I believed girls were annoying. She didn't even look at me—or anyone—when she took her seat, and I found that weird. Most girls stared at everyone and talked to everyone. All the time.

Mrs. Howlett told us to take out our history books and, realizing she didn't have a book yet, I slid mine over so it was over the crack where both our desks met. She finally looked up and I was shocked by her eyes. They're green. I'd never seen eyes quite that color before. A pretty light green color. And I was a little weirded out that I just thought anything about a girl was pretty. But they were also sad. She looked like Devin did last summer when he came back from hockey camp in Massachusetts and Dad told him his hamster, Thor, had died. It was that sad look that actually made me talk to her. Not tease, but talk.

"Do you watch hockey?" I whispered, asking her about the NHL because I had no idea what else to say.

It was the first time I'd ever asked a girl about hockey. I fully expected her to stare blankly. When she did, then I wouldn't feel so bad about ignoring her and her sad eyes.

"I used to watch the Sacramento Storm when I lived in California. My dad played for them once."

I blinked. "That is so cool!"

She smiled at my reaction but turned her sad eyes back to the textbook. I decided right then and there I'd be friends with a girl.

I'd woken with a start, and my brain had automatically continued down memory lane—without my permission. I thought about how my mother had reacted when I told her about the new girl in school—the tears in her eyes when she realized it was Jennifer Caplan's daughter. She told me Jessie's mom had been her best friend when she was in high school. I remember all the times that first year my mom invited the girls over and how weird it was at first to have girls in the house. My mom had actually pulled out her old dolls and Barbies from when she was a kid and kept them in the corner of the den for the girls to play with—next to our Hot Wheels and Legos. I had sort of dreaded having them over—especially when Dad insisted we share the backyard skating rink with them. Callie and Rose hadn't wanted to skate but Jessie did, and she volunteered to be goalie so my brothers and I could practice shooting. That's when I started to invite her over instead of waiting for my mom to do it.

When I fell asleep again, around three in the morning, I dreamed of her as a teenager. Of the way her hair got wavier and her hips curvier and her breasts fuller. Of the kind, patient way she would walk me through our English homework when I just wasn't getting it. I never saw the deeper, profound meaning in the books we were forced to read, but Jessie always did. She was a straight-A student, and the only reason I barely pulled off Bs was because of her unofficial tutoring. When I woke up at six from a dream where I relived the way it felt to finally touch her—really touch her, be inside her with no barrier for the first time in my life—I gave up on sleep altogether.

Now, already at the arena because I couldn't stand to be alone with my thoughts anymore, I finish lacing my skates and pull a practice jersey on. My cell phone starts buzzing beside me on the bench and I stare down at it menacingly.

Cole.

That's the second brother to call this morning. Devin had called earlier. And just like Devin's call, Cole's would go unanswered. I pick it up, hit the ignore button and carry it, along with my gloves, from the dressing room to the rink. Coach wants me to avoid deep conditioning until they know how the ankle will respond, but, with the frustrating night I've had, I need to feel useful. Skating full force across the ice a few hundred times and getting that puck to the net will accomplish that. I have to do it.

I grab a couple pucks and toss them out on the ice, then I grab my stick and glide away from the boards.

"Don't even think about it, Forty-four." Her voice echoes through the empty arena.

"Fuck," I mutter, and chop my stick against the ice. "You're not supposed to be here for another hour."

She's smiling triumphantly. "And if I didn't know you so well I wouldn't be."

"Jessie, it's just a couple pucks in the net," I start to rationalize.

"I know," she says with genuine sympathy. "But I have my orders and I have to follow them."

I sigh and toss the stick over the boards. She walks to the bench and calmly picks it up, propping it against the boards.

"So what am I supposed to do? Skate in circles like a five-year-old?" I know I sound like a spoiled child on the verge of a tantrum.

"Yes. Do you want me to get you a chair to push around for balance?" I glare at her and she stares right back, a bemused smile on her full, perfect lips.

As I do my painfully slow laps, I watch her. She's wearing yoga pants and a black long-sleeved running shirt. I can't help but ogle her body. I'd spent the last few years searching for a body shaped as perfectly as hers and hadn't been able to find it. I told myself it was because I'd been a horny, oversexed teenager and her body really hadn't been as uniquely amazing as I'd remembered.

But now I realize I was right all along. Her breasts are not large but work with her tiny frame, forming the perfect arc under her form-fitting top. She has just the right amount of curve to her hip and the roundest, tightest ass I have ever seen—even now after I have seen a lot of asses.

I feel my dick twitch. Traitor.

She pulls herself up and sits on the boards, her legs dangling over the ice.

"Jordan! I want you to pick up some speed and come around the corner. I wanna know if there's any discomfort."

I do what she asks.

"I feel nothing," I call out.

She nods, pleased. "All the way to the other side of the ice. Go to the net full force and hit the brakes."

I follow instructions. Snow flies off my blades. I remember the copious amounts of snow jobs I used to give her when my brothers and I conned her into playing goalie for us on our backyard rink. I smile at the memory.

"You're smiling so I guess that means it feels good," she calls out.

I skate by her at mock speed. "Yeah…it feels good."

"Relax there, superstar," she calls after me cautiously. "Lack of pain isn't the only factor here."

I fly by the net at the other end and then stop as quick and hard as I can, then turn and start back toward her quickly again. She glances over her shoulder as I blur by and shouts, "Your phone is ringing!"

I glide to a stop at center ice and watch her jump off the boards to pick up my iPhone. She smiles at the call display.

"Let me guess, it's Luc," I call out.

"Yeah!" She smiles. It's the first good, old-fashioned Jessie smile I've seen, and I'm amazed at how it still squeezes my heart.

"I'm not talking to him," I announced, skating closer and gliding to a stop in front of her as she steps onto the ice.

"What? Why not?"

I look down at her as she stares up at me. My skates make me feel like a giant next to her. She seems ridiculously far away. I forgot that they did that. She tries to hand me the phone, but I shake my head and skate backward. She rolls her eyes and grabs the front of my jersey, stopping my escape.

"Jordan." She says my name pointedly like she used to when she was annoyed with me when we were kids. "Why aren't you talking to Luc?"

"Because of you," I admit.

Her green eyes blink and her hand lets go of my shirt. "Me?"

I shrug, feeling a little self-conscious suddenly. "I know my brothers and Luc knew you were here, in Seattle, and they didn't say a word."

Her pretty lips tighten into a line and she shakes her head. "Are you a six-year-old, or what?"

"Admit it," I urge harshly. "They knew, didn't they?"

"Yes. They knew." Jessie says this quietly as she stares at my phone, which has finally stopped ringing.

I let out an angry puff of air and fold my arms across my chest. "Yeah. Well, if they can't be bothered to tell me important shit like that, then I can't be bothered to waste my time talking to them."

She steps forward and glares at me. "I hate to break this to you, buddy, but they didn't tell you because I explicitly said I didn't want you to know."

"But I should've been told," I argue. "And they're my relatives."

"Why? It's not like you missed me," she snaps. As I open my mouth to speak, she raises her hand and cuts me off. "And don't say you regret sleeping with me again. There is only so much my ego can take."

"I never said I regretted sleeping with you. God! I meant I regret hurting you afterward!" I bellow in frustration.

I skate closer to her again. She turns her face away from me and stares at my phone still in her hands. When she looks back up, I see a hard look in her eyes.

"I'm here for work," she tells me firmly. "This isn't the time or the place for this."

"So, have dinner with me tonight."

She looks at me like I have lost my mind. "No."

"Okay, have a drink with me."

"No."

"Coffee?"

"No."

"So, how are we going to talk about this?" I ask, feeling desperate.

"We're not, Jordan," she says quietly, but there's conviction in her voice. "I'm glad you regret it. It means there is still a little bit of that guy who was my best friend left in there somewhere. But the fact is... it's been years, Jordy. Years. And..."

"And that's why I'm so mad at everyone," I interrupt, taking the phone from her hand. My fingers purposefully graze her wrist and palm. "Because if they had just told me you were right here..."

"It wouldn't have made a difference," she states, all businesslike and closed off. "Let's get the skate off and see how your ankle is doing."

I want to say something. I want to keep talking, but she turns and marches that perky butt off the ice and through the tunnel to the Winterhawks' empty locker room.

I follow her and when we reach the locker room, I walk over to my designated space and pull off my jersey because it's a little damp with sweat. I'm not shirtless, I'm still wearing the spandex Under Armour shirt, but Jessie turns a little pink as she looks at me. It makes me want to smile. I sit on the bench under my nameplate and bend forward to unlace my skate.

After I pull my foot free and yank off my sock, Jessie crouches in front of me. Her reddish brown hair creates a curtain around her face, so I can't see what she's doing. I lean back, close my eyes and concentrate on the feel of her tiny but strong fingers as they probe my muscles and explore the mobility in my joints.

"You know, what's really got them freaked out is how angry this incision still looks," Jessie says softly.

My eyes flutter open and I see her gazing up at me. She pulls a jar out of her bag and opens it. Inside is a weird-looking greenish paste. I raise my eyebrows skeptically.

"It's a mixture of cucumber, tea tree oil, lemon juice and Indian gooseberry," she tells me as she scoops a little onto her finger and rubs it onto my scar. "It'll calm the skin and tissue around the scar and help it heal."

I say nothing, just concentrate on her hand sliding across my leg, wishing it would move upward. Jessie always had the best hands. She used to rub my shoulders and neck after practices if I was stiff and do this weird hand massage thing that would feel so fucking good. At seventeen she liked to practice methods from a reflexology book Callie had gotten her for her birthday and I was her willing guinea pig.

"I miss your massages," I can't help but mumble.

I see her smiling when I glance down. "I can still give you one, but now you have to pay for it. I'm a professional and everything."

I laugh.

Jessie finishes applying the cream and hands me the jar. "Put this on after every shower and before bed. By the time your team gets back, it should look much better, and maybe they won't be so nervous about playing you."

She stands up. "I have to head back to Sea-Tac. I have another patient in half an hour. After your shower I want you to go to the training room and do the stretches I gave you. Nothing else. No cardio. Just the stretches. Okay?"

I nod and watch her go, then start pulling off the rest of my clothes. I'm in nothing but my boxer briefs when Jessie comes charging back in. She sees me standing there half naked and covers her face with her hands.

"Sorry! Oh my God! Sorry!" She turns to face the door. "I forgot my bag!"

I grab her knapsack and walk up to her, putting my hand on her shoulder to turn her around. She's still got her face buried in her hands. This makes me laugh.

"Jessie, I've been interviewed wearing less," I assure her, and then pause, biting my lower lip for a second, trying not to let my smile grow. "And Lord knows you've seen me in less."

Her fingers part and I see her pretty green eyes peeking through. Her hands slowly drop and she reaches for the knapsack. She's less than half a foot away and I feel this need to reach out and pull her closer, pull her body against mine and press my lips to hers…

My phone buzzes from the bench behind me, making us both jump a little.

Before I can react or realize what the hell she's doing, she charges around me and grabs the phone off the bench. She smiles at the call display and punches a button.

"Hi, Devin! It's Jessie. How are you?"

I groan and roll my eyes, collapsing in defeat onto the bench.

"Well, it's a funny story. I'm treating him. Yeah. I know. Right? How's the baby? Ashleigh? That's great. Yeah, he's right here, but he's acting like a giant infant. I know. Some things never change. Okay. Sure. Yeah. Hold on."

She covers the phone with her palm and knocks my shoulder. I look up at her.

"Talk to your brother."

"Nope." I sigh loudly but take the phone from her hand.

She smiles triumphantly and grabs her knapsack. "See you tomorrow."

"Hey," I mutter into the phone as I watch that perfect ass disappear out the door again.

"She's your physical therapist now?" Devin asks, and I can hear the smile in his voice. "Are you getting rubdowns from her?"

"Did you know she was in Seattle and not tell me?" I change the subject, my tone the polar opposite of his.

The laughter gone from his voice, Devin says, "I just found out like a month ago, I swear. And Luc said she didn't want you to know."

"But *I* wanted to know!"

"Really, Jordy?" Devin says. To my surprise, there is surprise in his voice.

"What does that mean?" I demand.

"You haven't exactly been…lonely," he reminds me in his calm, factual way. "And you haven't mentioned her. You knew she was in Arizona. Did you ever try to contact her?"

"Yeah. Once."

"Once? So what about all the other women?" Once it's clear that I'm not going to answer him, Devin continues speaking. "Okay, whatever. It seems like you guys found each other again, despite everything. That's what's important."

"It's not that simple," I admit gruffly.

"It never is," he replies, then sighs audibly. "Listen, bro, don't get bitchy with us, okay? We are on your side. I promise."

"Fine. Whatever."

I hang up. So that's why my family hadn't bothered to tell me Jessie and I were living in the same city? Because I slept around? Is that what her problem is too? Was I supposed to be a fucking monk after she rejected me? Is this worth it? All this bullshit…is she worth it? I take a deep calming breath. Yeah. She is.

Chapter 13

Jessie

I hang up my office phone just as my text message notification dings on my cell.

"Okay, so who *hasn't* called you today?" Tori asks with a smile.

"My family is having a meltdown," I say, rolling my eyes. "I apologize."

What I don't tell her is that not only have Callie and Rose called and texted me, but Devin, Luc and Donna have as well. All this because I answered Jordan's phone the other day.

"I hope everything is okay."

"Yeah. Everything is peachy. My family's just crazy."

Tori glances at her watch and groans. "T-minus ten minutes until the manwhore."

I smile tightly and nod. Tori pulls out her purse and starts digging for the makeup bag she now carries constantly and applies at work. I don't know why she does it, but I still don't wear makeup at work so it kind of makes me feel like the ugly stepsister.

"So, I went to the Warren," she blurts out as she finishes applying lip gloss.

"The what?"

"Warren. It's a message board where puck bunnies send stories and pictures of hookups with NHL players," Tori clarifies, and stands up, holding her makeup bag and a brush.

"Because bunnies live in warrens. Clever," I remark wryly.

"Oh, puck sluts are nothing if not clever…and gossipy, hence the site." She pauses. "Did you know there are more stories posted about Jordan than any other player in the league?"

"No, I didn't know." I feel kind of nauseous about this information. "I've never been to the website."

"You have to be a member to see anything. And they don't let just everyone sign up," she says, leaning back in her chair and putting her feet up on her desk.

I raise an eyebrow at her. "But they let you sign up, I take it?"

She nods sheepishly and then smiles. "What can I say? I was curious. And they post information about what bars players like to hang out in and what hotels teams use on road trips. When I signed up it was because I wanted to meet a player…or two…or ten."

I give her a rueful head shake, but I'm smiling despite myself. Tori's expression changes and the sheepishness is replaced by something gloomier. "But then I met one and realized the puck bunny wasn't for me."

"Who'd you meet?" I can't help but ask.

"Does it matter? They're all shades of the same, I'm willing to bet," she counters, and drops her feet back onto the floor with a thump. "Jordan Garrison may be dirtiest birdie in the nest, but no one's feathers are clean, if you know what I mean. Luckily he won't be our patient forever."

That was true. Jordan was progressing nicely. His conditioning was getting better and the ankle was definitely structurally sound. It was just the incision from surgery that needed to heal up, and the cream I gave him should have that looking better in a week or two. The idea of not seeing him three times a week kind of makes me sad, as much as I hate to admit it.

"He should be here any minute so if you'll excuse me." Tori stands up to leave but stops at my desk as she passes, picks up a pen and scribbles something on a Post-it. She sticks to my computer screen. "Username and password for my Warren account. Because I know you're curious."

"No. I don't want to know any more gory details than I already see in the regular media," I state emphatically and shake my head so vigorously the end of my ponytail whacks me in the face. "I have to work with him thanks to you."

"Oh, come on...you know you want to check it out." She winks at me and walks out of the office.

My cell phone rings again. I glance at the name and number on the display and roll my eyes.

"Oh my God, not you too!" I bellow into the phone.

"Sorry, Jessie. I'm being forced to call. They all seem to think you'll be honest with me."

"Oh, for God sakes, Cole. I'm being honest with them. NOTHING is happening."

"Nothing?"

"I'm assisting with his therapy because I have to. That's it. I swear."

"Fine. I'll report back and tell them all to fuck off," Cole vows solemnly.

I laugh. "Don't tell your mom that. Just everyone else."

"Good point." Cole clears his throat and then I hear Leah talking in the background. "Leah wants to know if you're at least getting along."

"Some of the time," I admit quietly, and spin a pen between the fingers on my free hand. "When we avoid talking about our past, yes."

He repeats my answer to his girlfriend and I hear more talking. "Leah wants to know if you'll ever actually get past the past."

"Tell Leah that I have no idea. Maybe one day we can be friends, but right now that seems iffy."

He repeats the message and there is more whispering. I glance up and see Jordan standing there in the doorway staring at me. I sit up straighter and pull my feet off my desk, wondering how long he's been there.

"I can't believe you…no, I won't tell her," Cole says to Leah, and then sighs dramatically. "Fine. Leah says to tell you that the reason you can't be friends with him is because you're meant to be more than friends with him."

I stare at Jordan in front of me as Leah's words flow through Cole's voice.

"Please tell your girlfriend that I love her, but she's crazy."

"I tell her that every day. Nice to know someone agrees with me."

"I have to go, Cole," I say, and Jordan's eyebrows fly up. "I have a patient."

I hang up.

Jordan keeps staring at me, leaning casually against the doorframe, his six-two frame clad in a puffy black down winter ski vest, which is open, and a clingy light blue waffle shirt that makes his pretty eyes pop and also shows off the definition in his chest and arms.

"Cole? My brother Cole?"

"Yes," I reply quietly in case Tori is in earshot. "Apparently, answering your phone set off a shit storm."

"Oh, I know," Jordan replies, and rolls his eyes. "My mother called. And Luc. And even Callie."

"Callie called you?"

"Well, apparently when she called you, you hung up on her," Jordan explains, and gives me a smirk so sexy my stomach does a little dip. "So, since you wouldn't listen to her tell you what a scumbag I was, she decided to tell me what a scumbag I was."

"I didn't even know she had your phone number." I'm honestly shocked.

Jordan stares at me incredulously. "You're kidding, right?" he says, suddenly serious.

I glance up at him, confused to see shock in his face tinged with what looks to be anger.

"Callie has had my phone number for years," Jordan tells me frankly. "I gave it to her that first summer you were in Arizona."

"What?" Now it's my turn to be shocked. "Why would you give her your number?!"

"Why do you think?" he counters imploringly.

I had asked Callie about Jordan every time I talked to her the first year I was in college and Callie and Rose were still in Silver Bay. Every freaking call I asked if he'd come home to visit. If they had seen him. If he had asked about me. Callie always said she hadn't seen him. Once, the summer after I left—the one Jordan is talking about—she said she had seen him at a local pub. He'd been with Hannah and never mentioned me at all. That's when I stopped asking.

Jordan opens his mouth to speak, but I raise my hand. "Enough chitchat. Let's get to work."

I lead him down the hall to the training room. As he saunters along behind me, I get this weird feeling and glance over my shoulder and catch him checking out my ass. I frown. "Eyes up, Forty-four."

He falls in step beside me, a cocky grin making his dimple appear, and he shrugs. "Can't help it. You still have the best ass I've ever seen."

I stop abruptly as we enter the training room and level him with a hard stare, even though I feel a ripple of excitement and my cheeks flush from the compliment. "This is a professional relationship. Act professionally."

He rolls his eyes and the cocky smirk disappears. I run Jordan through the usual stretches, exercises and weights. He's quiet throughout but he's blowing through them with no trouble. When he's working on the lifts on one foot, I grab a ball from the rack and toss it at him. He looks shocked but catches it with only a wobble, which is good.

"Toss it back while staying on one foot," I command, but he doesn't toss it back. He just stands there smirking.

"You want it, then you have to answer a question."

"What part of professional relationship is confusing you?" I ask, and put my hands on my hips. "Throwing the ball is part of your therapy. It's balance training."

"I'll throw it. Just answer my question," he explains, and I glare at him. "Have you thought of me at all in the last six years?"

Wow. I stare at him as my brain and my heart bicker about what to answer. My heart says tell him the truth—that I thought about him every day. My brain says lie. Tell him he never crossed my mind. I bite my lip. He holds up the ball and wobbles slightly on his bad ankle.

"Yes," I confess. My heart won the battle, but as soon as I see the victorious smile that starts to crawl up his face, my brain adds, "Hard to forget you when every sports writer and gossip site likes to snicker about how you can't keep your dick in your uniform."

"What?" His blue eyes cloud over and the smile falls from his face.

"Ball." He tosses it back to me gently. "Everyone in my sports therapy program knew I was from Silver Bay. They all wanted to know about the superstar hockey players from my hometown. Especially the one who can manage to score fifty goals a season and still drink tequila out of slutty girls' belly buttons at bars every night."

He looks hurt by that comment. Good. It used to hurt me to hear about it. And then I remember Tori's comment about how Jordan has more stories about him on the gossip site than any other player in the NHL, and I realize it still hurts me.

He forgets his exercise and puts both feet on the ground. "We need to talk about things, like Callie having my number. A friendship between us might not be as iffy as you told Cole it would be."

I decide not to respond to that. Instead, I drop the ball back on the rack. "Treatment room," I bark, and march down the hall.

He hops up on the table as I grab the heating pad and look at the surgery incision. It looks much better than a week ago. I flex my fingers, which are tingling in anticipation before I even touch his skin. I would never admit it to anyone, I hate even admitting it to myself, but I love this part. Touching Jordan. He's lying back on the table, his left arm behind his head like a pillow and his eyes closed. When I grip his ankle and begin to massage it, he lets out a deep, heavy, completely sexy sigh that sends a shiver of desire through me. I'm so weak.

I force myself to be the professional I asked him to be earlier. I stare at his foot and mentally make notes. No swelling. Minimal redness. Minimal stiffness. Slight…

"Jessie." I look up at him. He sits up and leans toward me, his face so close his breath dances across my cheek. "I gave my number to Callie to give to you because I'd been away from Silver Bay for almost a year, and I realized when I came back the thing I missed most about it was hearing your voice."

There's a sharp knock on the door and as I jump back so quickly I almost fall over. Tori marches into the room with a tight smile plastered on my lips. She glances down at his ankle and holds up his file that she's carrying. "Things look great. I have a feeling your team doctor will clear you for play anytime now."

"Seriously?" He looks relieved. "That would be amazing."

"Uh-huh," Tori mutters, like the news means nothing. "I've emailed your trainers to update them on your progress."

"I'd really like to thank you for everything." Jordan smiles at her and I almost laugh. He's trying so hard to win her over because God forbid someone not be a member of the Jordan Garrison fan club. "How about I get you tickets to the next game?"

Tori's scowl quivers. She was just complaining last week how she hasn't been to a Winterhawks game all season because she's trying to save money and the tickets are just too expensive. "You don't have to do that."

I know it kills her to say that.

"I insist." Jordan grins that cute little grin he's been pulling since he was eight. The one that makes him look innocent and adorable but yet completely devious all at once. My heart is starting to melt, but this has to be out of habit. I don't actually feel anything for him again. Still. I'd have to be crazy to still have romantic feelings for him. "I'll get you ice-level seats, right behind the bench. I don't wanna brag, but I've got connections. How many do you need?"

Ice level behind the bench is an incredible offer but Tori doesn't crack. "Give them to Jessie. She's done all the work and besides, NBC is broadcasting it, her ex-boyfriend Chance Echolls will be there. By the way, he's totally hot. I Googled him."

Oh, fuck.

Tori smiles at me. "Maybe he'll bring you up to the press box. I hear they have amazing food up there."

I turn my attention to Jordan, who has completely lost that pretty little smile of his. "I don't need tickets, but thank you anyway."

"Yeah." He jumps off the table. "I'm going to head out."

"We've got heat therapy to do still," I blurt out.

"Sorry, I have an appointment I forgot about," he mumbles,

clearly lying—at least it's clear to me. "I have to get going. But I promise to put a heating pad on it tonight after I stretch it."

He disappears out the door, pulling on his vest as he goes. I fight the urge to run after him. I know he's upset I'm friends with Chance, but I'm not ready to explain to him how much easier it was to be friends with Chance and even talk about that failed romance because it didn't hurt anymore. I didn't want to tell Jordan how much it still hurt to think about us. Maybe it was pride. Maybe it was some weird survival instinct. I had promised myself when I was in Arizona trying to get over him, feeling like I would literally die from losing him, that I would never let him know how much he hurt me. And I would never, ever let him do it again.

Later that day on my lunch break, I head outside and dial my sister's number on my cell.

"Callie Caplan."

"You've had Jordan's phone number for five years and never gave it me?"

"You never asked for it," she replies simply.

"Callie, I asked about him every day for almost an entire year. Why would you keep that from me?!" I'm pissed. *Really* pissed. More pissed than I have been at her in years. She kept us apart. Maybe if…

"He showed up at O'Malley's while I was waitressing there one night," Callie explains with a hard edge to her voice. "He was with Hannah. I'd heard rumors she was visiting him in Quebec all season too. And to make matters worse, there were, like, three other girls that night who were hitting on him."

That news hurts. A lot. Did he really keep hooking up with Hannah when he was in Quebec? Was it really that easy for him? I was sitting in my dorm room in Arizona brokenhearted and he was banging his ex and flirting with everything who walked by—and badgering my sister for my number? What did he want to do? Add me to his entourage?

"He cornered me, drunk, and begged for your Arizona number," Callie goes on angrily. "I'd seen him a few times already that summer, but the only time he ever mentioned your name was when he was drunk."

I swallow. This news is ripping me apart.

"So I told him you had a boyfriend."

"WHAT?"

"You'd gone on some dates with that guy from your biology class, remember?"

"Charlie. From my kinesiology class," I correct, and grit my teeth before adding "And you shouldn't have told him that."

"He stumbled out of O'Malley's with his arm around a skank and never mentioned you again."

Callie pauses and her voice softens. "That's why I didn't tell you. Because you deserved better than him."

"What I deserve is not your decision," I snap.

"He gave me the number. It was my decision," she counters heatedly. "And tell me you wouldn't have done the same thing if it was me and some loser."

I look up and see Carl and Tori walking toward me on their way back from Starbucks.

Callie goes on softly. "Jessie, I did what I thought was best. Think about it. Really calm down and think about it. He had wrecked you and finally, after a year away, you were doing well. I had finally stopped worrying about you."

"I have to go," I say shortly.

"I love you."

"Yeah, so you say." And then I force myself to add "I love you too."

I hang up the phone and smile tightly as Tori and Carl walk by.

Chapter 14

Jessie

Later that night I'm curled up on my couch, watching the heavy rain hit my windows as my playlist titled "The World Sucks" blares from my iPod dock. It's full of angsty, brokenhearted ballads—everything from R&B to rock to country. I'm feeling melancholy tonight, and the gloomy Seattle weather is making me want to wallow in it. If my sisters were here, Rose would curl up with me on the couch and try to hug it out of me while Callie would give me a shake and tell me to "get over myself." She wasn't always so insensitive, but she'd know this current mood was because of our previous conversation about Jordan, and she had zero tolerance for Jordan Garrison–related wallowing.

I sip my blueberry tea—not the kind actual made from blueberries, but the one made from amaretto and Grand Marnier. Lately I've needed some help falling asleep at night. Hot toddies always seemed to work. I know Callie means well. I know she wasn't trying to make my life worse, but I can't help but wonder…would things be different between Jordan and me if she had given me his phone number five years ago?

She's right, I *was* dating someone—casually. As my first year at Arizona ended, a guy named Charlie Cohen, who was in my kinesiology class, asked me out. He was nice and it was comfortable, which is why I guess it somehow continued for several months. But it never really turned into anything serious. And if I'd known Jordan wanted to talk to me...

I sigh and pull my laptop off the coffee table, looking for some kind of distraction from the perpetual game of "what if" happening in my head. As I surf Facebook absently and Tori's status update appears in my news feed, I remember the conversation I had with her earlier.

Warren. Because bunnies live in warrens. Clever.

I type the name into Google. It pops up as the first link. My finger hovers over my mouse and my heart starts thumping in my chest, every beat feeling like an ominous knock on a front door in the middle of a horror movie. But yet, just like the idiots in horror movies, I open the door—I click on the link.

It's nothing but a pink page with little cartoon bunnies all over it. In the center is a space for a username and password. I didn't have the Post-it Tori had written it on but I didn't need to, it was seared into my brain. Username: Torilicious. Password: Winter4hawks4. I type it and hit enter quickly to avoid thinking about what I'm about to inflict on myself.

It's a pretty basic website with a collage of candid photos of NHL players at the top above the menu and a welcome message from whoever runs it. Under that is a list of every single player in the NHL, every name a link that clicks through to their dedicated "stories" page. I click on Devin's name first, because I don't have the courage to click on Jordan's. There's many more pictures than stories. Devin walking to his car at the airport after a road trip, ordering coffee at a Starbucks, at a park in Brooklyn with Conner, and there's even a one of him at the lake in Silver Bay, standing waist-high in the water, dripping wet and looking like an Adonis. The recent stories are about seeing him out but not doing anything with him, thank God. There are only two stories from girls who claim to have slept with him—one says it happened his first year in Brooklyn and that he has a giant penis. I scrunch up my nose at that because, ew...it's Devin. The second says it happened on a road trip to Kansas City after he was married to Ashleigh, but the more I read the more I know the poster is lying her face off. She's vague, and the details she does give sound like she stole them from an erotica book. Handcuffs and paddles? Not Devin's style. Plus she said he came over to her house from the bar, and it's common knowledge that although hockey players go out on road trips, they have to sleep at the hotel with the team. No exceptions. And the other posters call her out too, one of them explaining that Devin wasn't even on the road trip in question because he was injured at the time.

I click on Luc's name next. The pictures are much more compromising than Devin's. Mostly girls Luc kissing girls at bars or walking in and out of road-trip hotels with a variety of girls—sometimes more than one at the same time. A shot of him shirtless, standing on top of a bar holding a pitcher of beer in one hand and a short blonde's ass in the other, makes me roll my eyes. I don't read the stories, but there are quite a few. I feel like I don't want to know about Luc because I don't want Rose to see me look at him any differently. She's been crushing on him since she knew how to crush.

Then I do what I came here to do to begin with—I click on Jordan Garrison's name. The thread is seventeen pages long. Seventeen! Luc's was only five and Devin's was two. I start to feel cold despite the cozy blanket I'm under and the warm booze I'm sipping.

The next hour is a blur of stories and pictures—Jordan making out with two girls at once at a bar, Jordan making out with a girl in a cab, Jordan groping a willing girl in an alley outside a club. Jordan lowering himself into a hot tub across from two girls. The girls are topless and Jordan isn't wearing a suit—I know because his half his bare ass is visible. The stories are graphic and, sadly, I can confirm from my own knowledge that a lot of them are true. They describe his anatomy, the noises he makes and the way he moves with a clarity that brings back my own memories. Every single post seems to scorch little holes in my heart, like cigarette burns, but I don't stop reading. I click on the newest one, which was posted while he was in Silver Bay throwing himself back in my life. It's from username JustJackie111 and starts by thanking a previous poster for telling her the Winterhawks players like to hang out at the Barnacle down on the waterfront near the arena. Then she explains how they showed up after a preseason game and how adorable Jordan looked limping around in his air cast. She talks in great detail about the flirting and the drinking and how he invited her to some other player's condo after the bar closed. She then goes on to talk about the various positions and how many orgasms she had. She ends her kiss-and-tell session with "*You girls were SO right! He does not disappoint!*"

Under her little blurb is a selfie—of her giving a thumbs-up, lying in bed next to a sleeping, clueless Jordan, the sheets barely covering his naked body.

"Actually, he does disappoint," I argue at the unknown girl like a pathetic loser.

I log out of the website and close my laptop with a loud smack. I head to the kitchen to make another, stronger blueberry tea and wipe at the one tear that has managed to escape, despite my willpower, and slide down my cheek.

Callie did me a favor. This guy—the one on this site—I don't want him in my life.

Chapter 15

Jordan

I lace my skates for morning practice while my teammates yammer around me. Despite meeting the coaching staff the morning after they got in from the road trip, running drills for them and then practicing with the team yesterday, Coach still said I would be a game-time decision. I was frustrated. I needed to get back on the ice. Hockey was the only thing in my life that made me feel right. It used to be hockey and Jessie, but then I lost Jessie. It had been hockey and only hockey ever since. This was the first prolonged amount of time I didn't have it—couldn't have it—and that, coupled with her reappearance in my life and her complete and repetitive condemnation, was making my life pretty much a living nightmare. I had to play tonight. I just had to.

"Oh my God! There are two hot pieces of ass out there!" Alexandre announces as he wanders into the dressing room.

"You're late, Larue," Avery Westwood, ever the team captain, chastises him lightly.

"Sorry, I got distracted by *les belle filles*," he says with a lascivious wink.

Alex resorts to his native French whenever he's making excuses or lying his ass off. I think he thinks it makes him seem adorable. Chicks seem to think so anyway.

"Why girls here?" Igor asks in his broken Russian-English.

"I don't know." Alex shrugs. "They're talking to the trainers. They're smoking hot!"

"What do they look like?" our goalie, Mike Choochinsky whom we affectionately call Chooch, wants to know as he pulls his practice jersey over his head.

"There's a tall blonde with a big rack," Alex explains excitedly. "And then there's the other one. Tiny but with a phenomenal ass. She is the reason yoga pants were invented."

"Brunette?" Chooch asks. "I like brunettes in yoga pants."

I grab my stick and check the tape on it.

"*Chatains rouge*."

"What the hell does that mean?" I ask, not because I care about the girls but because I've never heard the French words he just used.

"Umm..." Alex is at a loss for the translation.

"Chestnut and red," Pierre, one of our French defensemen, pipes up as he gets up to head for the ice. "She has auburn hair."

I turn and stare at him and then Alex.

"What?" Alex asks confused by the look on my face.

"Great ass..." I repeat his words.

"Yeah, man. Like perfect."

"What is she doing here?" I wonder aloud, knowing without a doubt that he just described Jessie.

"You know her?" Alex asks.

I leave the dressing room without giving him an answer and head down the hall.

I peek into the training room but no one is there. When I make it down the tunnel to the rink, Mick, Tori and Jessie standing together in a huddle by the bench. I hit the ice and skate over toward them.

"Garrison!" Mick says as he sees me coming. "You remember Tori and Jessie."

"Yeah, of course." I try to keep my voice relaxed and unaffected.

"They brought me the notes on your treatment," he says as he holds up a file folder. "I invited them to watch practice."

"Great! Well, enjoy, ladies. Good seeing you again." I keep my eyes on Jessie the entire time, even while I skate, backward, across the ice to join the rest of my team who are filtering onto the ice.

Practice is light. Coach takes a lot more time with me than the others. I know his style—he's diligent. He wants to make sure I'm ready, not just physically but mentally. I do everything he asks and say everything he wants to hear. I need to play.

"Okay, Jordan, looking good," Coach finally says with a flicker of a smile on his road-worn face. "I'm leaning toward yes. Let's talk after practice."

I smile and skate over to the bench to grab my Gatorade. I suddenly feel happier than I have in months. Chooch is standing by the bench with his own water bottle. He looks at me and smiles deviously.

"Larue wasn't kidding, huh?" he says, and his eyes move to the girls sitting a few rows up from the bench. "They're fucking hot."

"Yeah." I say feeling that tight, cold clench in my gut I used to get when Chance would talk about Jessie in our high school locker room.

Chooch puts his water bottle down and his eyes grow wide as he nudges me. "Oh! She's moving. Look at that!"

I glance over and watch Jessie make her way down the stairs. She's moving fast and her perky little chest is bouncing lightly as her hips move side to side. Chooch makes a low appreciative growling sound, and it makes me think of the years and years I had to hear this from Chance and my other high school teammates. I like it even less now.

Jessie reaches the bottom step and, without looking at me, turns and heads down the tunnel, giving Choochinsky a perfect view of her backside.

"What a tail on her!" Chooch whispers. "Magnificent."

I shove him a little harder than I should. "That's her. The girl I told you I knew. From home."

Chooch thinks hard because, clearly, my fucked-up love life is not noteworthy to him. Finally, his eyes flare in recognition. "That's her?"

"Yep."

"Wow, man...I can see why you want that back."

Before I can respond Coach calls out and points to the net. "Chooch, in the cage! Shoot-out drill! Hurry up, the Storm has the ice in fifteen."

I glance down the tunnel where Jessie disappeared and wonder where she went as I skate over to take my shots on Chooch.

Chapter 16

Jessie

I'm making my way out of this place and away from Jordan's sexy, sweaty body and intense, sultry stare. Watching him out there, doing what he was born to do, what I've watched him do his whole life, was…hot. More than that, it brought up all the feelings I had for him when I used to watch him in high school, like adoration and attraction. And those warm feelings began to war inside me with the cold reminder of why they went away in the first place. It was too much. I needed to get away. I need to clear my head and think, but I'll be damned if I can find the goddamn door I came in. There's a whole bunch of other exits, but none marked 14B, which is the one I'm looking for. I don't want to try a different one in case I get even more lost.

As I follow the curving hallway, I hear a lot of rowdy male voices and I falter. It's got to be Jordan and the team coming off the ice. I spin and start walking in the opposite direction.

"Jessica?"

I know the voice, but it's not Jordan. He doesn't call me Jessica unless he's joking or trying to annoy me. I spin around and find Chance standing there in a slim-fitting charcoal suit, deep purple tie loosened just slightly at his neck. There's a guy behind him with a camera and he's holding a microphone. I realize he must have been doing an interview with a player. His ice-blue eyes are smiling at me as he hands the microphone to the camera guy and tells him he'll meet him upstairs.

"I have to say I'm surprised to see you here," he says once we're alone.

Awkwardly, I blurt, "I'm working."

I know what he's thinking—that I'm here because of Jordy. And in a way I am, just not in the way he must think.

"I don't care why you're here. I just want a hug."

I hesitate. But then I remember how cool he turned out to be back in Silver Bay after the funeral. I hadn't wanted him there, but when I burst into tears and started bawling after Jordy stormed out, it was nice to have someone to hug me. And that's all he'd done. Hugged me and told me it would be okay.

When I'd calmed down, we'd actually talked. A couple years ago, Chance had found me on Facebook, and I'd accepted his friendship. We sent a few emails, catching up on each other's lives, but that trip to Silver Bay was the first time we'd had a long, in-person conversation since high school. He told me about how hard it was to not make the NHL but how much he was enjoying his job covering games as a reporter. And he apologized for what had happened with Amber. I told him about my job in Seattle and assured him the Amber thing was old news. I appreciated his apology but I'd forgiven him long ago. What I didn't tell him was that I should have thanked him for cheating on me. I'd been dating him for all the wrong reasons, and the cheating made me realize that.

So, now I walk over and hug him. He squeezes me hard and lifts me off my feet.

"You're working for the Winterhawks? I thought you were at a private facility," he says, leaving his arm resting on my left shoulder as he looks down at me.

"I am, but we were hired to rehab Jordy." I give him a look that says I know how ridiculous it is.

He laughs loudly. "So, did you rehab the beast? Is he playing tonight?"

"They're calling him a game-time decision, but my money is on yes."

He looks serious for a minute. "Well, here's hoping he does something stupid so I can talk about it on national television."

I furrow my brow. "Come on, Chance. That feud between you two should be over by now. You're both adults."

Chance gives me a smile that says he's not buying what I'm selling. "I have a feeling seeing me show up in Silver Bay might have pissed him off."

"If he's mad you came to support an old friend, he's an idiot. He did the same thing."

"Jessica, I'm not stupid and neither are you," Chance begins softly, his eyes narrowing. "Garrison's had a thing for you his whole freaking life. He came to your grandma's funeral for more than just friendly support. He came for you. He still wants you. You're a prize he never got to claim."

Chance lifts his hand again and cups my face.

"And Jordan's pissed because he knows I went back to the Bay for the exact same reason." Chance takes a step toward me "To try and get you back."

"What?"

Chapter 17

Jordan

I wasn't even looking for her.

I had just assumed she'd headed back to work. Why would she want to stick around and watch me practice? She had done that a million times before as kids and she always seemed bored by it—and that was when she could stand me.

I'm heading to Coach's office, as per his request, to get the final yes or no about playing tonight.

I wasn't thinking when I headed west through the bowels of the building. I was just looking for the quickest route, and the fact that the media would probably be wandering that same hall after doing game-day interviews with our opposition hadn't even crossed my mind.

But then I look up just in time to see Chance standing in front of Jessie. His head is bent forward and his hands are on her face. It looks so intimate, and suddenly I feel seventeen again—and not in a good way.

The way he's got his hand against the side of her face makes me tingle with rage. I walk right up to them, ignore him completely and stare down at her. "I thought you were leaving."

She blinks up at me, stunned by my tone. I can tell I've hurt her, but I'm hurt too. Seeing her with him, here, hurts. Realizing she may have left my practice to go find him hurts even more.

"Gee, this is a surprise." Chance winks at Jessie and smirks at me. "Relax, Garrison. You can consider her my guest right now."

"This isn't your arena. You don't get guests," I snap, and stare him down. I take a step toward him.

"Chance, just go," Jessie begs from in between us. She reaches out and places a hand on each of our chests. "I'll leave, Jordan. Just back down."

"You need to let it go, buddy. Move on. Give it up," Chance says to me, and rolls his eyes like he's really annoyed.

"What the fuck am I supposed to be letting go of?" I snarl.

"Her," he clarifies, and gets a cocky gleam in his weird-ass eyes that are so light they look see-through. How Jessie ever thought that was hot, I'll never know. "She doesn't want you that way. She never has. After all these years, you think you would have figured that out."

I shake my head and smirk at him. "Is that what you think?"

"I know it," he replies confidently. "She hates you."

"Chance!" Jessie says angrily. "Stop."

"She hates me now, fine. But did you ever bother to ask yourself why, Echolls?" I say, taking another step closer to him. I feel her hand fall away from my chest, and she takes a sharp breath, but I don't look down. My eyes stay on him.

"Because you freaked out like a fucking stalker," Chance replies with a look that says he's convinced that's the truth. "That night

I brought her home from work, you lost it because you knew she didn't want you. Even after she dumped me, she still didn't want you."

Something in me snaps. After all these years, all this time, his superiority still gets under my skin, especially when it comes to Jessie. I'm so filled with rage I get tunnel vision, aware of nothing but his smirking, arrogant face. My brain shuts down but my mouth doesn't. "You never fucking loved her. You wanted her because all the guys thought she was hot and you wanted to be that one, the first to nail her. But she was too smart to take you back. And guess what? Even if she had, she wasn't going to give it to you. 'Cause she'd already given it to me."

"You fucking asshole," Jessie whispers, and stumbles back away from us. Her quivering voice breaks the bubble of rage I was in, and as soon as I see her cheeks tinge red and the watery look to her eyes, I realize I fucked up. Again.

"Jessie, I didn't mean..." It feels like slow motion but it isn't. In seconds, Jessie turns away from me and runs down the hall at the exact same time Chance raises his fist.

He goes to punch me, but I'm expecting it. Hell, if it was me hearing this, I would swing too. But that doesn't mean I'm going to let him do it. Jessie deserves to punch me over this, not Echolls. I duck but he swings again and lands one on my cheek. Fuck, he's gotten stronger.

I want to hit him back but I know I can't—not here. So I grab him by his suit jacket and try to shove him backward. I stumble, my left fist still tangled in his jacket. Someone yells. I hear feet slapping the concrete as people run to break it up. As he leans in to hit me again, he slips and crashes into me with his full body weight. I start to fall backward, with Chance coming down on top of me. I reach back to stop my fall, my right hand landing on the concrete floor to brace myself. I know right away it's not a good angle. And then Chance falls down on me and my hand takes all the weight of both our bodies. I feel a lightning bolt of white-hot pain flash up my forearm. Oh fuck.

And then Mick is yanking Chance off me and Seb is there, helping me to my feet. Chooch is there too and he lunges at Chance, shoving him and threatening him, like he would if I was punched on the ice. Teammate until the end. I'd thank him but the pain in my wrist is all I can think about. That and the fact that Chance is telling everyone he's going to report that I attacked him on national TV.

"Chance." The voice is hard and flat, like a stern principal talking to a delinquent student. I turn and realize Jessie's still there. She's across the hall standing against the wall. Her eyes are filled with tears but piercing as she stares at her ex-boyfriend.

He stares back at her defiantly. "After what he just said, you're going to defend him? He just made you look like a—"

"Chance!" She hisses his name again and he shuts up midsentence, thankfully.

Mick looks furious and completely lost at the same time. He turns to Jessie. "Miss Caplan, do you know what happened here?"

"Jordan hurt his wrist." She points to me but doesn't look at me.

Mick turns and realizes I'm holding my wrist. He swears, storms over to me and barks. "Come with me. Now."

I follow him, but my eyes stay on Jessie and hers stay on mine, until the curve of the hall makes it impossible to see each other anymore.

Forty minutes later I shove open the door to the reserved parking with my one good hand—the one not wrapped in a brace thanks to Chance Echolls—and step out into the cold, misty Seattle afternoon. Mick had diagnosed the severe sprain in seconds and spent the next twenty minutes screaming at me. Then he went and got Coach Sweetzer, told him what happened, and Coach spent another twenty minutes yelling at me before storming out of the room to call some producer guy he knew at NBC to do damage control.

He came into the locker room just as I was yanking my coat on. Although he looked furious, he seemed much less panicked as he barked, "Echolls isn't going to talk. But this isn't over for you. Expect a call from team management."

As I walk toward my car, a green Volkswagen Beetle parked a few cars away catches my attention even before the door swings open and Jessie gets out. She marches over to me, the hood on her jacket up.

"Jessie. I'm sorry."

She shoves me hard in the chest and when I stumble back, she steps into me, rocking up on her tiptoes and pointing an angry finger in my face. "You're a hypocrite, you know that?"

"What the fuck are you talking about?"

The wind picks up, the misty rain whipping us and causing strands of her long hair to blow into her face. She pushes them away angrily, causing her hood to fall back. "You think Chance was such a monster because he wanted to play me. You act like your intentions were so fucking different."

"They were!" I bellow.

"Really? Because you got what you wanted and moved on," she

shouts. "You're the one fucking half the free world, not Chance. You're everything you thought he was in high school."

She shoves me again, but this time I reach up and grab her hands and yank her to me. I bow my head so my face is inches from hers and our eyes lock. "He cheated on you. He broke your heart."

She stares up at me, green eyes blazing, her breath huffing out in rage-choked gusts. Her hair, damp from the rain, looks dark as it sticks to her neck. I let go of one of her hands and let my fingertips trail over her neck, then gently lift the hair away. I can see her shiver and I know it's not from the cold air. I fucking know it. It's from the same lingering desire she won't admit she still has for me. The same desire that makes me want to kiss her right now.

I lean forward, my hand slipping back to touch her neck, but she abruptly pulls back and slaps my hand away, her palm making a loud smack as it hits the side of the plastic brace I'm wearing.

"I'm nothing like Chance," I call out as she turns to walk back toward her car.

"No. You're not," she calls back as she keeps marching to her car. "You told Chance about our past because you thought he'd give up and go away. That's what you did so you figured he'd do it too. Well, he didn't. We're still friends. Such good friends that he's agreed to keep quiet about this as a favor to me. The NHL won't know you're a hot-headed idiot who picks fights with the media. You're welcome."

She reaches her car and yanks the door open. Before sliding behind the wheel, she looks up at me again. "And if that hand needs extra therapy, call someone else because I quit."

And then she's peeling out of the parking lot and I'm left standing there, rain-soaked and feeling like I've just been eviscerated.

Chapter 18

Jessie

I laugh—really, truly, deeply laugh. And it hits me I haven't even cracked a smile, let alone laughed, in the last five days since the disaster at the hockey arena. Man, it feels good. The bartender puts two more shots down in front of Tori and me. "These two are on me, ladies."

He winks at me and I smile back. He is so not my type—too short, his hair is too dark, and he's too meaty looking. But hey, free shots.

Tori and I giggle and clink glasses, powering through what are our fourth shots of the night. She's been picking the poison, throwing names like "broken-down golf cart" and "honey badger's foot" at the bartender. I have no idea what's in any of the things I'm pouring down my throat, but they're sweet and delicious so, whatever.

"I'm glad you made me do this!" I admit, and hug her spontaneously. When she first suggested a girls' night at her favorite bar, a place called the Nine-Pound Hammer, I was reluctant because I hadn't exactly been in a partying mood lately, but I was enjoying myself for the first time in months.

She hugs me back. "Well, you looked like you could use a night out. And I wanted to celebrate getting rid of Jordan Garrison."

I try to ignore his name. Ignore *him*. Thinking of Jordan would just ruin this night. I will not think of him.

I haven't seen him since that day he sprained his wrist. Either his trainers are handling the injury on their own or he had told them he wouldn't go back to Sea-Tac. I didn't care, I'm just glad to have some space. Now if only I can get him out of my head as easily as I've gotten him out of my physical space. I think about him all the time. I even found myself on the Winterhawks website, looking for updates on his condition. All it said was that Jordan Garrison was back on the injury list after "a freak accident at practice caused a severe wrist sprain."

An unknown number had popped up on my call display a couple times in the last week, but I didn't answer it. Although no one would admit it, I assumed someone in our shared group of friends and family had finally broken down and given him my cell, but I wasn't ready to talk to him again. I need to get my head straight and get my defenses back up. I'd almost let him kiss me in the parking lot, even though I was hurt and humiliated by what he'd said to Chance and how he'd said it. Chance was right, he'd made me look like a whore. What kind of crazy person wants to let a boy like that kiss her?

"I need to tinkle!" Tori announces, and adjusts her silky blue strapless top. It's barely keeping her ample breasts contained. "I'll be back."

She bounces off to find the restroom. A few seconds later, the bartender winks at me and places some kind of yellow frothy martini in front of me.

"Lemon meringue martini," he says with a smile, and nods his head toward the other side of the bar. "From him."

I glance down the bar and see a stocky brunet with a mischievous smile and nice blue eyes. Not Jordan nice, but nice. I scold myself for even thinking of Jordan. I can't help it though. I've been comparing men to him since I was a teenager. Even in those years when we weren't speaking.

I raise the glass toward him as a sign of thanks and he raises his beer back to me. That mischievous grin grows a little, as does the twinkle in his eye. I take a sip. It's sweet, tangy and delicious. I watch him walk over to me over the top of my drink.

"You like it?"

I nod. "It's good. Thank you."

"It's the best drink in the house. You look like someone who deserves the best," he says, and smiles.

"Wow." I nod and giggle. I'm getting very drunk. Not fall-down-barf drunk but flushed-and-flirty drunk. "That was quite the line."

He blinks, laughing. "Like I said, you deserve the best."

"I'm Jessie." I extend my hand and he takes it. His handshake is firm. That's hot.

"Finally! A name for the pretty face," he coos, and I'm not sure what he means by "finally." We've only been talking for six seconds. "I'm Alexandre."

He says his name with a heavy roll of the "r," and my drunken brain realizes he's French. His accent is similar to but heavier than Luc's. We stare at each other smiling and sip our drinks. I'm so not in any place emotionally to be flirting with a guy—any guy—but this one is adorable.

"You're Canadian."

His nice blue eyes flare in surprise. "Yes. How did you know?"

"The accent. I have a French Canadian friend," I explain, and sip the yummy drink again.

"Pretty and smart," he says. His praise makes me blush and giggle, playfully swatting at his chest. It's rock hard under his black T-shirt. I let my hand lightly graze down his taut belly as I pull away, and his smile gets larger.

"What are you doing all the way over here in Seattle?"

"I work here."

"What kind of work does a pretty French Canadian boy do in Seattle?" I ask as I gulp down more of my frothy beverage. If my brain wasn't doing the backstroke in alcohol right now, I would have known the answer to that. There's usually only one reason an athletic French Canadian boy would be working in Seattle. Before he can answer, there's another guy beside him. A shorter, even stockier guy with brown hair and brown eyes. He's clearly as fit and muscled as my new friend Alexandre.

"Dix!" Alexandre claps his buddy on the back. "This is Jessie."

Dix and I smile at each other and shake hands.

"Chris Dixon," he says. "Nice to meet you."

"Dix plays with me," Alexandre explains. "But he's not as good."

Dix rolls his eyes at that and Alexandre laughs. I smile and nod, but then I realize what he just said. I stop smiling. "Play?"

Alex nods as his eyes twinkle playfully. "Hockey. You don't recognize me? I recognized you."

"No," I say firmly. No, because I really don't recognize him, but it's also a giant "no, this can't be happening" to the universe. Because, seriously. No.

"Yeah. Winterhawks," Dix adds helpfully.

I put my half-empty martini on the bar. Alexandre uses the opportunity to reach for my hand. "Seattle Winterhawks. The National Hockey League. But you know that. You're a therapist, right? You worked on Garrison."

"I gotta go." I yank my hand back and push my way through the crowd, looking for the restroom so I can find Tori and get the hell out of here.

Alexandre and Dix are fucking Seattle Winterhawks. Just when I think my luck can't get any worse…

I see the restroom sign blinking neon above a doorway to my right and start toward it. As the crowd breaks apart making room for me, I see Tori. She's leaning over a small high-top table beside the restroom. She's face-to-face with someone, raising a shot glass toward them in a "cheers" gesture. The person in front of her is holding a beer bottle in a brace-covered hand. His blond head is angled so I can't see his face, but I don't have to. I know exactly who he is. I know even before his eyes find mine.

Chapter 19

Jordan

I can't find the guys. They were here a minute ago, but then I went to take a leak and now they're not by the pool tables where I left them. I do one lap around the overcrowded bar, but I'm too drunk to continue the search. Not fall-down drunk, but unfocused, lazy drunk. I order a shot of tequila and a beer from a waitress and find an empty table by the bathroom. Eventually one of the guys is going to take a piss.

I'd been in a shit-tastic mood since I hurt my hand. The team's general manager had a lengthy, angry discussion with me about the incident. He was furious, obviously. If it had gotten out that I was brawling with a reporter, it would have been a press nightmare, not just for me, but for the entire team and even the league.

He also said it's not a bad thing I was injured because he would have had me benched anyway. He wanted to know what it was about. I wouldn't give him details other than to say Chance and I had known each other a long time and this was an ongoing issue.

It was explained to me, in no uncertain terms, it was not an issue I was to bring to work ever again.

It was stupid and I deserved the scorn. I'd just…snapped. There was no excuse and no way to rationalize it. I was probably as angry with myself as Jessie was with me. I always wanted Chance to know what had happened between me and Jessie. I needed him to know he hadn't hurt her as badly as he thought he had; that he hadn't mattered as much as he thought he had. I also needed him to know that *I* mattered to her more than he thought I did. It was infantile and driven completely by my ridiculous ego, and I knew this. I wish I hadn't done it. I'd been trying to tell Jessie all of this, but she refused to answer the phone. And the one day I went by her work was her and Tori's day off. When I'd subtly asked the receptionist where she lived, she got suspicious and looked at me like I was a stalker or a serial killer so I'd backed off and gone back home to sulk.

I went to the arena every day to do cardio and skate in an attempt to stay conditioned. When this hand healed, I didn't want any reason not to get back on the ice immediately. I was on my best behavior. I barely spoke to anyone, and when I did it was only about hockey. Coach seemed relieved. Still pissed, but relieved.

On my off time I was going out way too much. I'd go out with any teammate who had the urge. This week alone I'd been out four nights. I hated sitting at home. When I was home alone, all I could think about was Jessie.

The annoying part was when I was out in public, no matter where I went or how many women were flirting shamelessly with me, all I could think about was Jessie. And then I would go home and jerk off—my thoughts on Jessie in her yoga pants. Or how it had felt to be inside her the one and only time I'd ever been inside her. I felt like a giant loser.

The game the Winterhawks had played tonight hadn't been an easy win, but I'd managed to convince Alex and Dix to come out despite the fact they had practice tomorrow and then had to get on a plane for the next away game. As I sit here now, by myself, I wonder briefly if they all went home. And as I sip my scotch, I think maybe I should just leave. Every time a pretty woman walks by, it reminds me how much prettier Jessie is. I should just go home, jerk off and feel pathetic again.

Then suddenly, before I can register what's happening, I hear my name being called and there's a big-breasted, tall blonde towering over my table.

"Hey, Tori!" I say, slightly glad it's someone I know, but only slightly because, as usual, this girl has a dirty look on her face as she stares at me. "How are you?"

"Better now that you're not my patient," she snaps.

"What the fuck is wrong with you?" Maybe it's the booze or just the way my life has been going lately, but suddenly I've got no patience and no subtlety when it comes to this woman. "You've been cold and rude since I met you, and I have no idea why."

She stops and stares at me incredulously, blinking her big blue eyes. The waitress comes over and places my shot and beer on the table between us. She winks and says, "On the house, superstar."

I give her a grateful smile—the innocent kind that makes them think this has never happened to me before. The fact is, there's at least one waitress or bartender in every bar in every town with an NHL team who comps a drink or two as a way of flirting. She's beaming as she wanders away.

"Whatever I did to offend you, I'm sorry," I tell her because she's friends with Jessie. She could be an ally, and right now I need all the allies I can find. I slide the shot glass toward her. "Let's drink to a truce."

She steps closer, her eyes go to the shot glass, and a bitter smile flickers over her features briefly as she picks it up and stares at the clear liquid inside. Then she leans across the table. "The first time we met I wasn't rude or cold to you."

I frown as my mind goes back to the meeting in her office. I'm about to shake my head to argue when she continues. "The first time I met you, I was downright giddy because I thought you were the hottest thing I'd ever seen and the most talented player in the NHL. And you were so charming. You liked my dress and the fact that I knew the difference between a slap shot and a wrist shot. You bought me one of these...actually you bought me two. And a couple margaritas. I was nice to you. I was a total fucking sweetheart all night long."

Is she crazy? Is Jessie's coworker an escaped mental patient? What the hell is she talking about? I stare at her—really stare at her—my brain pulling out any fuzzy, confused memory in every corner of my mind. Did I meet her before? I can't for the life of me remember.

"You made it clear it was a one-night stand and I was fine with that. I really was." She looks at me sincerely. "I thought one night with you would be a fantasy come true. I've had one-night stands before. They're just good clean fun. But I haven't had so many that I don't remember."

Oh fuck. A fuzzy memory surfaces from the recesses of my mind. Tori in a Capitol Hill martini bar with slightly shorter hair and a tight red dress. Then I remember Tori out of the dress.

I open my mouth but she lifts her free hand and holds her palm out in front of my face, commanding me to shut up. "No, seriously. I was fine with the one-night stand. I was even looking forward to joking about it with you when I found out we'd be working together. It was only when you looked at me blankly and I had to introduce myself that I regretted it."

And just when I think this night can't get any worse, my eyes catch a glimmer of auburn hair and there is Jessie watching us from a few feet away. Then she's standing beside us. Her hair is loose and wavy around her face and shoulders. She's wearing makeup—not a lot, but enough to make her eyes greener and her skin glow, and her perfect fucking lips are glossy and wet-looking. She's wearing a slinky black tank top and I can see the outline of her black bra through it. Her low, painted-on jeans and high-heeled black leather boots give her a few extra inches in height—plus, they tilt her ass just so, making it look even more amazing and perky.

"What's going on?" she asks Tori, not me.

"Nothing much," Tori says quickly, and nods her head toward me. "Just finally explaining to our ex-patient here why I hate his guts."

"Tori, I don't know what to say," I croak out lamely.

"I do!" She raises the shot glass in a toast. "Here's to being such a manwhore you don't even remember the women you slept with!"

She downs the shot, slams the glass on the table and storms away. I close my eyes, run a hand over my face and let out a long, humiliated breath. When I open my eyes again, Jessie is still standing there.

She says nothing. She just stares at me. I stare at her. I can tell she's furious and I can also tell she's had a lot to drink. "Jessie, please say something."

"I was just at the bar. I met a great guy. Alex. He's hot and bought me a drink."

"Alex?" I repeat, the nervous ball in my stomach turning to dread.

"Yeah." She smiles but it's mirthless. "You know him. French guy. Your hot teammate. I think I need to be with Alex."

She turns on her heel and storms back through the crowd. My blood starts whirling through my body, too fast, too hot. Jessie disappears around a pillar, out of sight. I turn and begin to push my way through the crowd toward Jessie and the dirtiest, horniest teammate I know.

Chapter 20

Jessie

I find Alexandre standing playing pool with his buddy, Dix. I walk right up behind him and slip an arm around his waist. He doesn't even look shocked. He just grins a mischievous grin that I am one hundred percent sure has charmed the pants off a few hundred women.

"I thought we'd scared you off," he says in a husky voice.

"I don't scare easily," I tell him, and bat my eyelashes. "And besides, I owe you a drink."

I turn and order a beer and another martini from the waitress, then turn back to Alex. This time he slips his arm around my waist. With a little tug he pulls me flush against him. Clearly, he thinks he's got the green light from me. This is fine, even though it makes me feel kind of sick.

"Are you trying to get me drunk?" he whispers against my ear.

"Something tells me I don't need to," I purr. Alex laughs and I feel his lips brush my earlobe.

This is doing anything but turning me on. It feels completely horrible and wrong. But then I see Jordan storming toward us. His blue eyes fill with fire when he sees us together, and that's all that matters. Alex leaves my side, walking around the pool table to survey his next shot.

Jordan walks right up to me, standing so close I can feel the heat of his skin through his thin cotton shirt. He dips his head and whispers, "Jessie…we need to talk."

"I'm not here to talk to you," I snap, and walk away, over to Alex. My phone buzzes and I pull it out of my purse. It's a text message from Tori saying she's sorry but she had to get out of there. I send her a quick one back telling her it's okay, we'll talk tomorrow…Even though the thought of her with Jordan makes me feel sick to my stomach, I don't blame her for this. She didn't even know me when she was with Jordan. She did nothing wrong.

The waitress comes back with the drinks, and as I go to pay her, Alex pushes my hand away and tells her to add them to his tab. I smile and lean over, kissing his cheek. It's light but lingering. I want to make sure Jordan sees it.

"*Merci,*" I tell him, using one of the only French words I know.

"*Mon plaisir,* Jessie," he replies in French, and I have to admit it's sexy as hell. I'd swoon a little if the red-hot rage running through my system wasn't so all-encompassing. Alex reaches out and brushes my hair from my face.

Jordan is watching us intently. He runs his braced hand through his hair, sending it off in too many different directions, and gives me a pleading look, like he wants me to go over there, but I ignore him. I focus on Alex, putting my hands on his broad shoulders. God, I have to admit I love hockey players' bodies. So strong and so tight.

"I need to get out of here," I say to him quietly. "Do you want to come with me?"

Alex nods.

Jordan's eyes fall on me. They're full of something I haven't seen from him in a long, long time—pain.

"Don't," he mouths to me with a slow shake of his head.

I turn toward Alex, who has just finished signing a bill for the waitress. He grins at me and it's no longer mischievous. It's feral. Expectant. Horny.

"Let's go, *ma belle*." Alex pulls me close to him.

We turn to go and as we weave our way through the crowd, his hand on my lower back slides to my ass. I'm sure he's a nice guy, and I know I've given him every reason to think I'm just some puck bunny who wants a ride on his hockey stick. He's just trying to give me what he thinks I want. And of course it's what *he* wants. He's young, rich, single and horny. He has every right to want meaningless sex.

Of course I have no intention of having meaningless sex with him. I just want him to leave the bar with me so Jordan thinks I'm doing that. I know he'll eventually find out nothing happened. I can tell Alex is the type of guy who will bitch in the locker room about the tease who wasted his time, but tonight Jordan will have to go home and picture me riding his teammate all night long.

I want that pain for him more than I want anything else in the world right now. Mostly because *I* have already lived through that pain repeatedly—and now I'll be living through it again every time I look at my coworker.

"One second," he whispers, and leaves me standing by the restroom as he goes into the men's room.

As I wait for Alex, I turn and see Jordan shoving his way through the crowded club, heading toward the door. He doesn't see me. He probably thinks I'm already in a cab with Alex. Good. I should just stand here and let him go home and hope that he's gutted. This is exactly what I want. But for some stupid reason, I find myself following after him.

Chapter 21

Jordan

I look around the parking lot frantically but don't see Alex or Jessie anywhere. They're gone. Knowing Alex, he already has his tongue in her mouth and his hands on her tits and…

"Fuck!" I yell, tearing my hands through my stupid hair. I feel a wave of sadness wash over me. It's overwhelming, and it's followed by an insurmountable anger. My eyes get moist and my face gets hot. I can't get the images of him touching her out of my head.

"How's it feel?"

I'm so lost in these sick visions that I don't recognize the voice. I spin around, and there she is. By herself. Standing behind me rigid with anger. The hard glint in her mossy green eyes falters for just a second when she takes in what must be a devastated look on my face.

"How does it feel?" she repeats, the hard edge coming back as swiftly as it left.

"You didn't do it." I can finally pull air into my lungs. I hadn't even realized I wasn't breathing.

"Not yet" is her short response.

"Please don't," I say gruffly, and shake my head.

"Why?" she asks, tilting her head so her auburn hair falls over her shoulder. "Because you don't want to think about me screwing your buddy?"

I swallow. "No. I don't."

"It sucks. I know," she replies with a bitter smile. "To know when you're home alone he's going to be touching me and tasting me. And you're going to be able to imagine exactly what that feels like for him. What I'll say. What I'll do. What noises I'll make. "

"Stop it," I demand.

"Don't worry, Jordan," she quietly assures me. "If I do this, it'll be a one-time thing. You won't have to lie in bed at night wondering who I'm fucking a week from now or a year from now. Wondering if I'm telling some stranger I love him the way I told you. I went through that. So let's even the score. If I go home with Alex, you won't be able to avoid that pain either."

Her words cut through me. They hurt but they don't gut me because I'm clinging to four simple words she said: *If I do this.*

And one other thing…

"You never said you loved me," I tell her flatly.

"What?" she barks, annoyed.

"That night we were together. Or any other night for that matter…you never said you loved me." This is the truth, and it's always been clear in my mind. "I told *you*. You've never said it back."

The hard glare in her eye dies and she shifts on her heels uncomfortably.

"Did you love me?" I ask, but she doesn't answer. She just stares at the cold concrete beneath her feet. I take a step toward her. "Because, if you loved me—if you ever did, even just a little bit—please don't do this now."

"I don't owe you anything, Jordan," she replies defiantly, raising her face to mine. "Why should I do you any favors?"

"Because it would kill me," I confess to her in a choked, thick voice.

"You killed me," she spits back, her voice equally clogged with emotion. Her pain feels like a knife in my gut.

Without a word she turns and charges back toward the club. I follow but the crowd swallows her up before I can reach her. Desperate for air, I head back outside. I stand on the sidewalk, motionless. My face flushes and my vision blurs.

I hear Dix call out to me. "Garrison! Your turn to get your butt kicked at pool! I need a new victim now that Alex took off with the hottie."

I don't answer and his footsteps get closer and closer until he comes around and stands in front of me.

"What the fuck?!" Dix gasps, shocked. "Jordan...what happened?"

I shove him and turn away. I lean on a parked car and try to will myself to stop fucking crying. What the fuck is wrong with me? I'm a fucking disaster.

"Dude...I...why? What can I do?" Dix is confused because it's unfathomable that I would be a sobbing mess. He grabs my shoulder and turns me around. "Jordan! What the hell?"

I hear a guy on the crowded patio a few feet away say "Hey! Isn't that *the* Jordan Garrison?"

"Yeah! And Dixon! Hey, guys!" Any second these fans will be walking over asking for photos and they'll see me losing my shit and by tomorrow morning it'll be all over the sports news.

"I gotta go," I say, and clear my throat to take a deep breath. "I gotta go."

"Dude!" Dix calls, but I just keep walking as fast as my legs will carry me.

"I'm fine! I gotta go."

I get into a cab and the driver gives me a stunned stare. I sniff and say "allergies" and then give him my address.

Eight days later, I walk into the treatment room at the Winterhawks' arena, trying to act laid back.

Charles, our team doctor, follows me to the back where there's a free treatment table. Dix is sitting by a therapy table, his ankle in a bucket of ice and water. He tweaked it in the last game, so now he's joined me—sitting in the bowels of the arena while our team plays on the ice just down the hall. It's particularly frustrating when we score and the roars of the cheering crowd rumble down the concrete hallways.

Dix looks surprised to see me and I notice trepidation in his gaze. I haven't seen him since my meltdown outside the bar. He texted me from their road trip a few times. I kept telling him nothing was wrong. I was fine. Don't worry about it. I thought about texting Alex, but what the hell would I say? Did you bang the girl from the bar? The one I've been in love with since I was fourteen? They'd have me committed. So I didn't do a fucking thing. I stayed home. I drank. I sulked. I stewed.

I sit down on the other side of the table from Dix. Charles takes my hand out of its brace and starts to manipulate the joints carefully.

I was supposed to be on the ice tonight, but my wrist is stiff and sore and it starts to swell any time I take a few shocks with a stick. Nobody wants to risk it. Nobody but me. Charles continues his poking and prodding for a few minutes longer, then tells me he'll be right back and heads into his office.

Now, alone in the treatment room, Dix turns to me. "Dude, seriously," he starts in a low voice. "What the hell happened to you that night?"

I smile awkwardly. "It was my time of the month."

He laughs but shakes his head, not willing to let it go with a joke. "You freaking cried, Jordan."

"I know. I was there."

"I told Chooch about the night and he said it must have been over that girl Alex was trying to bag," Dix goes on, making me cringe. "She was your girlfriend in high school?"

I shake my head. "She wasn't. She should have been but she wasn't, technically. It's a long story."

Pulling his foot out of the ice bucket and wiping it dry with a towel, Dix says, "She bailed on him, you know. He said she just jumped out of the cab at a red light few blocks from the club and took off. He was moaning and bitching about it the entire road trip. Until he laid some chick after the game in Vegas, that is."

I feel like I've been wearing a lead suit and someone just took it off me. I take a deep, relaxed breath. Thank freaking God.

"Dude, I can't imagine anything so complicated that I'd lose it like you did," he remarks, but there's no condemnation in his voice, just concern. "Scared the shit out of us."

"I just need to get back on the ice," I mutter.

"Tell me about it," Dix agrees, and his round, normally jovial face turns sour. He hops off the table and I watch him leave.

Alone, I lie back and close my eyes as I wait for Charles to return with the X-ray results.

Jessie is the only woman I have ever cried over. And the humiliating part is these waterworks weren't the first Jessie had caused. I'd shed tears over her when she left me at eighteen too. That's what had set me off—the powerlessness and pain of losing her the first time is why I'd decided I would never let someone in like that again. I hated being so hurt then—feeling so out of control—and I hate it now. The only difference is now I know that blaming her and running from my feelings—even the painful ones—aren't going to fix anything. I know that because that's what I've done for the last six years.

I close my eyes and lean back on the medical table as my mind wanders back to a time I have tried adamantly to block out.

Chapter 22

Jordan

Six years earlier

Slow the fuck down, Jordan!" Cole complains as he struggles to keep up. He's dragging Leah along with him.

"I don't need to slow down, you need to hurry up!" I complain.

We'd just gotten back from the draft. The plane was half an hour late and then Mom had insisted on stopping at the grocery store for milk, and then Cole had insisted we drive all the way across town to pick up Leah. Now it was almost midnight.

Luc had gotten a text from Rose before we left Minnesota saying that tonight was the first bonfire party of the summer. Bonfires on the beach in the summer were a Silver Bay teenage rite of passage. My dad said they'd even done it when he was a kid. I can see the ball of fire flickering and jumping. It's not very big anymore; I can only see maybe twenty or so people milling around. If she isn't here, I'll freak.

Four days earlier I was drafted by the Quebec City Royales. I did it. I was going to be an NHL player on a historic team. The Royales were one of the oldest teams in the league, and they were still one of the best. I thought finally being drafted and having a team would mean all the pressure I'd been feeling would disappear. It had only gotten worse.

Now I actually had to make the team. All players were drafted and given a fifty-thousand-dollar contract. That only went up if you made it through training camp in the fall and earned a spot on the team. Most rookies spent a year or more on the junior team—or the farm team, as it was sometimes called. I didn't want to be most guys. I wanted to make the big team and play in the big leagues right out of the gate. Now that a team had picked me, I had to make that happen.

The draft was supposed to be one of the most special, happiest days of my life. And it was; only all I could think about was how I wished Jessie was there with me. And how upset I was that Hannah was there. I hadn't invited Hannah, but she had bought a plane ticket and flown out there all by herself to "surprise" me. She just showed up at my hotel the morning of the draft.

My mother had taken me aside and said to just "deal with it" because I had bigger things to focus on. She was right, of course, but I prayed the whole time the TV coverage hadn't shown her. I knew Jessie was watching.

As soon as the general manager of the Royales called my name, I had to go up on stage and put on one of their jerseys. Next, I had to take photos and do interviews with television stations—me. On TV. So weird—but once that was done, before even going back to my family, I ran to the bathroom and called Jessie.

She didn't answer. I left her a message, anyway.

I wanted to catch the next flight back to Silver Bay, but I had to spend four more days there meeting with team VIPs and doing media interviews with the other Royales draft picks. Everyone wanting something from me and yammering advice at me. As my stress grew, so did my need to see her because she wasn't answering any of my texts, phone calls or emails.

I reach the clearing and feel the rocky shoreline under my feet, glancing around frantically. I see Rose and Luc.

"Luc!" The jerk said he wasn't coming here but clearly changed his mind. And he got here before us! Luc's sitting on a log leaning over Rose who is cross-legged on the ground in front of him.

I walk over to them and Rose jumps up, squealing as she throws herself into my arms. "You did it, Jordy! You did it! I'm so proud of you!"

"Thanks," I reply, and smile genuinely. Already, I feel myself start to relax a little. Everyone notices me now and starts coming over, slapping me on the back, high-fiving me and hugging me. I thank everyone but grab Rose's hand again.

"Where's your sister?" I ask urgently. She glances around and gives me an exaggerated shrug.

"Umm..." Her perfect little face squishes up like she smelled something bad. "Oh, wait, you screwed up. I'm not supposed to like you anymore."

I glance at Luc. "Is she drunk?!"

"I think so, yeah," he replies, and raises his hands innocently. "I don't know who gave her booze. I just came here when she called me and she was slurring her words."

"Rosie! You're fifteen!" I say with condemnation, ignoring the fact that Jessie and I were fifteen the first time we tried beer.

"It's no bigs, Jordy! I just had a couple," she explains, and then covers her mouth with her hand to stop herself from speaking. "I'm not allowed to talk to you."

"I'm going to find your sister. Luc will get you home." I wander around searching faces on the dark beach.

I walk to the edge of the sand heading west because I see two people—a guy and a girl—standing by the water. Standing really close together—too close. If she made up with Chance, I swear, I will just lose it completely. But as I get closer, I realize it's Callie and a guy named Bobby. They're making out. Hard core.

"Callie." I clear my throat.

She turns around and frowns. "What do you *want?"*

Clearly, Callie knows about Jessie and me, and she's not as drunk or as forgiving as Rosie.

"Do you know where Jessie is?"

"Why would I tell you that?"

I feel a huge wave of despair for the first time that night, but it wouldn't be the last.

"Callie, please, I really want to make this right."

She stares at me with hard eyes and pushes back her narrow shoulders.

"Where's Hannah?" she asks bitingly. "She was here looking for you earlier."

"I don't care," I say. "I broke up with her. I just want to see Jessie."

"She didn't look like your ex with her arms wrapped around your neck on national television while my sister's heart broke." Callie glares at me, and now my heart is breaking.

This is bad. Really bad. I start to panic so badly I'm sweating.

"Callie, honestly. I need to see Jessie."

She sighs and rolls her eyes as she steps away from Bobby, closer to me. She pokes me in the chest with her finger. Hard. I don't even flinch. I deserve it—especially since Jessie knows Hannah was at the draft.

"I love you like a brother, Jordy, but let me make this very clear." She holds my gaze for a long moment. Her mouth is pressed into a tight line, her eyes are like stone. "I'm going to tell you where she is but if you screw up, that's it. No more help. No more chances. Hurt her again and I'll punch you."

I nod solemnly.

Callie points to a place where the beach curves and the lake gets wider. "She's in Arizona."

"What?" I can't breathe.

"After the draft I called Grandma Lily, told her Jessie got into Arizona, and she bought her the plane ticket. Finally the cow did a good thing. She left this morning," Callie says, and I can see the slightest flicker of sympathy in her eyes. "What else was she supposed to do, Jordan?"

"Give me your phone," I demand. "She doesn't answer when she sees my number. Give me your phone."

Callie hesitates but finally pulls her cell phone from her pocket and hands it to me.

"Thank you." I hug her quickly and start to walk farther down the beach, adding over my shoulder, "By the way, Rosie is drunk."

"What?!" she yells in shock, but I keep moving.

I walk around a giant rock as I scroll through Callie's contacts and hit Jessie's number. I lean against the rock and hit call.

"Hey, Cal." Her voice is soft and she sniffs a little like she has a cold or she's been crying.

"Hey," I say softly. There's a long moment of silence so I beg, "Please don't hang up on me."

Tersely she replies, "I don't want to talk to you."

"I didn't know she was coming," I blurt, my voice desperate and rough. "I didn't invite her or anything, I swear!"

"But you didn't ask her to leave either, did you?"

"I wanted to."

"But you didn't."

"Look, just come back. Come here and we'll work this out," I beg. "Trust me. We can work this out."

"I've decided to start in the summer session here," she explains quietly. "I was going to decline because you promised me we'd be together, but then, when I saw Hannah there..."

"So, you don't want to be with me," I say. It isn't a question, it's a statement. An acceptance. A defeat.

"You kissed her! On national television!"

"I told you I loved you!" I yell.

"Jordan!" The voice cuts through the air around me like a butcher's knife.

"What the hell are you doing?"

"She's there?" Jessie's voice turns cold and hard.

"Who are you talking to?" Hannah asks.

"Go away!" I snap at Hannah.

"Jordan. I'm done. Don't call me again."

"No! Jessie, wait!"

Out of nowhere, Hannah grabs the phone from my hand. "What the hell did you do to him? We're in love and you're trying to screw that all up."

I reach for the phone, but she pushes me away. I don't know what Jessie says, but a bitter, twisted sneer takes over Hannah's features. "So you ruined my life for nothing then? I HATE YOU!"

Hannah screams those last words so loud that Callie comes running over. I finally managed to grab the phone back. "Jessie? Jessie?"

I hear a short beep and look at the screen to see the call has ended. Jessie's gone.

"I warned you," Callie hisses, and I glance up in time to see her fist hurling toward my gut. I buckle, winded.

Luc and Rose come running over. Luc grabs Callie by the waist and lifts her up, hauling her away. Rose chases them. I'm having trouble catching my breath, but it's not from the punch.

"Jordan?!" Hannah says my name in a high-pitched, frantic tone. "Are you okay? Oh my God. Jordan!"

"Leave me alone," I warn, and turn my back and start down the beach back toward the rocks, away from everyone. Tears are filling my eyes and I choke back a sob.

"Jordan!"

"Fuck off!" I scream at her, and continue to stumble away.

I get to the rocks and feel my stomach clench up, and I want to punch something so bad my fists ache. And then there's a hand on my shoulder. I spin and see Hannah's concerned face.

"I didn't want you at the draft! I didn't want you to be there for me," I blurt out harshly, reminding her for the millionth time that I didn't plan a future with her even though she planned one with me.

"No, because you wanted her all along," Hannah spits out, and tears start to fall down her cheeks. "You left me for that fucking orphan and she doesn't even want you now! You ruined everything between us for nothing!"

She turns and starts back down the beach. I watch her go for a minute and think about it. I had told Hannah I loved her when she first said it to me months ago. I didn't do it to lead her on. I did it because she was the first girl I had sex with. I thought that was love. I didn't know how much more I could feel for someone because I hadn't let myself feel things for Jessie. Now that I had, I knew that what I felt for Hannah wasn't love. It was like and lust. It was painless. Thanks to Jessie, I knew love felt like pain. Deep, cutting, dying-inside pain. I storm up the beach toward the parking lot. Fuck this. Fuck her. And above all else, fuck love.

Chapter 23

Jessie

How was your trip?" I ask Callie as I sit in the waiting area outside my gate at Seattle-Tacoma International Airport with my phone to my ear.

"Fine. Long. Annoying."

"Is Rosie there?"

"She got in last night but disappeared immediately," Callie says with a sigh.

I smile. "Luc's back too, then?"

"Yep. He swung by the house roughly forty seconds after her car pulled up." Callie sounds irritated. "They went out for drinks and I think I heard her stumble in around three. She's still sleeping."

"Are you sure she's alone?"

"Don't even joke, Jessica Caplan!"

I shake my head and laugh. "Callie, Luc isn't Jordan."

"He's a reasonable facsimile," she argues hotly. "Tall, hot, cocky hockey player, horny."

"If she loves him, she should be with him," I say honestly.

"Thank God I don't have any more sisters professional hockey players can decimate." She pauses and her voice changes and becomes less bitchy. "So, have you talked to him?"

"Not since that nightmare at the bar," I reply. I'd told her all about that, a few days after it happened.

"He's turned into a real disaster," Callie proclaims. "They've shown him at games, in the press box with that thing on his wrist, and he looks like a kicked puppy. And he mumbles his way through interviews like he has a speech impediment. And what the hell is with that hair? He's really let himself go."

I'm shocked and even amused. "You're watching interviews he does?"

"Yeah. So? Whatever," she mutters defensively. "I want new material to make fun of him."

"Flight 412 to Boston will begin boarding," a voice crackles through the waiting area. "We'll start with first-class passengers and those with small children or needing extra assistance."

"Gotta go, Cal," I tell her. "We're boarding. See you soon."

"Okay, have a safe trip. And just one more thing—we're having Christmas dinner at the Garrisons'. Love you! Bye!"

The line goes dead.

I want to be angry but I can't do anything but shake my head and laugh to myself. I wonder when she accepted that invitation on our behalf. Being able to eat Donna's amazing turkey and stuffing again is worth putting up with Jordan again for a couple of hours—if he even shows up.

This is going to be our last Christmas in Silver Bay. Seeing the Garrisons, the ones other than Jordan, will help make it perfect. I doubt Jordan will even be there. He should be back on the ice any day now. The Winterhawks are playing tonight and will play again on December 27 so if he's healthy, he would have no time for a trip home.

I turn my phone off and shove it back into my purse, pulling my ticket out. I glance up and see the first-class line is dwindling fast, so I stand and get ready to get in line with the rest of the regular Joes.

And then I see him running up to the gate in his black wool jacket and his black wool cap. He's got a black laptop bag on his shoulder and his ticket in his hand, which is wrapped in a tensor bandage instead of the brace I last saw him in. Of course he's on this flight. Of fucking course.

I look heavenward and whisper, "Really? Really?!"

A middle-aged woman standing nearby hears me and gives me a funny stare. I sigh, smile and shuffle off to the left, away from her and out of Jordan's sight line. Not that he's looking around. He's busy smiling at the gate attendant, who is beaming back at him, the way girls do with him. Then he disappears through the tunnel with the rest of the first-class passengers. That means I have to walk right by him to get to my seat.

"Now boarding rows fifteen through thirty-one. Please have your ID ready."

I glance at my ticket. Fifteen A. Here we go.

My heart starts beating faster and harder as I walk through the tunnel to the plane entrance. Why, oh, why does this have to happen? I don't know what to say to him. God, that scene outside the bar was so messed up.

The flight attendant greets me at the door and smiles. I nod and glance down the aisle ahead of me. He's not hard to find. He's standing up, in front of the second-to-last row in first class, shoving his coat into the overhead bin.

There's a string of five people in front of me waiting patiently for his perfect butt to stop blocking the aisle. I try my best to hide behind the overweight bald guy in front of me. I see Jordan smile apologetically at the first person in the line and slip into his row. He sits down in the aisle seat and starts fiddling with his iPod. I can only hope he doesn't look up again.

I shuffle down the aisle and I'm almost directly in front of his row when it happens. It always happens on every plane I'm on, but usually once I'm settled and trying to sleep. A baby starts to wail. The sound comes from behind me, and Jordan's eyes dart up.

He sees me. He blinks. And blinks again. And then his eyes close tight and his lips move upward like they do when he's about to laugh. He does laugh—hard.

"It *is* rather hysterical at this point," I say to him, and can't help but smile because what the hell else can I do? "See you later."

I continue to shuffle down the aisle, past the curtain that divides him from the rest of us mere mortals, and I find my seat. It's the window seat in a three-seat row. There's already a friendly-looking guy in the middle seat and a tiny gray-haired woman in the aisle seat. I smile at them and thank them as they let me shuffle in.

I shove my bag under the seat in front of me and shrug out of my puffy knee-length parka, keeping it on the seat under me in case I get cold later. As I reach for my seat belt, I look up and I'm shocked by the wave of happiness that ripples through me when I see Jordan standing in the aisle. Before he can say anything, the guy beside me looks up and his face lights up.

"Garrison, right?" he asks with excitement in his voice.

"Umm…yes," Jordan says with a tight smile.

"Dude! I'm a huge fan!" he gushes, and stands up in front of his seat so that all I can see now is his butt. "I grew up in Queens and I've followed the Brooklyn Barons since I was a kid. I was so psyched when we drafted you. You're great!"

I start to laugh—loudly—and duck my head, unable to look at them.

"I'm not that Garrison," Jordan clarifies. I can tell he's smiling by the sound of his voice. "I'm the one that plays for Seattle. The Winterhawks."

"Oh? Really? Wow, you two look alike!"

"But, hey, if you're a fan of Devin's, I have a proposition for you," he says, and I stop laughing and look up. Jordan has a devious glint to his blue eyes. I'm suddenly nervous.

"Give me your address and switch seats with me for this flight, and I'll send you one of Devin's game-worn Barons' jerseys—I'll even have him autograph it."

My mouth falls open. I can't see it, but I'm fairly certain the other guy's does too.

"You want to sit here?" He looks down at his cramped middle seat. "Where's your seat?"

"Fourth row, aisle, in first class."

"You're giving up a first-class seat *and* you'll give me a jersey?" The guy is astounded. Frankly, so am I. I have no idea how he's going to wedge his giant frame into this seat.

Jordan nods. "That girl beside you is an old friend of mine and I'd like to catch up."

The stranger glances down at me and grins. "You must be a very good friend."

"I've never met him before in my life," I lie.

Jordan rolls his big blue eyes but smiles his perfectly imperfect, crooked smile—the one that makes his dimple show and my insides melt. The guy looks completely confused, but he grabs his stuff and follows Jordan back to first class. A few minutes later Jordan is carrying his bag and his coat walking back toward me. He's wearing an untucked white dress shirt under a thin, black V-neck sweater, and as he reaches up to shove his coat and bag in the overhead compartment, a sliver of skin above his belt appears. As I stare at his flat, hard stomach and the beginning of his blond treasure trail, my mouth waters. I wrench my eyes away and swallow hard as he slides into the seat beside me. His knees are wedged up against the back of the seat in front of him and his elbows are hanging over both armrests. The little old lady beside him looks annoyed, but we both ignore her.

"Hi, Devin Garrison." I giggle.

Jordan rolls his eyes. "I get that a lot and I never understand why. I'm way better looking."

"And you have a better slap shot. And your team is way better," I declare.

He smiles at that. "Your hockey opinion is always good for my ego."

"Not always," I shoot back. "I still think you're an idiot for not wearing a visor. I mean, you had to wear one in junior, so why take it off? And I used to say what is it going to take, a puck to the face? You should wear a visor."

"Messes with my sight line."

"You know what messes with your sight line even more? Losing an eye."

He smiles at that. God, I love his dimple. I shouldn't, but I do. We both fall silent. The flight attendants begin locking down the cabin and going through emergency procedures.

"I didn't give away a first-class seat to talk about the pros and cons of a visor," Jordan finally says a few minutes later.

"You just couldn't wait until Christmas Day to fight with me?" I retort, only half joking.

"I'm kind of shocked you're going home," he admits. "You haven't been home for Christmas since high school."

"Rose begged us. She wants one last Christmas together in the house," I explain. "And your mom invited us over for Christmas Day dinner."

He smiles and turns his head so we're looking right at each other. Suddenly oddly self-conscious, I reach up and play with my hair, smoothing it down and tucking the left side behind my ear.

"I don't want to fight on Christmas, Jessie. That's why I'm going to spend the entire flight with my knees at my earlobes. We need to talk this out."

I nod but say nothing. He just stares at me. Once the plane is barreling down the runway and the front end is lifting into the air, I swallow hard and take a deep breath.

"I'm sorry about the Alex thing," I blurt out quietly.

"I deserved it." He pulls the black wool cap off his head. His overgrown blond hair is all over the place, and he tries his best to smooth it down.

"No, you didn't deserve it." I sigh and lean my head back against the seat. "I just wanted to hurt you. It was completely immature of me. I swear to you we didn't have sex. We didn't even kiss. I went home alone."

He nods and then turns his gaze to his hands in his lap. "I'm sorry for my meltdown. I just…the thought of you…I mean, I want you to be happy. But he wouldn't have made you happy. And I just didn't want to have to hear about it in the locker room."

"The way I have to hear about it at my work," I can't help but say. He looks instantly embarrassed, his eyes shifting downward and his stubbly cheeks turning a pale red.

"I feel horrible about Tori," he whispers gruffly. "I do remember what happened between us…now."

"I don't want to know the details, Jordan," I warn him. "I don't ever want to know."

He nods. "Just know I intend to apologize to Tori. And I want to start over with you."

"What do you mean…start over?" I whisper, but I'm not breathing.

"Look, Jessie," he says in a deep gravelly voice as he picks at the edge of the bright blue tensor bandage that's on his right hand. "I just want to be friends again."

I feel a pain in my chest. I do not even want to deal with what that means. He looks up at me, holding my gaze, his blue eyes so light, so round and so earnest.

"You were so much fun to hang out with," he says in a hoarse whisper. "Remember how much fun we had? And how easy it was to talk to each other? You were like family to me. I miss that. I just want to get it back."

I turn my head to look out the window. A year ago—hell, even a few months ago—I would have told him to go to hell and that I never wanted to see him ever again. But…this hate is exhausting. Maybe it's impossible to get over the pain of what happened when we moved past the friendship. Maybe I'll never have the answers I want when it came to why he did what he did afterward. But maybe I should just stop asking the questions and let go of the pain and get back what mattered to begin with—our friendship. When it came to friendship, Jordan had never disappointed me.

"We are adults now. I guess there's no harm in acting like it," I say with a small smile. "And I really do miss your family."

He smiles at that. "So…Friends? Again?"

I hesitate but nod. "I'll give it a try if you will."

"I will."

We stare at each other for a long moment, and it suddenly seems way too intense on this plane.

"Besides," I begin, trying to lighten the mood, "I have a feeling that my sister is completely in love with Luc. So, our lives are probably going to cross more, not less."

Jordan laughs. Really laughs. Like he did that day in the therapy room. And this time I let myself completely revel in the sound.

"I really hope you're talking about Luc and Rose."

"Who else would I be talking about?"

"Callie and Luc?" he tells me, and I make a barfing sound. "What? You know with Callie anything is possible! I mean, if she can hook up with Devin, why not Luc?"

"Are you drunk?" I ask completely taken aback. "She never slept with Devin."

He giggles. He actually freaking *giggles.*

"The year after I was drafted, he signed that big contract extension and we had a big party," Jordan explains with a smile. "You were already gone to Arizona, but Callie and Rosie came. Callie and Devin got drunk and totally hooked up. I walked in on them in the barn at the back of our property."

I study his face intently. "You're lying."

"Jessie, I don't lie to you," he says, and he means it. He means it so much the atmosphere around us starts to get intense again.

"That little slut." I shake my head and laugh. "I can't wait to confront her on this one!"

Jordan puts that hat back on his head and shifts in his seat. He looks so ridiculously uncomfortable. As if to prove that, he groans in misery.

"You know you can go ask for your seat back now. I won't mind," I tell him.

"Nah. It's fine." He shrugs and gets that big mischievous grin on his face that makes his dimple appear and the cleft in his chin look deeper. "Besides, I can't kick your ass at Scrabble from first class."

I laugh loudly at that. "Really? Jordy, you have never, ever beaten me."

"No, but I've had years of road trips to practice since we last played." He pulls out his iPhone and opens his Scrabble app. I try hard to focus on how good it feels to be friendly with him and not how weird it feels.

But as we get settled in our game and I start kicking his ass, what I feel the most over the weirdness is contentment.

I just love being around him again.

Chapter 24

Jessie

It started snowing," Rose says gleefully, clapping her hands.

I glance out the kitchen window, over her shoulder and smile. "When Jordy gets here I'll make him start a fire."

"When Jordy gets here blah-blah-blah," Callie mimics in a totally annoying whine. She's been a barrel of bitchy monkeys since Jordan and I walked out of the Arrivals gate together earlier this afternoon. I stare at her as she rummages through a dusty box of ornaments we dug out of the attic earlier. She looks up at me, defiant.

"It's Christmas Eve," I remind her. "Stop being Scrooge and show some Christmas spirit because I invited him and Luc over to help us with the tree."

"Of course you did. Bah, humbug." Callie shakes her head and pulls a bag of brightly colored bulbs out of the box. Rose rolls her eyes, annoyed.

"If she can forgive him, who are we not to?" Rose demands, and I nod emphatically.

Callie looks at me skeptically. "You forgive him, do you?"

I falter. "I do. I guess. I mean, I just want to stop being angry with him."

"Why?"

I go to the fridge to check the progress of a bottle of white wine we put in there earlier to chill. Lord, I need a drink suddenly.

"Because I miss being his friend," I reply as I dig in the drawers for the wine opener. "He was a great friend."

"Friendship?" she says as though she's never heard the word before. "You honestly think you can go back to a friendship?"

I find the wine opener in the drawer by the stove. Turning to her, I smirk and say, "Why not? You and Devin got along just fine after bumping uglies."

Callie looks like I just dropped a dancing gorilla into the middle of the room. Her jaw drops and her eyes look like they might pop out of her head.

"WHAT?!" Rose squeals excitedly.

I just laugh.

"Who the hell told you?" Callie demands, her porcelain skin quickly turning crimson.

"Who do you think?"

"That little fucker!"

As if on cue, the front door opens and his deep baritone fills the house.

"Hey! We're here!"

Jordan turns into the kitchen from the entryway, just barely avoiding the plastic Santa Callie hurls at him.

"Whoa!" He looks at me with wide blue eyes. "What did I do now?"

"It's not what you did." I laugh and reach out to block the ball of tangled lights Callie is now throwing at Jordan. "It's what *she* did. With your brother."

"Oh my God, SHUT UP!" Callie screams, but she's laughing, totally embarrassed.

Luc is stunned. "You slept with a Garrison brother? Wait, which one?"

"Devin!" Rose yells, still laughing. "Gross!"

Jordan chuckles. "I'll be sure to tell him you called him gross."

"You're not going to say anything to anyone ever again," Callie instructs him. "Ashleigh doesn't need to know. It happened before she entered the picture. And it wasn't really sex. You should have kept your yap shut!"

"Sorry," Jordan tells her honestly. "I didn't know it was a secret."

He looks over at me and his eyes slide to my shirt. Well…his shirt. He stares at the Silver Bay Bucks logo, and I know he knows it's the one he left on kitchen floor so many years ago because when his eyes find mine again, they're soft and his voice is deep. "Nice shirt."

Callie marches up to him and shoves him. "Come make yourself useful and help me get the tree out of the truck."

I watch as she pulls him back out the door. Jordy throws me a glance like "Help me!" because he's probably worried she's going to run him over with the truck. And I'm not sure she won't. But I just give him a shrug and hope for the best.

Chapter 25

Jordan

Callie marches to the back of the truck while I stand on the porch and take a deep breath. The night sky is navy blue and peppered with stars. The air is that kind of clean, crisp cold that turns your cheeks pink upon contact. I hesitantly step onto the ground, snow crunching under my boots, as Callie pulls down the truck's tailgate. I peer over the side at the bushy green spruce lying there, covered in a light dusting of snow.

"I can't believe you guys are going to this much trouble for a few days," I can't help but observe aloud.

Callie glances up at me, her face as stern and dark as always. There was a time when she didn't look at me with condemnation, but I can barely remember it.

"It means a lot to Rose," she explains quietly. "Out of all of us, she probably has the fondest memories of the Bay. And if she wants one last Christmas tree, I'll give it to her. My sisters should get what they want."

"You didn't always think that." The words leave my mouth before I can stop them, creating a foggy puff of air between us.

She stares up at me. The hard look in her eyes tell me she heard exactly what I said, but she questions it anyway. "Excuse me?"

"Never mind. It doesn't matter now," I say, and smile at her as a peace offering. "Look, I get why you didn't want to give her my number that first summer I came home, even though I begged you to do it. But I want you to know that I just want to be her friend now. I promise."

She huffs then walks around to the open tailgate. She starts pulling on the trunk of the tree as she speaks.

"You know, it's weird. When we were kids, I swear you were the most honest guy we knew. Then you had sex with my sister and bam! Everything you say to me is a complete bag of shit."

"Come on, Callie," I complain, and then move her out of the way because that tree isn't going to budge for her. "What do I have to do to get you to trust me?"

"Stop lying."

"I'm not lying."

I tug, and half the tree slides out of the bed. I glance up to find her staring at me with a somber look on her face.

"Tell me you don't love her."

I blink. "Callie."

"Tell me you don't love Jessie. Tell me that you feel nothing beyond sisterly love for her now." Her hands land on her slim hips. "Tell me that and I will cut you some slack. I'll be your best buddy and biggest fan. I'll make a freaking 'I love Garrison' sign for the next hockey game."

"You're such a freak." I shift my weight, the snow under me

crunching, and I roll my eyes. Callie is making me really uncomfortable right now and I don't like it.

She sneers and a gust of air billows from her lungs, making a white cloud in front of her. "You still love her."

"But I'm willing to let that go," I say sincerely.

"Don't you get it, Jordan? That's why I hate you!" she says, raising her voice in frustration. She plants her hands on the front of my coat, trying to give me a little shake. I don't move an inch.

She hip-checks me out of the way and tugs on the tree again. It starts sliding out of the truck—and it doesn't stop. I grab Callie's arm and yank her toward me so the tree doesn't slam her into the ground and land on top of her. The bushy pine hits the driveway with a thud. Callie looks up at me, and for the first time in a very long time, she doesn't look angry. She looks...dejected.

"Jordy, you give up on her too easily," she whispers desperately. Her eyes dart toward the house to make sure she's not overheard. "You know why I didn't give your number to her that summer? I saw you about five times that summer and the only time you ever brought my sister up was when you were drunk. And after that night, you never brought her up again."

"You said she was seeing a new guy at college. She had moved on," I argue. I will never forget Callie telling me that, even though I was drunk at the time. The pain of it had been sobering. I hadn't tried to contact Jessie after that because of Callie's words.

"She was seeing a guy, but it wasn't serious. But what *was* serious was how much she'd healed since moving to Arizona," Callie informs me sharply. Her mouth—so similar to her sister's—presses into a hard line for a minute before she continues. "She was starting to try to be happy again, and I knew one phone call from you would destroy that."

As Callie moves to the tip of the tree, her eyes fix me. "She loves you, Jordan. She always has. But you didn't deserve her then and you don't deserve her now. Jessie isn't perfect. She's got issues. Our childhood gave them to her, and she has every right to have them."

"I know," I reply because I really do know.

"And yet you still walked away every single time she needed someone to do the opposite."

"What?"

She sighs loudly. "You want Jessie. I know you still do, so then work for it! Show her you're not King of the Man Sluts anymore and then give her the time she needs to actually believe it. Be there and don't give up."

We stare at each other, the tree between us and the snow falling all around us.

"You guys need help?" Luc calls as he lumbers down the porch steps.

Callie breaks our stare and turns to my best friend with a smile. "I'll let you two do all the work."

"Did you let Dev do all the work too?" Luc quips, and wiggles his dark eyebrows, grinning.

She starts back to the house but stops in front of him and shoves him ass-first into the snowbank by the porch. I see Rose and Jessie on the steps smiling. Jessie's eyes meet mine and suddenly, I can't swallow.

Two and a half hours later I'm kneeling in front of the massive brick fireplace in the living room placing another log on the fire, Callie's words still bouncing around my head. She had marched off to bed shortly after the tree was decorated, claiming jet lag, and Rose and Luc had gone to Last Call to meet up with Leah and Cole. Jessie had asked me to make a fire, and as I dug around for a match in all the weird ceramic boxes and bottle Lily kept on the mantel, Jessie asked me if I was hungry.

"Starving," I'd replied, and she disappeared into the kitchen.

Now as I lean back and admire my work, the delicious scent of bacon wafts into the room. She turns the corner with a tray full of grilled cheese and bacon sandwiches and two beers. My face lights up as Jessie places them on the old pine coffee table. "Donna used to make a loaf's worth of these for you after practice. You loved them."

"I can't believe you remember that!" I say, walking over and plopping down on the plaid couch beside her. I reach for half a sandwich and she grabs the other half, and we sit in silence and eat, her eyes on the fire and mine on her.

"You know, this place kind of feels comforting tonight," she murmurs as she reaches for her beer and her eyes move to the Christmas tree. "I bet once we get rid of all of Lily's ugly junk, it'll actually be a nice place and buyers will be able to see its potential."

"I always liked the place," I confess. "Bad plaid, gaudy sunflowers and all."

She laughs and then, as I devour a second sandwich, she reaches out suddenly and pulls my Winterhawks cap off my head. I reach for it self-consciously.

"What's with the hair, Jordy?" she playfully demands as she puts the hat on her own head.

I shrug. "I've never had long hair. Why? You don't like it?"

She reaches out and runs her hand into the floppy mess. Her fingers graze my scalp. It sends a ripple of electricity down my spine and up my cock. I should pull away but there is no fucking way I can make myself do that.

"I don't mind it, but I'm used to you with shorter hair. You look so much like my Jordy when it's cropped and neat," Jessie replies, and my stomach flips at the term "my Jordy." "Callie says the long hair makes you look like you're letting yourself go."

"Tell Callie to bite me," I retort with a smile. She laughs under her breath.

"I think you're going to miss her giving you a hard time after we sell this place," Jessie muses. "Because you know once it's done she'll never leave California again. She loves it there too much."

I open my eyes. She's smiling at me, but it's sad. Sad because she sees the potential in this place—the warmth, the possibility—but she'll never get to enjoy it, and I hate that. I also hate that if a stranger moves into this house, Jessie won't have a place to stay in Silver Bay. Why would she ever come back?

"Speaking of houses...I need a place. And you're selling a place..." I let my statement trail off and hang between us. Her body tenses. She looks ridiculously adorable in my hat and my shirt from when I was eighteen. Her eyes land on mine. I stare back.

"You want to buy my house?"

I can't tell by her tone if she likes this idea or not. When she stands up and walks to Christmas tree, I start to feel panic bloom in my gut.

"Yeah," I say, and shrug like it's no big deal. I stand and walk up behind her. "I mean, it's near Dev's new place, it's big enough. It needs some renovations, like a new kitchen, and I'd add a bathroom to the master. Oh, and I would totally get rid of that heinous

Pepto color in your room. But, yeah. I like the place. I want to buy it."

She turns to face me. Her pretty features are twisted into a mask that's equal parts confusion and shock. She shakes her head, then she smiles—then she shakes her head again.

"It would be weird," she confesses quietly, her eyes on the floor between us.

"What's weird about it?" I ask, worried that she's going to say no. "I'll pay fair market value."

Jessie walks over to one of the windows that faces the front porch and stares out. "So what? You're just going to…live here? Like your summer bachelor pad or something?"

I can tell by the way she says "bachelor pad" that she's thinking of me bringing girls back to her house. I want to tell her that the only reason I want her house is because I want her to live in it with me when I come home for the offseason. Not random girls, just her. But that's too much honesty for her to handle right now. Plus, I promised to be her friend, and that's not a friend thing to say. So I keep my response light. "I just want a place to live that doesn't involve my relatives. And if I buy it, you and your sisters can crash here anytime."

"Jordy, it's a dump," she whispers, and an embarrassed flush crawls up her cheeks. "Lily never maintained it. The roof leaks and the plumbing sucks. And it's not very big. You could buy something much nicer. Or build something new."

"I don't want new," I say firmly. "I want old. I *like* old. Old has character. Old has history. It feels right."

I catch her reflection in the window. She holds my eye for a long, hesitant moment. I hope she's contemplating the meaning of my words. I hope she knows I'm not talking about the hundred-year-old farmhouse.

"I guess it would be cool to know it went to someone we know," she muses, her back still to me so I can't read her expression.

I stand up and walk over to her. She turns around and seems shocked that now I'm standing right there. She looks up at me, her eyes sweeping slowly over my chest, neck and face before they lock with my stare.

"Well, think it over. There's no rush or anything. Talk to Rosie and Callie," I say, and rub her shoulders. "I won't buy anything else until you decide."

"Okay, sure," she says, equally as casually. "I'll run it by them after Christmas and everything. Ultimately, if they're okay with it, I'll be okay with it."

"I should get going."

She follows me to the front door where she leans against the kitchen counter—the one I first kissed her on—and stares at me, arms crossed over her chest. God, she's fucking beautiful.

I step forward, uncross her arms and pull her into a hug. "Night, Jessie."

"Night, Jordy."

She's so warm and soft in my arms. I love how she feels, so I keep one arm around her back, to keep her close while I reach up and take my cap off her head with the other. She tilts her head and looks up at me with a soft smile. Impulsively, I kiss her forehead, pressing my lips softly to her skin for a long moment.

Just as I start to slowly pull back, I feel her shift. She gently, almost unnoticeably, shifts her weight to the balls of her bare feet and pushes up, making herself taller. Her cheek is next to my lips now. If she tilts her head just a fraction of an inch…Jessie tilts her head just a fraction of an inch.

The sound of footsteps bounding down the stairs fills the room, and I step back as Jessie drops her arms from my neck and turns away. Callie walks into the kitchen in red flannel pajamas with cats in Santa hats all over them. She looks from me to Jessie and then rolls her eyes and continues on to the fridge.

"See you tomorrow," I call, and head out into the snowy night. The cold air envelops me and calms the fire coursing through my veins.

Friendship, I tell myself. Friendship isn't supposed to light your insides on fire and make your dick throb in your pants. *Get it together, Garrison.*

Chapter 26

Jessie

After parking the truck at the curb in front of the Garrison house, we follow the shoveled path around the side of the house. There, in the backyard, are the battered boards for the old skating rink that Devin, Jordan and Cole grew up practicing on.

It was a treat. Wyatt hadn't put the rink up for a few years, since the boys were gone all winter and Cole didn't skate anymore. I was so excited when Jordan mentioned last night that we should bring our skates today.

Wyatt sees us first and waves. "Caplan girls are here! Now it's officially Christmas!"

I feel a swell in my heart that gets even bigger as everyone yells welcomes and Jordan grins at me like a big goofball. We all quickly lace up and then hit the rink.

Devin is at one end of the ice, bent over with his hands hooked under the armpits of the snowsuit of his son, Conner. Conner, on his first set of skates, is the most adorable thing I have ever seen.

Ashleigh and Leah are skating backward in front of the duo,

clapping and cheering for the little rugrat. The blond munchkin is grinning from ear to ear. Donna is just outside the rink recording the whole adventure on her phone.

Cole and Luc are at the other end of the ice with hockey sticks trying to steal the puck from each other. Rose skates over to them and does a delicate, graceful spin.

"No figure skating allowed. This is a hockey rink," Luc warns her gruffly, but he's smiling brighter than the sun as he wraps an arm around her neck and pulls her in for a rough, loving hug.

I skate over to Jordan who is standing mid-boards looking helpless. Because of his hand, all he can do is skate—no stick and no roughhousing for him. I do my best boy-style stop, snow flying up at his shins. I'm actually impressed I can still do that without falling on my ass.

He reaches down and hugs me, lifting me off my skates, and whispers in my ear, "Merry Christmas."

I ignore the delicious shiver running down my spine. "You too, Jordy."

We play an impromptu game of hockey with Rose, Devin and Leah on one team and Luc, Callie, Cole and Ashleigh on the other. Jordan sits with Conner on his lap in the corner of the rink, and they cheer us on.

I can't stop staring at the sight. Jordan is still so similar to the sweet, goofy preteen I first met with his long limbs and yellow-blond mop and happy blue eyes—but now he's got stubble growing over his chiseled cleft chin, proving he's no longer a boy. Now he's a man with a tow-headed, smiling toddler curled into his chest. The image is crushingly sexy. I can't believe how it inexplicably turns me on.

Donna calls us in for dinner at four and, thankfully, Ashleigh skates over and swoops up her child, allowing me to shove away that beautiful image of Jordan with a child and the forbidden thoughts it encourages. Thoughts that do nothing to help me forget that I totally almost kissed him last night.

We pile into the modest dining room with the antique oak table and cram ourselves in around it. Dinner is a feast: mashed potatoes, sweet potatoes, green bean casserole, broccoli, cranberries, gravy and a giant turkey cooked to a golden color. I shamelessly stuff myself. We all do. And there's so much laughter. Everyone is so happy. God, I missed this so much.

Rose looks positively euphoric as she sits beside Luc, laughing at something Wyatt said. Donna is beaming as she impulsively kisses the side of Jordan's head while she reaches for the gravy. Even Callie is grinning as she tells Leah some story about a commercial she worked on.

I glance up at Jordan sitting beside me as he shovels some mashed potatoes off my plate and into his mouth. He always used to do that—just eat off my plate, even though his plate had plenty of food.

"Thank you," I say quietly. He looks confused. "For letting me have this again."

A serious, almost sad expression flickers across his face and then he reaches out, wrapping his long arm around my shoulders, and squeezes.

"Thank you for wanting it back." He presses his lips to the top of my head. It's a brotherly gesture but still makes desire spark inside me.

Inwardly, I chastise myself.

After dinner, Ashleigh puts Conner down for the night and we all settle into the living room for board games. This has always been a tradition, but now that we're adults it involves drinking. We start with Jenga but Luc keeps losing. For a guy with such smooth hands on the ice, he's a complete klutz off it. We move on to an old high school favorite—Cranium.

We take a break halfway through Team Jordan and Jessie kicking every other team's collective asses to refresh everyone's beverages. Donna and Wyatt announce they're exhausted and going to bed.

I head to the kitchen with Jordan and Callie, where we all watch my sister put her bartending skills to use with Donna's blender.

"Where did Cole and Leah go?" Rose asks, wandering in with Luc behind her.

"Off for a quickie?" Luc suggests, prompting Rose to smack him in the chest.

"He took Leah out to the rink," Devin says, pointing to the window above the sink that faces the backyard.

I glance out the window and see two parka-clad figures moving cautiously out to center ice in their snow boots.

"What on earth is he doing?" Callie questions but before anyone can answer, Cole is lowering himself to the ice—on one knee.

"Oh my God! Oh my God! Oh my God!" Rose starts chanting excitedly.

"No fucking way!" Jordan breathes, clearly shocked.

I glance at Devin and Ashleigh, who are both smiling knowingly.

"Donna!" I yell at the top of my lungs. "You need to get out here!"

Donna's bathrobe is tied tight around her as she comes charging in, demanding to know where the fire is. I point out the window just as Cole slides a ring on Leah's finger and Leah squeals joyfully.

The room erupts in cheers. Donna fights tears. She knows better than to cry in front of her boys—they're not comfortable with it. Wyatt joins us as Cole and Leah come back in, and he rushes to the garage for a bottle of champagne he was saving for the next Stanley Cup winner.

The next few hours are full of bubbly and laughter.

Ashleigh and Devin are the first to head to bed, knowing Conner will wake them up early. Wyatt and Donna follow soon after as Cole takes Leah home and declares he'll be staying there. Jordan puts Luc to bed because he's completely sloshed.

We're in no condition to drive home either, so Callie and Rose grab sleeping bags from the hall closet and head down to the den.

I gather the last of the champagne glasses from the living room and decide to give them a quick wash before I head down to the den so Donna has one less thing to do tomorrow.

I'm carefully placing a glass on the drying rack when a sliver of light appears in the hallway. Jordan's childhood bedroom door creaks open. I glance up to see Jordan padding down the hall in nothing but a pair of navy blue flannel pajama pants.

"Water," he says, smiling slightly.

I watch him make his way to the fridge, taking in his body. It's quite the sight with all that perfect porcelain skin wrapped around tight, hard, lean muscle. He takes the Brita pitcher out of the fridge and then turns back to me. I blink and give my head a small shake.

"Hangover prevention," he explains, holding up the pitcher.

"Ah," I say, trying as hard as I can to look at anything other than his smooth, muscled chest. Or at his toned shoulders and arms, which have always been my favorite physical part of him.

He walks right up to me, standing only a few inches away. I can feel the heat from his bare skin through the fabric of my sweater. I tilt my head up as he reaches behind me with one of his impossibly long arms and pulls out two glasses from the cupboard above my head. Still smiling his lopsided, dimpled smile, he places the glasses on the counter to my left, then takes a small step in that direction to fill them both with water.

He hands me one of the glasses. Our fingers brush and I feel a tingle shoot up my spine as my belly clenches. I take a big gulp, almost choking. I'm suddenly feeling completely out of sorts—sure, I've had a couple of daiquiris and a glass of champagne, but I don't think this feeling is from the alcohol.

I put the water glass down next to the sink and turn back to the last champagne flute. Jordan jumps up and sits on the counter beside the dish rack.

"So, Cole and Leah," he says, and sips his water. "Another one bites the dust."

I laugh. "Those two have been in love since they were sixteen. It makes perfect sense."

I place the flute in the dish rack and look up to find him staring at me with really intense eyes. I have a feeling I look the exact same way. The air in the room feels thick and heavy all of a sudden. I avert my eyes and notice he's flexing and unflexing his hand.

I reach out and touch it tentatively. "Is it still sore?"

He nods wordlessly. I carefully remove his tensor bandage and turn his big mitt so the palm is facing up. I start to massage him gently. His eyes close and he sighs.

I work diligently on his thumb joints and the pad of his hand and then move to the fingers. I'm swiftly slammed with the memory of how those fingers felt inside me so many years ago. Not just the pleasure of it but the comfort of it—the way he felt so incredibly…right. All these years later, even after all the pain and drama, I still can't forget that feeling…

"I don't know how they did it," I hear him say softly, pulling me from my thoughts.

"Did what?" I ask as I move my fingers to his wrist.

"How they didn't fuck the whole thing up when they were teenagers."

I realize he's back to talking about Leah and Cole.

"*I* fucked it up," he says.

My hands stop moving along his wrist. I stare at the soft blond hairs on his arm, unable to look up. I'm terrified I'm reading way too much into his words. I don't want to look at him and have him see how hopeful I am. I don't want to admit I'm hopeful.

I swallow and shrug, fighting to calm down the hormones raging in my body. "They really love each other. They just never forgot that, I guess."

"But I really loved you," he says in a voice so deep and angst-ridden I barely recognize it. "And I've never been able to forget it either."

I watch as he wraps his fingers around my forearm and starts to pull me by it. I take a step and close the short distance until my body bumps the counter between his long legs.

Don't look up at him, I warn myself. *Don't look up. Don't look…*

I look up.

He's leaning forward. His face is inches from mine. And then it's just...happening.

Jordan is kissing me.

The second his tongue pushes its way into my mouth, I whimper and my knees get weak and my heart explodes. I suddenly want him more than I even knew was humanly possible. I wrap my arms around his neck and tangle my fingers in his overgrown hair, holding onto to it. He stands, pushing his thick, hard body into the space between me and the counter. My whole body is pressed tightly against his; his bare skin is so warm, it's making me dizzy.

His hands slide from my waist to my ass and he cups it, scooping me up. I wrap my legs around his waist, feeling the tip of his cock under the pajamas as it pushes against the denim covering the space between my legs.

And then he's walking. My shoulder clips the doorframe as he moves us into the living room. He drops me down onto the couch and climbs on top of me. We're dry humping wildly, like our lives depend on it. Our lips move over every piece of available skin. I kiss his neck, he licks at my earlobe, I suck on his collarbone. He nips my jaw.

He pulls my sweater off my body and starts unbuttoning my jeans with his good hand.

I know we should talk. We should say something. Talk about what we're doing and why we're doing it and what it means. We should communicate, not fornicate. But all I want in the world right now—in the *entire* world—is for him to push himself inside of me. For him to own me like that again.

I start pushing down his pajama pants as his hand finds its way into the front of my jeans, sliding right into my underwear and then into me. I buck my hips and muffle a groan of pleasure into his shoulder. My hand is in his pants and I wrap it around his length. So long and hard—all because of me. He wants me again as much as I want him.

"Jessie," he whispers against my lips, in the middle of a kiss.

"Please," I whisper back, and he understands. He knows.

He pulls himself to a sitting position, his pajama bottoms still bunched at his bent knees. He yanks my jeans and underwear off in one forceful tug. The only light in the room is the twinkling, multicolored lights of the Christmas tree glowing in the corner by the fireplace. It's enough that I can make out the hard-muscled edges of his beautiful pale skin and the perfect shape of his sizable length pointing toward the ceiling.

His eyes take in my naked body and he smiles down at me. He has that same mesmerized look he had so many years ago, but now it has a glimmer of something he didn't have at eighteen—something voracious. Neither of us is an inexperienced, confused kid anymore. We know what we're doing and how to do it. We know exactly what the consequences are this time, and we're doing it anyway.

I reach up and wrap a hand around the back of his neck and pull him toward me. His body is heavy against me. If I had air in my lungs he'd have pushed it out, but I don't think I've taken a breath since our lips met in the kitchen. He uses his forearms on either side of my head to pull himself upward, every part of him rubbing against every part of me.

"Please," I whisper as he pushes against me again, his tip slipping over my opening as I wrap my legs around his lower back.

That's all the encouragement he needs. He pushes into me.

The feel of him inside me again is euphoric. Jordan shudders slightly when he's as deep as he can go and then kisses me hungrily, moaning into my mouth as he starts to move inside me. Neither one of us closes our eyes. We both want to see this—see what we're doing to each other. We both tip our heads to watch where he's moving in and out inside of me, like we both need to see it to believe it's actually happening again.

It's almost completely different this time.

He's much more aggressive, pulling my breasts free from my bra, covering them with his mouth, sucking and nipping as his thrusts continue, sharp and deep. I'm much more assertive than the first time. I roll my pelvis with every push of his hips and tug his hair and nip his neck. He grunts and moves his lips to my neck as I pant and dig my nails into his shoulders. What's the same is how we fit together—perfectly. No one else has ever felt like this—the way he fills me completely, the perfect, tight pull as he slides out, and the way he keeps his pelvis low, sliding over mine, creating that delicious friction against my clit.

My fingers slide lower, over his toned back. Every muscle under my fingertips is taut, like a wire pulled tight about to snap. His lips part and I kiss the dimple in his chin before I whisper, "So close."

And then he pushes in as deep as he can—once, twice, three times—and I claw at his back as I drown in my orgasm. He rides me through the ecstasy and then he chokes back a guttural moan and trembles, coming hard before collapsing on top of me.

We're both heaving like we've run a marathon. Luckily the sound of our rapid breathing does not mask a thud in a room down the hall or creaking sound of a door opening.

Jordan jumps to his feet, grabbing his pajama pants and pulling them up. I grab the knitted throw off the back of the couch and cover myself as Jordan kicks my discarded clothes under the couch.

Luc staggers into view. I snap my eyes closed and pretend to sleep.

"What are you doing?" he slurs to Jordan, clearly still drunk from the celebration.

"I was getting water," Jordan mumbles. "And Jessie is sleeping on the couch."

Luc mutters something but the only word I can catch is "Rose."

"She's downstairs with Callie in the den," Jordan says, and I can hear him move, walking over to Luc, I assume. "You need to go to bed. Sleep it off."

I steal a peek with one eye and see Jordan holding his best friend by the shoulders, guiding him back into their bedroom and shutting the door behind them. I wait a few minutes and then reach for my clothes, quickly getting dressed.

I lie back down on the couch and wait, but Jordan doesn't come back out. At least I don't think he does. My body and mind are suddenly exhausted, and before I know it, I fall asleep.

Chapter 27

Jessie

It's the smell of bacon that first starts to pull me back to the world. And then it's the sound of Conner's giggle. I shift and stretch.

"Hey, sleeping beauty," I hear from somewhere to my left.

I open my eyes, squinting against the morning light. Cole is sitting in the recliner with a *Sports Illustrated* on his lap and a coffee in his hand. Devin is sitting on the floor cross-legged with Conner across from him. They're playing with the brightly colored trucks we bought him for Christmas.

I realize I'm in the Garrisons' living room, on the couch. There's a blanket across me—a duvet. Jordan's duvet.

Jordan.

I slept with Jordan!

I bolt upright and my head spins as I glance every which way, trying to find him, trying to get confirmation that it wasn't a champagne-induced dream.

"Jessie, you okay?" Devin asks, turning his attention from Conner to me. His brow is furrowed with concern.

I nod. "Yes. I'm fine."

"Really? Because you look like you might barf," Cole observes with a smile on his face.

I have no idea why the hell he's smiling. Who grins like an idiot when they think someone is going to be sick?! I look around again. Ashleigh is in the kitchen in front of the stove. She's cooking the bacon I smell, but I don't see anyone else.

"Your sisters are still asleep," Devin tells me. "Luc got up to dry heave and then went back to bed."

"He better learn to handle champagne," Cole mutters. "Or else what's he going to drink out of the Stanley Cup if he wins one?"

"Ha! Let him concentrate on making playoffs for once," Devin teases.

I curl my knees to my chest, pulling the duvet up higher. It smells like Jordan, and my heart flutters. I try to muster up enough courage and composure to ask casually where he is, but before I can, Devin volunteers the information.

"Jordan's flight was first thing this morning. Mom and Dad are driving him there now."

"He left?" I can't keep the horror from my voice.

Ashleigh starts giggling from the kitchen. Devin laughs too. Cole is still grinning mischievously.

"He said you might freak out," Ashleigh tells me as she walks over with a mug of coffee. She hands it to me before going back to the kitchen.

"Thanks," I say as I blush. I wonder what the hell else he told them.

"He's got practice this afternoon. I think they're going to try to play him in the next game," Devon explains. Then he then he points to a folded piece of paper on the coffee table between us. "He left you something."

I reach out quickly and grab the paper. I unfold it and read. And then reread.

J,

If I'd known that last night was going to end the way it did, I would have pushed back my flight. But it was too late last night to do anything about it and I have to join the team for practice. I hope you understand.

I need you to not think about anything until we see each other again. I know you and you'll freak out. Don't, okay? It wasn't a mistake. At least it wasn't for me.

Call me as soon as you're back in Seattle.

Love,
J

His phone number is at the bottom of the page. When I look up again Cole is grinning at me—even bigger than before.

"You read it, didn't you?" I accuse with a narrowed glare.

"Of course I did," Cole says honestly. "The kid is my brother. I always invade his privacy. It's my God-given right. So, what happened last night that's going to freak you out?"

I sip my coffee. "None of your business."

He smiles. "My first thought is that you two totally…you know, did the deed."

I thank God he's keeping it PG with Conner in the room.

"Cole!" Ashleigh interrupts disapprovingly. "It's not your business, first of all. And second of all, where the heck would that happen? The house is filled with people. There's no privacy."

I keep sipping my coffee.

Cole glances around the room. "I wish I had a black light. Then I could check for fluids and tell you exactly where it happened."

We all make various noises of disgust. Callie and Rose come wandering up the stairs from the basement.

"Hello, family." Callie yawns and glances around. "What's with the moans and groans?"

"Cole is a pig," I reply, folding up Jordan's note and putting it in the back pocket of my jeans.

Cole tries to look innocent. "Hey! All I know is Jordy was smiling when he left here. He looked the happiest I've seen him in years."

I try not to react to that news, but it's impossible.

"Why are you smiling?" Callie asks absently as she tries to smooth her bed head.

"I'm happy that Jordan is happy," I mumble, and shrug like it's no big deal. "I like to see my friends happy."

Callie stares at me for a long, contemplative moment. "What did you do to make him happy?"

Cole laughs. So does Devin.

"You're all being ridiculous!" I say, pushing my hair back over my shoulders. I stand up, put my mug on the coffee table and then begin to fold up Jordan's duvet.

Rose cocks her head at me, steps closer, smiles and covers her mouth with her hand.

"What?" I ask, startled by her reaction.

I glance at everyone and they're all smiling and snickering—everyone but Callie.

"You've got a hickey on the side of your neck," Devin says, pointing. "It's huge."

"About the size of Jordan Garrison's fat mouth," Callie mutters.

I look down, not that I can see it, and then quickly move my hair forward again over my shoulders to cover it. I start to blush furiously.

"So, was it awesome?" Rose asks giddily. "As awesome as you remember? 'Cause you look like it might have been awesome!"

Devin and Cole both groan.

"Don't answer that in front of me!" Cole begs.

"Or me," Devin adds.

"You can tell me later." Ashleigh winks and then walks over to pick up Conner. She carries him into the kitchen for breakfast.

"I am not going to talk to you freaks about anything," I announce before someone else can ask something I don't want to answer—or don't have the answer to, like what the hell we were thinking. "So, please stop asking. I mean it."

We all gather around the breakfast bar and grab forks, everyone diving into the big platter of scrambled eggs and bacon Ashleigh left there. We don't bother to divide it up on individual plates, we all just start going for it.

"Maybe there'll be two Garrison weddings this year," Rose says quietly.

"Shut up. Seriously. Shut up," I tell her, panicked.

The way everyone is jumping the gun is freaking me out. I have no idea what will happen with Jordan. At this point, *anything* could happen... It could either all work out great, or it could all go horribly awry again.

Half an hour later, as we get ready to leave, Callie grabs the keys out of my hand.

"She still insists on driving?" Devon smirks and wraps Callie in a headlock. "Little Callie Control Freak."

I laugh. He hasn't called her that in years, but it's still accurate.

"I'm going to check on Luc and say good-bye," Rose announces, and then skips down the hall.

"Make it a quickie," I snark. I'm fed up with all the jabs coming my way and decide someone else deserves it.

"I'm pretty sure that's all Luc is capable of." Cole snickers.

Devin laughs at his youngest brother's joke as he finally releases the struggling Callie. He gives her a proper hug her good-bye. I hug him too and then move to Cole, who wraps his arms around my waist and picks me up.

"He's crazy about you, J," he whispers in my ear seriously. I nod even though his words make me panic.

Callie pushes me out of the way and hugs Cole as I move on to hug Ashleigh. Rosie suddenly appears in the hallway. She waves at everyone.

"Bye, everyone. Love you all," she says in a forced jovial tone and heads straight out the door.

Luc comes storming down the hall. "Rosie?"

"She left," Callie says, giving him a suspicious stare.

"Oh. Okay," Luc's hand moves to his bare stomach and he turns suddenly pale. "I need to lie down again." He wanders back to the bedroom.

We all exchange awkward glances. I'm just happy the focus is off Jordan and me.

Chapter 28

Jessie

I make my way through the airport slowly, trying not to freak out about being back in Seattle.

I've been trying not to freak out ever since Jordan left Silver Bay five days earlier. It was easier once Luc went back to Las Vegas and Devin went back to Brooklyn. My sisters didn't tease me mercilessly like they did. Callie just stared at me with hard, skeptical eyes, and Rose looked at me like she was secretly planning our wedding and naming our babies.

Now being back in Seattle—knowing he's here and I will see him again—is basically causing a panic attack. I know his note told me not to freak out, but how can avoid it? I mean, just last week we weren't even talking, and the next thing I know we're having sex.

Sex.

Holy hell, that was great. I blush as I meander toward the exit.

When Jordan took my virginity, it was beautiful and it was hot—as hot as two eighteen-year-olds can be. But sex with adult, experienced Jordan was just a heightened version of sex with young, barely experienced Jordan. Mind-blowing. No work, no awkwardness, just pure intense pleasure.

I walk out of the Arrivals gate and glance around for signs to tell me which exit has the taxi stand. But, instead, I find him.

He's standing there in dark, worn jeans and a form-fitting black turtleneck sweater under his black wool winter coat. He's hatless, his growing blond hair actually styled for once. He's wearing black leather boots that make him even taller than his already towering height. I notice he hasn't shaved, and the stubble on his chin and jaw is sexy as all hell.

He smiles at me. It's soft and gentle and so completely the real Jordan—the one not many people see. I blush furiously and feel that panic attack I've been trying to squelch start to bubble up again. He just took away the one thing that was keeping me from freaking out—the time I thought I would have today to find the confidence to face him and whatever it was we'd done. I was headed straight to work from here so I thought I would have all day. Now there's no time. I have no choice but to walk up to him, since running in the other direction would be a little dramatic.

He wraps his arms around my shoulders, dips his head and his lips make contact with my forehead. I force myself to look in his eyes. He's looking at me with such…tenderness.

"I called Rosie and she told me when you were coming in," he says with a wink. "I figured I'd save you the cab fare. You heading straight to work?"

I nod and let him take my bag as we walk toward the exit. "Don't you have practice?"

"This afternoon," Jordan says as we approach his black

Mercedes SUV. He loads my bag into the backseat and then opens the passenger door for me.

I climb in as he walks around the car to get into the driver's seat. I watch his face as he maneuvers his way out of the parking area. He glances over at me with an expression I can't quite read. I used to be able to read everything Jordan was thinking in his face. Not because he was more obvious about it, but because I knew him that well. It makes me realize that we might have a few new things to discover about each other.

"So, tonight..." he says softly. "Do you want to celebrate New Year's Eve with me?"

"New Year's Eve?" I repeat like I've never heard of it.

"My goalie, Choochinsky, and his girlfriend are having people over to his place. I thought we could go. You could meet the guys."

I suddenly feel dread. Meeting more of his buddies and hanging out with a bunch of people I don't know would be uncomfortable enough, but doing it while not knowing where we stand seems daunting. But I can see in his face that he really wants this, and I don't want to pull him from his teammates; his injuries have done that long enough.

"Sounds good." I smile.

His pretty blue eyes light up. "Great!"

As we make our way down the I-5 toward downtown, he starts to tell me about how awesome Chooch's parties always are and about all the guys on the team he wants me to meet. I ask him about his wrist and how his first game since the injury went yesterday. I'd watched it with Donna and Wyatt and he played well, but I wanted to know how he felt. The conversation is easy and light but the heavy, tense feeling inside me doesn't lift. It feels like the elephant in the room is sitting directly on my chest.

He jumps out of the car and walks around to my side as I open the door to get out. Jordan pulls my bag out of the back and then stands in front of me, trapping me on the seat with my legs dangling above the pavement.

His hand reaches up and cups the side of my face as he leans in to kiss me. It's slow and tentative for a second—but only a second. I can't keep it casual, and neither can he. His tongue pushes against my lips, which I part willingly, eager to deepen the kiss.

He grabs my hips and pulls me to the edge of the seat, stepping between my legs. My hands push their way inside his jacket, my fingers skimming across the heavy knitted cotton of his sweater and slipping under it to wrap around his strong neck.

I pull back reluctantly. "I have to go to work."

He groans, but he's smiling. And I'm grinning too, like an idiot. I can't help it. I push him out of my way and hop out of the car, taking my bag from him. I kiss his cheek again and then walk swiftly toward the front door of my building. If I do it slowly, without conviction, I'm likely to turn around and haul him into the back of his SUV and have parking lot sex. I'm that attracted to him right now. As I glance back from the front door, he's leaning on the side of his car, his eyes on me. He gives me a quick smile. He looks so happy. And I feel happy. It makes me nervous.

Do we even know what the hell we're doing?

The day seems to fly by way too quickly. I text Jordan my address, head home after work and the next thing I know he's knocking on the door to my tiny, humble apartment. I'm not ready. I spent way too long trying on everything I own and fussing over my hair, which I decide to curl. I still have to find the right shoes and the one lipstick I actually like.

I stumble out of the alcove I call my bedroom, drawing the gauzy curtains that separate it from the rest of my studio apartment, and rush to the door. I pull it open and find him already leaning in for a kiss, his arm resting above his head on the doorframe.

I don't even manage a hi before our lips connect. I think it was meant to be a peck but the contact is like two sticks that have been smoking, smoldering and finally catch fire. Everything in me flares with desire. My mouth opens and his tongue slides against mine. Now the kiss is deep and a little rough. He moves his lips to my jaw. The scrape of his unshaven face against my neck makes me shiver, and I can feel him smile against my skin. "Are you going to show me your place or make me come in my pants right here in your hall?"

I laugh and reluctantly step away, grabbing the front of his shirt and tugging him across the threshold.

"I have to finish getting ready anyway," I say, and make a grand sweeping gesture with my hand. "Welcome to my palace. Something tells me your place is bigger."

I don't bother to look at his reaction. I know my place is tiny, but it's cheerful and clean so there's that. I leave him walking toward the three large windows that are the front wall of my living room and disappear behind the bedroom curtain.

"It's nice," he calls out, and he sounds like he means it.

"It'll do," I call back from the bathroom as I dig through my makeup bag for that damn lipstick. "I picked it for the windows. It has really great natural light. And the location is not as scary as the other places I could afford."

I find the lipstick and start carefully applying it.

"I like the wide oak floors, and it's got great ceiling height," he says, and I glance over and see his form, through the curtain, walk toward the tiny kitchen tucked into the opposite corner from the bedroom.

"You would notice that because you're a giant and everything," I call back as I finally find the pair of heeled boots I was looking for under my bed. I drop onto the bed, which is covered in discarded outfit choices, and start to tug them on as Jordan pulls back the curtain. "Hey, nosy boy. This room is off limits."

He stares down at me with a cocky grin. "Don't worry, beds aren't our thing anymore. We've moved on to couches, remember?"

I shake my head and fight the heat that wants to erupt on my cheeks. His eyes move up and land on the frames on the wall behind my bed. Three children's drawings in matching cherry wood frames. He walks over and studies them, leaning over me and my messy bed.

He looks at the one on the left, which is of a giant dog with purple fur and three stick-figure little girls standing in front of an orange house next to a blue tree. Scrawled at the bottom is the name Rosie.

"She drew that in kindergarten," I explain quietly. "It was the first thing she drew after our mom died that wasn't bleak and sad."

He nods and I follow his eyes as they shift to the next frame. The work inside is a sketch done with colored pencils. It's of a tree and a lake and a dock. It's not fine artwork, but it's definitely got a lot of artistic value. At the bottom it says C. Caplan.

He smiles and glances at the next one. I watch his blue eyes widen and then he flushes.

"Oh my God, I remember this."

"My first Valentine from a boy." I smile softly. He touches the edge of the glass on the frame as if trying to touch the ridiculous red construction paper card that's pressed behind it. He had drawn the backyard rink at his house with me on it in full-on goalie gear and him taking a slap shot at me. In the drawing he's absurdly bigger than me with one giant arm and one tiny one, and I have giant disproportionate feet. The message across the top in black marker is "Happy Valentine's Day."

"I remember sitting at the kitchen table with Devin and Cole with all the paper and markers strewn out in front of us and being pissed that my mom wouldn't just let us buy the premade kind from the store," he explains, eyes still glued to the card. "Devin made them for everyone in his class—girls *and* boys. Cole made them only for the guys because at seven, girls were still gross. I had made them for all the guys in my class and you."

He finally tilts his head downward and finds me staring up at him. His smile is warm and maybe even a little embarrassed. "Do you remember what it says inside?"

I nod. "To the best goalie I know. Your friend, Jordy."

He laughs at that. Well, I think it's just at that but I'm not sure.

"You think I'm a sentimental fool, don't you?" I ask self-consciously.

"I think..." He pauses and his tongue darts out and wets his lips, which is so fucking hot I think I might pass out. "I think we need to get to this party before I change my mind and fuck you so hard those frames fall off the wall."

"Jordan Garrison!" I gasp, smiling, as he takes my hand and pulls me off the bed and out of my apartment.

My dread from earlier this morning when he first asked me to go to the party starts to build as we drive. By the time we pull up to a large, ornate Victorian home in the affluent Capitol Hill area, I almost ask him to turn the car around. But he looks so happy as he hops out of the car I can't bring myself to do it. So I jump out nervously before he can make it all the way around to open my door.

He grins down at me. "Have I told you how amazing you look?"

I shake my head and try not to blush. His compliment makes the struggle I had earlier trying to find something to wear to a party full of NHL players and their stunning significant others worth it. I decided on the dark-washed designer jeans Callie found at a secondhand store and gave me for my birthday. I paired it with a loose, basically see-through, off-the-shoulder silver-gray top with a little sparkle to it and matching gray camisole underneath. It was a little hippie-ish, but kind of sophisticated too.

It is so strange to be this nervous and concerned over my appearance with Jordy. When we'd first ended up together, impressing him with my looks had never been a consideration. He'd seen me at my best and worst. Heck, he'd seen me go through awkward puberty phases. But now, for some reason, I am struggling to impress him and his friends, which adds to that jumpy feeling consuming me. Jordan takes my hand in his and leads me to the front door. He rings the bell.

The door flies open and a tanned, exotic-looking brunette is standing there. She's in a tight white strapless top and a pair of low, hip-hugging black pants. Her bronzed, taut midriff is visible along with her diamond navel ring that matches the large diamond hoops in her ears.

"Jordan!" she says, delighted. She hugs him tightly. "Happy New Year!"

"You too, Ainsley." Jordan smiles and reaches back to take my hand. "I want you to meet Jessie. Jessie, this is Chooch's girl, Ainsley."

I smile but she doesn't, at least not warmly.

"Hi," she says tersely. Her dark brown eyes land on our attached hands before she spins back toward the living room, which is crowded with people. "Jordy is here!"

There are a bunch of cheers and some guys and girls come forward, kind of swarming us. It's hard to keep track as Jordan goes about introducing me to people. There are the guys from the bar that night—Dix and Alex, who gives me a secretive wink. I think he still thinks I'm crazy, but what can you do?

I meet Chris Dixon's wife, Maxine, and Jordan's team captain, Avery Westwood, and his sister, Kate, who he brought as a date. They all seem genuinely friendly, although they're obviously shocked that Jordan brought a date.

There's a gaggle of girls with resting bitch face against the wall of windows, tucked in where the kitchen and den meet. Ainsley is there with them, and they're in a bit of a huddle until we walk in. Then all their eyes land on us and they slowly break apart, sort of like sharks circling chum in the water.

Chooch and another guy I think I met briefly in the living room call me over to the breakfast bar. It's covered with bottles of alcohol and a blender. I wander over, leaving Jordan to continue talking to Igor, his Russian teammate, and Oksana, Igor's very blonde, *Playboy* model–looking girlfriend.

"What can I get you, little lady?" the new guy asks in a thick, charming French Canadian accent.

"Anything would be great right now," I confess, relieved at the sight of alcohol. "The stronger, the better."

"This is Sebastian, in case you haven't met yet," Chooch explains, grinning, which makes him look very young and adorably dorky. "He's our best defensemen, and he also thinks he's our best bartender."

"I don't think. I *know*." Sebastian winks at me and I notice he has impossibly long, thick dark lashes—the kind I can't even fake with mascara. "Call me Seb. I've heard a lot about you. You fixed Garrison, in more ways than one, I hear."

I blush at that but smile. Chooch gives Sebastian a small hip check.

"Let me make this lady a drink," he announces, and smiles, his nose crinkling and the freckles on it coming together like a blob of ink on the bridge. "One Chooch special, coming up!"

Seb shakes his head vigorously, his thick, shaggy dark brown hair falling into his eyes. "And I'll make you a Seb-tini. His drinks taste like battery acid."

I decide I like these two guys best of all the teammates I've met.

"How about I just drink both?" I reply hopefully.

"Not afraid of booze. I like it." Sebastian smirks at me.

I watch Chooch as he blends vodka, gin, lemonade, ice and frozen blueberries into the blender. He stares at me over the swirling blades.

"So, you and Jordan...you're no longer fighting?" Seb asks casually as he shakes together some alcohol and juice in a martini shaker.

I nod. "We've called a truce."

"That explains why he is so happy lately," Chooch observes, and I smile. "You got back together in Silver Bay, right?"

"Back together? No. I…well, we…I don't know if I would…I mean, we decided to be friends…" I am stammering like an idiot.

Sebastian is staring at me with a cocked eyebrow and an amused smirk. He has the kind of intense, exotic look that I'm sure is menacing to his opponents on the ice, but I'm equally sure women find it sexy and mysterious off the ice. "He called you his girlfriend yesterday at practice."

"He did?" I'm shocked. But that warm feeling blooming in my belly and crawling onto my cheeks also feels like happiness. And that kind of makes me panic. Sebastian laughs and pours his green concoction into a martini glass, which he then slides across the bar at me.

"So, you two haven't had 'the conversation' yet?" He uses his fingers to make air quotes. I shake my head sheepishly. "Poor Garrison clearly has no idea what he's doing."

Chooch gives Sebastian another shove. "What the hell do you know about conversations? The only one you ever have with a woman is 'your place or mine?'"

"That's the best conversation to have!" Sebastian argues sincerely, and then watches me take a sip of the melon-flavored drink he created. "Good, right? Better than that blueberry sludge he made?"

I laugh at both of them, feeling at ease for the first time tonight. But then I glance behind me and I don't see Jordan anywhere. I slip off my stool and give the boys a quick smile. "I'm going to find Jordan."

"Conversation time?" Seb asks with a wink.

"Something like that," I murmur, and head down the hall toward the living room. He's not there either. I start to panic. Where did he go? The last time I lost a boyfriend at a party was Chance in high school…I see Alex coming down the ornate carved oak staircase. There's a tall, thin blonde beside him in a skimpy, hot pink bandage dress. She's got her hand on the railing and he's got his hand on her ass. He smiles at me.

"Have you seen Jordan?" I ask quietly.

"He was upstairs. I just saw him by the bathroom," the blonde tells me, and then turns to Alex. "That was him, right?"

Alex gives her a nod.

"Thanks." I push past him and make my way up the stairs, my heart pounding harder with each step. My mind flashes to climbing the stairs six years ago…a different party, a different house, a different boy.

Please may the result be different.

Chapter 29

Jordan

As I exit the guest bedroom, I see Jessie coming up the stairs. Our eyes lock. She's got a weird look on her face, one I can't read and that makes me uncomfortable. I smile at her, trying to ease the tension.

When she reaches the top, she stops. I notice her delicate hand is gripping the railing so hard her knuckles are white. I don't know what to do so I simply place my hand on top of hers. She tips her head, her hair swinging softly behind her. My free hand tingles at the prospect of tangling itself in that thick auburn mass, but I stick it in my pocket instead.

"You okay?"

"Yeah, I guess." Her focus moves from me to the hallway, eyes darting around as if looking for something.

Before she can say anything, I bend down and kiss her. She isn't expecting it and her body freezes for a second. I'm gentle and soft. I fight the urge to just overpower her like I feel I've been doing with every kiss we've ever shared. The blood in my body boils as I fight to restrain myself.

"How were drinks with Chooch and Seb?" I ask when I finally come up for air.

"Hysterical," she says with a smile on those perfect, full lips. "They remind me of your brothers and Luc."

"Yeah, they're idiots just like them," I joke.

She laughs and the sound is an aphrodisiac. I suddenly regret taking her to this party because I want nothing more than to be alone with her right now. Alone and naked.

"Were you using the bathroom?" she asks.

I nod.

"Show me where it is," she says.

I take her hand in mine and lead her into the guest bathroom, which is in the guest room.

I stop and push open the door to the attached bathroom, reaching around to flick on the light. The room, done in pale green glass tile and off-white marble, fills with light that spills into the guest room.

Instead of going into the bathroom and closing the door, Jessie rocks up onto her tiptoes and kisses me. Her lips are soft but urgent, and her tongue is in my mouth before I can protest. Not that I was planning on protesting.

Everything inside me roars to life and I grab her sides, just below her breasts, and push her up into the wall, laying my whole body flat against hers. I use that pressure to keep her up as she lifts her legs and wraps them around my waist. I cup her ass and push my hard-on up into the space between her legs.

"Jessie..." I whisper into the kiss. It's a warning. I'm warning her that she's started something I will have a lot of trouble stopping.

"I know. It's not the place...and we're not eighteen," she murmurs, and starts to put her feet back down. "This isn't a Silver Bay house party."

"So, what?" I reply, and yank her legs back off the ground.

I back away from the wall and she wraps her arms around my neck to keep from falling back. I carry her into the bathroom and turn, using her back to push the door closed, then press her up against it.

I don't want this to end—ever—so I tell her that.

"Let's get naked and stay in this bathroom forever," I murmur, and kiss my way from her ear to her collarbone.

She laughs and twists a little, which grinds her core against the throbbing in my pants. I groan and push into her. I use my upper body to pin her to that door and snake a hand in between us to pop the button on her jeans.

"Jordy..." she says breathlessly, but she doesn't move to stop me, so I don't stop.

Her hands tangle in my hair as I tug down her zipper.

"There are people everywhere," she says, but again, no call to stop.

Her arms slip down my chest and her fingers curl under the hem of my shirt. I feel her knuckles graze the flesh below my belly button, making me quiver like a virgin. Damn. She owns me.

"Yeah, but not in here. We're alone here." I gently push my hand into what feels like lacey underwear, but I'm too busy kissing that awesome spot just under her ear to actually look.

She takes in an audible ragged breath as one of my fingers slides through her slick folds. Both her hands skim the waistband on my jeans and she follows my lead, popping my button.

"We're not horny teenagers," she reminds me, and then gasps

a little as I push a finger up into her. She's so wet, it's making me crazy.

"We were once," I counter. I try not to quiver as her fingers push into my underwear and lace around my shaft. "We're picking up where we left off."

Her hips start to work with my fingers, which are moving in rhythm with the hand wrapped around me. I fight against the urge to come. You'd really think I'd never done this before. I'm both in awe and fearful of the power she clearly has over me. Still.

Her beautiful lips part, her mouth forming a tiny O as I guide my thumb to the spot every woman wants a man to find. "Jordy, I'm..."

I cover her mouth with mine before she can finish the sentence and smile into the searing kiss as her body clenches and pulls at my fingers. She's quivering against me as her orgasm fades and then, before I know what's happening, she's sliding down the wall.

I watch her drop to her knees, her hands pulling my pants and underwear with her.

"Oh God, Jessie..." I hold my breath as she wraps that perfect mouth around me, fulfilling a fantasy I've had since I was old enough to have fantasies.

Chapter 30

Jessie

We walk back downstairs holding hands, and I'm smiling. Sure, we still haven't talked and I don't know where this is going, but I feel like, right now, living in the past is just fine. This night, that little romp in the bathroom, this is how things should have been with us when we were kids. This is what I've been missing.

Someone calls Jordan's name. It's Chooch. He's in the great room by the foosball table, waving frantically at Jordy. "Come! Unless you're too scared I'll kick your arse." He's trying to be tough but he's got such a baby face, he just looks goofy.

Jordan looks down at me. "I kicked his ass at foosball last party."

I let go of his hand and give him a push. "Go. Defend your title. I'll find Seb and get him to make me another drink."

He grins and kisses my forehead before walking to his teammates. I scan the room, finding Sebastian exactly where I hoped I would—back at the monstrous island in the kitchen, pouring liquid into the martini shaker.

When I plop myself down in the bar stool across from him,

he grins at me and winks. "You want another of my drinks, don't you?"

"Yes, I do."

"Because it's a magical, fantastical concoction way better than Choochinsky's?"

"I didn't say that," I reply.

"Well, you better say it or no drink for you!" He grins mischievously but slides a full martini glass my way anyway.

I take a big gulp of the frothy drink he just placed in front of me. "Delicious," I confirm, and he smiles knowingly.

"It's all about the lemon zest," he tells me secretively and adds, "And if you tell your boyfriend and my teammates I know what lemon zest is, I'll cross check you."

I choke a little at that and he reaches across the counter to pat my back. Boyfriend. Is Jordan actually, really, finally my boyfriend? I guess he is. I take another sip and notice Ainsley slinking toward us, like a jaguar hunting its prey in tall grass. She's being trailed by two other girls in her pride.

"Sebastian, *vein avec moi, s'il vous plait.*" A willowy blonde in a low-cut tank top loops her arm through his as she whispers these words to him in broken French.

Seb raises his dark eyebrows just a little, clearly impressed. "You speak French?"

"I do a lot of things in French," she replies suggestively.

Seb lets her guide him away, leaving me with Ainsley and a busty brunette I haven't met. I meet Ainsley's cool stare. I try to remember the feel of Jordan's hands on me and the way he looked at me after he came in my mouth upstairs; that gives me confidence. He wants me here. I belong.

"Having fun?" Ainsley inquires, but her tone suggests she doesn't give a shit.

"I was."

"You must feel like you've won the lottery," she surmises. She starts dropping fruit into the blender, tipping vodka in after it. "A rich, talented boy takes you out on the town and another rich, talented boy makes you drinks."

I take another sip but don't respond. Because if you have nothing nice to say…

"Where did he meet you again? A bar? At the restaurant you work at?" Ainsley's dark eyes are hard.

"Let's see…" I put my glass down on the marble counter between us. "I think it was Mrs. Howlett, our third-grade teacher, who first introduced us."

She looks perplexed. Her slutty sidekick looks downright confused. But Ainsley isn't new to this mean-girls routine and recovers quickly.

"Funny, Jordan never mentioned you. Ever," she says with a shrug. "I guess you don't matter that much."

The brunette sidekick reaches for the vodka and starts looking for a clean glass. Ainsley hands her the martini shaker with the last mouthful of what Sebastian had concocted for me.

"Have some of Jessie's drink," Ainsley tells her friend, smiling. "You've shared men, you might as well share drinks."

I really wish I could appear unaffected, but I can't. That jagged little revelation is cutting through my heart like the blade of a serrated knife.

"Jordan's good, isn't he?" she asks with a smug smile. "At least he was for me. Every time."

"You're not the first, Jenny," Ainsley says, leaning over the counter so she can hiss it at me. I'm sure she got my name wrong on purpose. "And even if you stick around, you won't be the only."

Without a word, I take my drink, slip off my stool and walk away. There is nothing else I can do. I can hear Ainsley and the other slut laughing at me. It takes everything in me not to turn around and punch them both in the throat.

I wander through the house, feeling like I've been shot. I must look like it too, because Jordan abandons his foosball battle and walks over. Chooch screams, "Forfeit!" but Jordan ignores it.

"What's wrong?"

I shake my head. "I'm going to go."

"What?" He's upset now. "Why?"

"I don't belong here," I tell him quietly, and then put my drink down on the coffee table. I start toward the front door. He follows me. When we get to the front hall, he grabs my shoulders and spins me around. It's not rough, but it's insistent.

"Jessie, talk to me. Please. What's going on?"

"I don't know what the hell I'm doing here," I confess in a choked whisper. "I mean, what the hell are we doing, Jordan?"

"We're dating again," he insists, his hands sliding to my upper arms in a loose grip.

I laugh, but it's mirthless and cold. "We never dated to begin with, so we can't be dating *again*. All we did was have sex. Then and now. That's all we did."

I pull my arms out of his grip and jab an accusing finger toward the living room. "Just like you did with her."

His blue eyes shift in the direction I'm pointing, and he sees the brunette across the room sipping her martini and smirking at both of us.

"Bethany?" he says.

"Oh, so you remember sleeping with this one?"

He ignores the dig completely. "That was...nothing. And the last time it happened was a year ago."

I shake my head. "She wanted to compare notes."

"That's because she's bitter I'm picking you, not her," he whispers hotly, reaching out for my hand.

I pull away. "Look, I don't regret having sex with you," I tell him honestly. "Not then and not now. But we're just not good at anything else."

"How can you say that?" he questions angrily. "You've never even tried."

"I haven't tried?" I fire back, furiously pushing my hair back from my face. "I would have tried way back when, but you and Hannah—"

"Tried from where, Arizona? Because you left, remember?"

"Hey! It's almost midnight!" Chooch calls out, unknowingly interrupting our fight. "Everyone get in here! We've got champagne!"

We stare at each other for a long heated second as people walk by us heading for the living room where Chooch and Ainsley are handing out noisemakers and tiny bags of confetti. Without a word, he takes my hand and starts to drag me back to the party.

"I want to leave," I quietly plead.

"And I want to stay," he returns. "I'm bigger, so I win."

His old argument still rings true. I know if I pushed hard enough—both verbally and physically—he'd let me go. But I don't.

I just stand beside him as his teammates and their partners and Ainsley's slutty friends start counting down to the New Year. They reach one and everyone cheers. Confetti flies. Noisemakers wail. People start hugging and kissing.

Jordan turns to face me and wraps an arm around my waist. He lifts my chin and tilts my head upward. Before I can protest, his lips are on mine. It's a hot, deep, needy kiss. I lose myself in it completely. All my anger, frustration and humiliation melt. And then I hear whistles.

"Easy, Garrison," Seb calls out. "Keep it PG, buddy!"

Avery laughs and calls out, "Get a room!"

"There's a guest room upstairs if you need it!" Chooch happily suggests, garnering chuckles and claps.

I break the kiss, flushed from the heat of it and also embarrassment at such a public display. My eyes fall instantly on Ainsley and Bethany, who are both shooting me death stares. Jordan refuses to let go of my hand.

He drags me over to Chooch and tells the goalie we'll be heading out. We then make our way around the room saying good-bye to various people. Well, Jordan says good-bye. I just wave, nod and smile.

Seb reaches for me and hugs me good-bye. "Women all over Seattle are going to be crushed you took this boy off the market. Well, at least the three or four who haven't had him."

I know he's just teasing. He doesn't mean to hurt me at all, so I try not to frown. I let Jordan lead me through the house and out the front door. As soon as we reach his SUV, he pushes me against the back bumper and puts his hands on either side of my head, staring down at me.

He brings his mouth close to mine—hovering maybe half an inch away—and then he just stops. My eyes are glued to his lips; his tongue slides out to wet them slowly. I have always loved Jordan's lips. And the cleft in his chin. And the cool azure color of his eyes.

I hold my breath and look up into those eyes. He's looking at me with so much desire, it's radiating off him. I can *feel* it. I can't handle being this close to him. I can't resist the need to touch him. I tilt my head and push up on my toes, pressing my lips to his. He kisses me, his hands moving to my hair, grabbing onto it, tilting my head back farther so my mouth opens and his tongue can gain entrance.

I push my hands into his open coat and under his shirt. His skin is warm contrast to the cold night air. He flattens me against the back of the car, his body pressed firmly against every part of mine. My hands slide up his back. His groin pushes against my hip. He's hard. I can feel it. And I'm wet. I can feel it that too. And then he does the unthinkable—he pulls away.

"Tell me you don't want me," he says in a hoarse whisper, fighting to catch his breath.

"I *do* want you," I tell him quickly, and then take a breath to clear my head. "That's not the problem."

"Then what the hell is?!" he demands, his breath making white clouds in the winter air between us.

"We don't even really know each other anymore," I mumble as he pushes himself off the car and away from me.

"Are you different?" he asks in a hard tone. "Is orange no longer your favorite color? Have you finally stopped listening to nineties pop and started listening to hip-hop? Are you no longer scared of spiders? What's changed?"

"*You're* different."

"Me?" He shakes his head dismissively. "I'm not different at all."

"Really?" I say, and now it's my turn to have the hard tone. "The Jordy I knew didn't fuck random puck bunnies."

He stares at me for a long moment, then rolls his eyes. "I slept around a bit. I won't deny it and I'm not ashamed of it. I like sex, Jessie. I blame you for that. If it wasn't so fucking perfect with you, maybe I would have been satisfied with one of these girls. By the way, no one—nothing—has ever made me feel as good as you do."

I say nothing. I mean, what do you say to that? "Thank you" seems a little ridiculous.

He cocks his eyebrow. "Are you trying to tell me that you haven't had sex? You've been a born-again virgin since our first time?"

"*My* first time," I bitingly correct him, reminding him I was the only virgin in the room that night. "No. I've had sex. Just not with everything that walks by."

"I would have just had sex with you this entire time, Jessie, but you left me, remember?" he says sharply, jamming his hands in his pockets. He kicks at the snow at the edge of the sidewalk in front of Chooch's house. "You *left* me."

"What was I supposed to do, Jordan? It felt like everything you said was a lie!" I ask angrily. "I didn't trust you and I couldn't risk my whole future on you. I just...couldn't."

"I've never lied to you a day in my life, Jessie." His voice is low and deep, thick with anger and pain. "But somehow I'm always the bad guy."

"You let Hannah—"

"There is no Hannah!" he yells, cutting off my words.

"There *was* a Hannah," I correct him. "And a Tori and a Bethany and a million others. Ainsley reminded me of that."

"Fuck Ainsley!"

"I'm surprised you haven't."

He swears under his breath, runs a giant hand through his hair and then balls that hand into a fist. His cheeks are turning red with anger, not from the cold.

He opens his mouth and points at me. His eyes are blazing with anger and something else... rejection? Sadness? Something painful and dark. But before a word leaves his mouth, he drops his hand and presses his lips together. And once again, he's that eighteen-year-old kid who can't—who won't—process his emotions.

We stare at each other in silence. Jordan moves around me and opens the passenger door. "Get in. I'll take you home."

I get in.

We drive most of the way in silence. I keep glancing at him trying to figure out what he's feeling and what he's thinking. I have no idea. It makes me realize once again how much has changed. He pulls up in front of my apartment building and turns to me as he shuts off the car.

I close my eyes and lean my head back against the seat. His words back there had left me colder than the winter air around us. I was chilled to the bone by the realization of how my actions had affected him. I picked Arizona because I was too scared to trust him. I needed to protect myself, and I really never stopped to wonder how that made him feel—because I'd convinced myself I had no other choice.

"I'm sorry I felt I had to go to Arizona," I whisper. "I'm sorry that it hurt you."

"It didn't hurt me. It destroyed me."

"Then why do you want this again?" I can't help but ask in a desperate, hoarse whisper. "Just go back to your women and your fun and forget this."

"That's what you want, isn't it?" I open my eyes and look at him. He's staring straight ahead at the steering wheel, his hands twisting in his lap. "For me to just drop you, or play you like you thought I was doing back then. Like you *still* think I did back then."

His words are hard and heavy, dropping between us in the car like bricks. I'd spent my whole life acutely aware that I could be let down at any moment—by anyone. Jordan had never failed me until I saw Hannah at the draft. He said he didn't invite her, acted like he wasn't a guy who would do that. I'd run anyway. So when I found out he'd gone on to treat his bedroom like a fast food drive-through, I assumed it was all the proof I needed that he *was* a bad guy. Was it? Was I just another one of the billions served, or was I different this time? Had I been different all along? I honestly didn't know, and that was the problem.

"Jordan, I'm incredibly attracted to you," I confess quietly. "I've never been so attracted to anyone in my entire life. But…I don't think I can just let that be everything."

I feel hot tears pricking at my eyes. He nods now, still staring straight ahead, still wordless, his fingers still tangling with themselves. Finally he mumbles, "So, this is happening? You're leaving. Again."

"No!" I say a little louder than I mean to. He finally pulls his eyes from the steering wheel. "I just need some time. I want to be friends. I need to get to know you again."

He looks away again.

"Please," I beg softly.

Finally, after a long time, he nods. "I'll try."

I feel a wave of relief wash over me. If he had said no I would have been devastated. I impulsively reach out and touch his hand in his lap. I feel his fingers seize and become stiff. "Have a good road trip. Call me if you want, okay?"

He nods, but I can't help wondering if he actually will.

I step out of the car and force myself to walk to my door. Glancing back once, I see him watching me through the window, his expression dark. As I put my key in the lock and pull open the door, I hear his tires peel away.

Chapter 31

Jordan

I skate over to the face-off circle left of Chooch's net as the TV network comes back from a commercial break. Devin is gliding along behind me. It's another Garrison against Garrison draw. The media loves this shit so whenever we're playing each other and Devin's on the ice, Coach's orders are I take the draw. Even if Westwood, arguably the best center in league, is out there too. Because the league isn't just about winning, it's about ratings, like any other televised sport, and brother against brother gets ratings.

"What are we at, Mac?" I asked the ref, Iain Macintyre, a silver-haired, gruff Canadian guy who had been in the league "since I was a gleam in my father's eye," as he once told me when I questioned one of his calls.

"He's won five. You've won three," Mac informs me about the draw count between Devin and me. "You gotta pick it up."

Devin grins cockily at me as he skates into position. "Yeah, little brother. Pick it up."

"Why don't you stop worrying about the draws and start worrying about your team's inevitable loss?" I shoot back cockily as I lean over and lift my stick, eyes glued to the puck in Mac's hand.

Devin does score in the dying seconds of the game, but it's not enough to win. The Seattle Winterhawks beat the Brooklyn Barons 3–2. More important, I beat Devin. It feels great, like it always does, but my first thought is to text Jessie about it. I love to gloat to her because I love how she loves to put me in my place when I do. But I'm not ready to text her yet...as her friend anyway.

The locker room is loud and boisterous. We really needed this win. We'd lost our game in Atlanta last night in the shoot-out, which was a shitty way to start a road trip. Tonight's win made us at least a little optimistic we could face Boston next, a team we hadn't beaten once so far this year.

As I'm shrugging into my suit jacket, my phone buzzes in the pocket. I figure it's just Devin telling me to hurry up, but it's Jessie.

Tell Devin I say hi.

I smile and type back, *You mean the loser? Yeah. I'll tell him.*

A second later she responds. *Easy, egomaniac. That loser won six out of nine draws against you.*

I laugh. *Whatever. Drinks are still on him.*

I head out of the locker room still smiling and glance up from my phone as Devin turns the corner. His dirty blond hair is damp from a shower, and he's wearing his pregame suit including the ice-blue tie. "Are we going to church or a bar? Lose the tie."

He sneers at me and gives me the middle finger before tugging his tie off and shoving it in his pocket. I find it hard to believe he's a married dad. He still looks so much like the big, scared eighteen-year-old who had moved to Brooklyn by himself and cried when he hugged our parents good-bye. I wonder how that big ball of dork managed to get someone to commit her life to him when I couldn't even get Jessie to commit to being my girlfriend.

As we make our way out the players' entrance and to the private drive where cabs are waiting, my text message alert sounds again.

Oh...you're going out. Well, be safe. Night.

I stare at the screen. Devin glances over and reads it as we slip into the cab and he gives the driver the address of the bar. "Is that Mom? Is she texting now? Please don't say she knows how to text because the phone calls three times a week are more than enough."

"It's not Mom," I explain as I text back a quick "goodnight" in response. "It's Jessie."

He balks at that. "Be safe? That doesn't sound like a girl who lets you give her hickeys."

I lean my head back and groan. "Why can't she just say something like 'miss you'? Or 'wish you were here'? Or 'come back from your road trip and fuck me again'?"

"Thanks for that visual." Devin's face scrunches up in disgust. "So you guys haven't...since Christmas?"

I shake my head, not bothering to mention Chooch's bathroom because I want his face to go back to normal. "She says she needs to be friends again. That she needs time. She's had six fucking years."

I stare out the window at the snow-covered Brooklyn scenery.

"A committed relationship nowadays is work. A fuckload of work," Devin explains as he rubs the back of his neck thoughtfully. "If you and Jessie aren't sure that you're in the right place emotionally to take that on, then don't. Ashleigh and I love each other, but sometimes with this job and Conner and everything...it's just not all shits and giggles. It's actually probably better you didn't rush into that as kids."

The cab pulls to stop in front of the Counting Room. Devin pays the driver and we get out and make out way across the icy sidewalk and into the bar.

I push Devin out of the way and walk in first, explaining "Winners before losers."

Devin smirks. "Sure. But the winner should also buy the drinks. I have to save my money for the All-Star game coming up. You don't. You weren't invited."

We make our way downstairs to the spirits lounge because Devin only drinks whiskey after a loss, a stupid little ritual he developed when he made the NHL. He said it's because he hates whiskey. I don't get the logic, but whatever. No one understands why I only wear red underwear on game days. We all have our quirks.

We walk up to the bar and I order a Crown Royal for Devin and a spiced rum and Coke for myself. Then, drinks in hand, we make our way to a free table near the back of the room. We talk about Cole's upcoming wedding and how Luc and his team are dead last in the entire league. Neither one of us can figure out why he's struggling.

"You know it's fucking killing him too," I say sympathetically as I take off my jacket and hang it over the back of the chair.

"You've got a hot blonde completely checking you out," Devin informs me, an amused smile on his lips.

I stop rolling up the sleeves on my dress shirt and glance over my shoulder. Sure as hell, there is a tall blonde in a pair of painted-on skinny jeans and a low-cut sparkly gold top batting her heavily eye-shadowed eyes at me. She's pretty—tanned skin and brown eyes and a ski jump nose. A year ago…hell, a few months ago... there would be no question that I would end the night with her on my cock. Now there was zero chance. But I turn back to him and grin. "What can I say? I'm hot."

"You're a watered-down version of me," he retorts, and sips his rye whiskey.

"Is that the lie you tell yourself?" I laugh and shake my head at his delusion.

"Incoming!" Dev pipes up a second later.

I turn to find the blonde standing right behind me.

"Hi," she says with a bright smile. "Let me buy you a drink."

I'm about to politely decline when she takes my hand and drags me toward the bar. I realize she wasn't asking me, she was telling me. Again, this would have been hot a few months ago, but now, it is a complete turn-off.

The blonde slides herself into a small space between against the bar between two groups of people, takes my hand and pulls me in next to her. "I'm Erica."

"Hi, Erica," I say, subtly stepping back and bumping a girl behind me in the process. "I'm Jordan."

"Jordan Garrison. Number forty-four on the Seattle Winterhawks," she replies with a deep, sultry grin. "I know. I'm from Bangor originally. Everyone in Maine knows the Garrison brothers."

Speaking of brothers, I glance over at mine. He's alone, nursing his drink and looking down at his phone in his hand with a scowl.

"This place is crazy busy," Erica says, still smiling suggestively. "You know, I have a fully stocked bar at home. My place is just around the corner."

"I'm sorry, I have to go." I pat her shoulder and, without looking back, make my way to Devin.

"Oh, fuck. What did you do?" Devin asks with a smirk when I get back to the table. "How'd you blow that? It looked like a sure thing."

"Have I mentioned I love the confidence you have in me," I snap, and make a face at him like I used to when we were kids. "I'm not interested in sure things. Apparently I'm only interested in impossible things."

He stares at me, glass hanging halfway to his open mouth. "You aren't filling the void, are you?"

"What?"

"Keeping busy with substitutes?'

"What the hell are you talking about?" I bark, annoyed.

"Scratching the itch?" he asks again.

"Huh?"

"You haven't been fucking other chicks, have you, Jordan?"

"The only thing on my goddamn dick is my hand," I reply angrily. He must see the sexual frustration on my face because he seems to believe me. "I haven't touched anyone else since I laid eyes on her at Mrs. Caplan's funeral."

"Have to admit I did not see that coming," he says, amazed, which annoys the fuck out of me. "So you're serious about her this time."

"I was always serious, asshat," I say angrily. I take a deep breath and then say, "But I want it to be different this time. I want her to believe me."

"Okay. Well, if you don't want to die of sexual frustration, you're going to have to do something you won't like," he warns me, and puts his glass down on the table as he leans closer to me.

"I'll do anything at this point," I confess, and I mean it. I'm desperate.

"Make a grand gesture," Devin advises, giving me a big, dopey smile. "Pull out all the stops. Do something romantic and embarrassing and completely out there. Girls love that shit. It makes them realize you're vulnerable, and they trust vulnerability."

"You're kidding, right?" I feel nothing but despair at his idea; I despise vulnerability and I'm romantically clueless. "I offered to buy her house. That's a big thing."

"You're going to buy the Caplan farmhouse?" Devin blinks and gapes in disbelief. "That gesture screams financial incompetence more than romance."

"Fuck you. It's a good house. It just needs to be fixed up," I state firmly. "And besides, I thought if I owned it maybe she would still feel like it kind of belonged to her and she would still want to visit Silver Bay. That's romantic, right?"

"No," he replies flatly. "Not if you didn't tell her that when you offered to buy it."

"I didn't."

"Of course you didn't." Devin nods and sighs at my hopelessness. "Valentine's Day is coming up. Do something related to that."

"I don't want to wait that long," I mumble, feeling defeated again.

Devin lets out an annoyed huff and picks up his glass again. "Okay, then. Give up. Invest in lube."

"You're useless," I tell him, even though he's not. He gave me a solution. I just have to figure out how to do something big and romantic while hundreds of miles away from her on a four-game road trip. Also, figure out what big and romantic even is. I never got the chance to do anything romantic for Jessie in the past. I went from being the handy friend who lit the pilot on a burned-out furnace or chased raccoons from under her porch to the guy who slept with her and punched her ex in a jealous rage. Nothing romantic about either of those things. And it's not like I learned from other relationships. After Jessie...well, romance wasn't something I wanted to share with anyone who "filled the void," as Devin had crudely called it.

Devin must sense how high my stress levels are over this because, as he finishes his drink, he reaches over and cups my shoulder, giving it a small squeeze.

"Don't worry. It's Jessie," he reminds me with a quiet confidence in his voice that actually soothes me. "You'll figure something out and it'll work."

"Thanks, Dev."

"Sure, Jord." He lets go of my shoulder by giving it a little shove. "Now get me another drink."

I decide he's right as I wave a waitress over and order us two more drinks. I need to lay it out there—once and for all.

Chapter 32

Jessie

Despite the fact I only got four and a half hours sleep, I'm feeling cheerful and oddly content as I pull into the parking lot at work. Just like the last four nights since Jordan left on his road trip, I had trouble sleeping last night, but it wasn't because of the usual conflicting feelings that had been warring in my heart since New Year's. This time it was one clear emotion keeping me up—doubt. He had said he was going for drinks with Devin, which meant he was probably going to some sexy, hip watering hole in Williamsburg filled with beautiful, single, eager women. He was single. We were friends. He could do whatever he wanted, but it would still break my heart.

Against my better judgment, when sleep refused to come, I'd picked up my tablet and surfed the net, hoping it would make me drowsy. It didn't, of course. In fact, I was wide awake when I typed that stupid puck bunny website into my search bar and waited for it to load. I clicked right through to his section, and my heart sank when I saw a brand-new post, only a few hours old, by someone with the username E_Cat14. The subject of the post was "Double Garrisons..." It glared at me, bold and bright, taunting me to click on it. So I did. Because I was weak and pathetic, I clicked.

The first thing that loaded was a continuation of the subject. Now it said: "Double Garrisons...aren't double the fun." Underneath that, she'd loaded a picture. It was of Devin and Jordan sitting alone at table in a dark bar, both holding tumblers with dark liquid, both deep in conversation with each other, unaware of anyone around them. My body relaxed and my eyes reluctantly pulled away from the two handsome brothers to the message underneath from E-Cat14. She wrote, "*So I finally ran into Jordan Garrison, which should have been a dream come true if all the stories on this site are to be believed. I got up the guts to ask if I could buy him a drink and got him to come to the bar with me. He seemed nice at first but before I could even order, he told me he was sorry and ran back to his brother. I get that Devin blows chicks off 'cause he's married, but Jordan is supposed to be DTF. Conclusion: I think you're all making the sex stories up. Dude is clearly gay.*"

After that I'd had trouble sleeping because I couldn't stop laughing. I'd even woken up and reread it. A couple people had commented on it with a few "LOLs" and a few "better luck next times," and one even bitched she'd run into him a few weeks ago and he'd blown her off too.

When I open the door to our office, Tori is standing in the reception area with a crooked, slightly crazy-looking smile on her face. It reminds me of a cross between a hyena and a high school cheerleader on uppers.

Suspicious, I ask, "What on earth is going on that could cause that look on your face?"

She grabs my hand and pulls me to the reception desk. Kelli, our bubbly nineteen-year-old front desk girl, is grinning just as maniacally. She points to a huge bouquet of flowers on the desk beside her.

"Someone has a secret admirer and it's not me!" Kelli says in an excited singsong voice. I turn to look at Tori again. The flowers must be for her.

"Sadly, it's not me either," she tells me with a quick frown, but the hyena smile comes back a second later. "It's you! These came for you!"

I look at the flowers again. They're lilacs in shades of white, purple and blue. Lilacs have been my favorite flower for my entire life. We had a bush outside the barn and when it bloomed in June, I would cut every flower I saw and fill the house with vases of them, completely ignoring Callie's hay fever.

But it's winter and lilacs aren't in bloom. Whoever sent these must have known my affinity for them and spent a ton of cash to get them off-season. Kelli unsticks the card that's taped to the side of the vase and hands it to me.

"Find out who it is!" Kelli demands. "Unless you know. Do you know who sent them?"

I swallow. I know who I want to have sent them, but Jordan wouldn't do this. He has no reason to send me—his friend—flowers, right? I shake my head, indicating I don't know, and stare at the big white envelope in my hand. It's not like a typical flower card; it's the size of a real card, which is weird.

I'm nervous as I open it with all these eyes on me. I pull the card out of the envelope and my heart melts—it's homemade. The drawing on the front is in pencil and ink, and it's a replica—albeit a much more detailed and less crude version—of the card framed on the wall in my bedroom.

He's written "Happy Early Valentine's Day" on the front. I try to keep my hands from trembling as I open it to read.

J

I didn't feel like waiting another month to tell you…

You're not the best goalie I know anymore, but you're still my favorite.

Yours,

J

I feel my heart swell and my grin stretches to the point that my cheeks hurt.

"J? Who the hell is J? And when were you a goalie?" Tori asks, reading over my shoulder. "Is that from Jordan Garrison?" She just about screams his name.

"Shhh!" I command.

A patient in the attached waiting room looks up at the commotion. I smile in apology and reach for the flowers.

Kelli is positively bursting with excitement. "Jordan Garrison is sending you flowers? Are you two dating?"

"No. Just old friends."

"Boys don't send flowers to just friends," Kelli informs me matter-of-factly, like I'm an idiot. "No matter how old."

I walk away, heading back to my office with the beautiful, aromatic display wobbling in my hands. As I place them on my desk, I can't resist taking a moment to inhale their beautiful fragrance. My eyes flutter closed. I remember being young and how stressed and scary it was most of the time—being alone and responsible for my siblings—and then I remember this smell calming me. This smell and the smile of my best friend—Jordan's smile—are my fondest teenage memories.

I grab my cell off my desk and send him a thank-you message. *Got the flowers and card. You're adorable! Thank you.*

I sigh and stare at the flowers. I miss kissing him. I miss having sex with him. I think about it all the godforsaken time.

Tori walks in and when she sees my face, her smile falls.

"Are you okay?"

Tears blur my vision. I blush, embarrassed, and wipe them before they can fall.

"Yes. I'm fine." I nod. "Sorry. I'm fine."

"Turns out I got something from Jordan too," She holds up an envelope and smiles. My heart lurches in my chest and I feel the blood drain from my cheeks. Tori must see it too because blurts out. "Nothing romantic like yours. Just a pair of tickets and VIP access passes to the next home game and an apology."

"Oh."

She pulls out a piece of paper and starts to read from it. "Dear Tori..."

"You don't have to." I shake my head.

"You want to hear this, Jessie," Tori insists, and continues. "Dear Tori. I'm not sure what to say other than I'm sorry. You have every right to hate me. There's no excuse that justifies my not remembering you right away. But I hope you know it reflects on my lack of character, not yours. These tickets don't make up for anything, but

I hope you'll take them and maybe even bring Jessie. I'm hoping time will prove to both of you that I'm not that guy anymore. Sincerely, Jordan Garrison."

She folds the paper and looks up at me. "I'm thinking I'm going to forgive him."

"Really?"

"I knew it was just a one-night stand when it happened. I also knew he was really drunk that night. It's embarrassing he forgot me but he regrets it. That's all I can ask." Tori shrugs and gives me a small smile. "How about you?"

"Me?"

She points at the flowers. "You say you two didn't date in high school, but it's been clear since the beginning that something happened between you two."

Mr. Howard, our next appointment, appears in the doorway just as my phone starts to ring. "I'll get started. Join me when you're done," Tori says, and turns and smiles at our patient. "Mr. Howard! How's the hip today?"

As she ushers him down the hall toward the training room, I glance at my screen, disappointed to see Callie's name, not Jordan's.

"Hey, li'l sis," I say.

"You need to say that twice," I hear Callie's voice.

"What?"

"Rosie made me do a conference call," Callie explains.

"Hi, Jessie!" Rosie says happily.

"Why are we three-waying?" I ask.

"Because we've talked over the house thing," Callie says, her voice terse. "And we've decided you can sell it to Big Bird."

"Callie," Rose says with scorn.

"What?" Callie argues defensively. "This is as nice as I get."

I roll my eyes and smile, but I'm skeptical. When I first presented the idea to them, Callie was dead set against it. Even Rosie seemed a little uncomfortable with the idea, although she didn't yell "Over my dead body" like Callie.

"Are you guys sure?"

"He's going to pay what we ask," Callie states. "No haggling."

"I'm sure he'll have no problem with that," I say.

"Okay, then," Rose says. "What now?"

"I guess I'll tell him we'll sell to him. He gets back from a road trip tonight and he's playing the Royales tomorrow afternoon, so I'll let him know after that," I say. An expected sadness starts to sprout in my belly. I guess I'm going to miss the house more than I thought. "I gotta go. I want to put fresh water in my flowers before my next client."

"Flowers?" Rose asks, a tinge of excitement in her voice because the girl was aptly named. She loves flowers.

Callie snorts. "I'd ask who from, but I think I know the answer."

"You know the answer," I confirm.

"Barf," she says.

Then Rose quietly says, "I kind of have a date tonight."

"WHAT?" Callie and I say in unison.

"A guy in my English lit class asked me out," Rosie tells us in a robot voice. "I said yes."

"Why would you do that?" I can't help but ask.

"Why wouldn't I?"

"Because you're in love with Luc," Callie states in typical, blunt Callie fashion.

"That's what everyone keeps telling me," Rosie snaps in a harsh tone that's totally out of character for her. "And I wish you would all stop."

"What did he do wrong?" Callie says.

"He didn't do anything wrong," Rose replies. "He has a girlfriend and there is nothing wrong with that. So, please just let me move on from my ridiculous childhood crush already."

Callie and I remain silent for a long time. The pain in Rose's pretty voice is heartbreaking. I want to pepper her with questions about what happened between now and Christmas when she and Luc were basically fawning all over each other, but I know it's not the time.

"Okay, then," Callie finally says. "So, one hockey jock is out and the other one is in. Again."

"Jordan is not 'in,'" I blurt out.

"I love you, Jessie," Rosie says in a despondent tone, like a mother talking to her problem child. "I love you so much, but you're such a complete idiot."

I hear a click.

"Rosie?" I say, but there is no answer. "Rosie?!"

"She hung up on you," Callie announces with awe in her voice. "Go, Rosie!"

"Why the hell would she do that? What's she so pissed about?"

"Maybe it's the fact that you have a boy completely and utterly in love with you and you won't do a damn thing about it, when she would sell her perfect little soul to have Luc care about her half as much as Jordan does for you." Callie takes a breath. "Or maybe she's just PMSing."

I say nothing as my eyes land on the card on my desk; I inhale the sweet lilacs again.

"Maybe I was wrong," Callie muses softly. "Maybe you don't love him anymore."

Instantly I say, "I've always loved him."

"No, Jessie, I mean *love* him," Callie argues. "That horrible think-about-him-all-the-time, forgive-him-anything, need-him-to-be-happy, can't-think-of-touching-another-person kind of love. That thing I hate that I hope never happens to me. Maybe you don't love him like *that*."

I say nothing.

"You need to tell him, J," she says a bit sadly. "If you don't love him like that, you have to tell him. I mean, if you can't or whatever, it's okay—it is—but he needs to know. Then he can move on. You may lose your friendship, but it's one-sided right now anyway because he does love you like that."

And then she follows Rose's lead and hangs up on me, albeit gently.

Chapter 33

Jessie

The loud, obnoxious Quebec City Royales fans behind us are jumping up and down and high-fiving each other, clearly oblivious to the fact that everyone hates them. Either that or they just don't care. I'm guessing Winterhawks fans would be just as belligerent if they were in the Royales arena and were embarrassing the home team.

"What the heck is happening?" Tori stares at me with confused blue eyes.

"They're melting down." I explain what I know she already knows. "No rhyme or reason. Sometimes a team just shits the bed."

"Well, did they have to do it the day I got free tickets?" Tori huffs, and I give her a half-smile at that before turning my eyes back to the ice.

Jordan is skating around by center ice, waiting for puck drop. His eyes are glued to his skates. He's beyond frustrated. I can tell by the scowl on his rugged features.

He still hasn't returned my texts or calls since I received his early Valentine's Day present. I was starting to panic about it. Maybe he's given up on me. As wrong as I thought it felt to give into my feelings for him again, because I was still hurting over his past, it felt much worse thinking that he was actually moving on.

When we first got to the arena, Tori went off to investigate the VIP room, and I sat in the stands and watched warm-up with all the other fans. He had a delicious scruff peppering his strong jaw and dimpled chin—and his hair is gone! He cut it off! He looked devastatingly handsome. Sure, he was hot with the longer hair, but in a rougher, unrefined sort of way. Jordan with short hair is downright model handsome. It makes him look younger too—so much like the boy I'd fallen in love with. It made my breath catch and my heart flutter. His eyes looked bluer in the bright glare of the arena lights off the ice and, just like when he was a kid, he glided around the ice with this intoxicating mix of grace and intensity. He is such a big, intimidating force out there—I'd be lying if I said it didn't turn me on.

Throughout the warm-up his eyes scanned the arena seats. The crowd wasn't huge at this point, and most people were plastered around the glass instead of in their seats, taking pictures of their favorite players. Finally, as the horn sounded indicating the end of warm-up and the players made their way off the ice, Jordan stopped to toss a puck over the glass for a kid and his eyes found mine a few rows up in my seat.

I smiled softly and gave him a small wave. He blinked, nodded and headed down the tunnel back to the locker room. The reaction was disconcerting to say the least and that dark panic I'd been trying to contain suddenly exploded and wrapped around my heart.

Luckily Tori returned from the VIP room and distracted me with stories of all the free food and wine she'd consumed.

The first period had gone horribly with the Winterhawks turning over the puck repeatedly and the Royales capitalizing on it. Chooch was having an awful game and was pulled in the second period after he let in an easy shot from the blue line, making the score 4–0 Royales.

By the time the third period started, the game had gotten rough. The frustrated Winterhawks were playing aggressively because they clearly couldn't play well, so there was an onslaught of penalties for late and cheap hits, hooking and tripping. Jordan had just gotten out of the penalty box for getting into a shoving match with a Royales defenseman after the whistle. While he was there the Royales scored again.

"The Winterhawks can't score to save their lives. They're hitting the post, shooting wide, breaking their sticks on breakaways. It's like they pissed in the hockey god's cornflakes," Tori announces, and sighs dramatically.

I smile at her analogy but shake my head in frustration. The ref drops the puck again and the game resumes. Avery Westwood gets slammed into the boards near our seats and loses the puck. The Royales' forward skates away with it. Tori covers her face with her hands.

"Ugh. I give up. I can't watch the rest of this train wreck. Distract me!" She peeks at me through her fingers and smiles. "Tell me you're going to take Carl's offer of a full-time job."

I smile at her. Yesterday our boss had come into our office and offered me a full-time position when my internship was over next month. He'd given me the weekend to think it over.

When I first took the job here, I'd never entertained the thought of staying in Seattle permanently. Even after I got settled in and realized this was a great facility with great people—both the patients and the staff—and that Seattle itself had a beautiful charm to it, I hadn't considered staying longer than the internship required. It was Jordan's home and I hated Jordan. When I started this job, the idea that I could run into him at any moment was so nerve-wracking, so suffocating. There was no way I could willingly live like that any longer than I had to. But now the idea of moving back to Arizona—or anywhere that Jordan Garrison wasn't—that's what was suffocating.

"You would leave me?" Tori pouts dramatically. When I just roll my eyes, she tries a different tactic. "You would leave Jordan?"

Before I can answer, the crowd lets out a collective gasp and the ref's whistle fills the arena. I turn to the ice and see Jordan at the far end, near the Winterhawks' goalie, doubled over with his gloves to his face.

"Oh my God! What happened?" I whisper, and jump to my feet for a better view.

"He got a puck to the face," the burly overweight guy beside me explains and points to the Jumbotron above center ice.

Tori and I both glance up in time to see the replay. In the video, the puck is being passed around between Royales' players. Jordy is on the ice, but not near the player with the puck, who is pulling back his stick for one hell of a slap shot. The puck sails forward and hits the stick of Jordan's teammate, Seb, who is trying to keep it from reaching their net. After the tip, it redirects to the right at a weird angle and nails Jordan in the face. He crumples to the ice instantly, and I gasp and throw my hand over my mouth.

My eyes return to the ice. Jordan is still covering his face, and I watch in horror as red drops start to leak out from behind his glove and hit the stark white ice.

"Why isn't anyone helping him?" I shout, and Tori puts a soothing hand on my shoulder.

Finally, a trainer hustles onto the ice with a towel and Jordan holds it over the left side of his face. He starts to make his way off the ice. My feet are already moving—led by my heart even before my brain realizes what I'm doing. I'm climbing the concrete steps two at a time and I'm already in the concourse area before Tori reaches me.

"Where are you going?" she asks as she latches onto my arm.

"I'm going to see him. We're his physical therapists. We can help."

"The Winterhawks have a team physician and incredibly qualified trainers. We can't do anything about a puck to a face, Jessie."

I march toward the main elevators, not even sure if that's where I need to go. I have no idea how to get down to the private staff area where the medical rooms and locker rooms are located. I've been there before but from the players' private entrance, not the public area. I put a hand to my chest, pressing on my galloping heart, trying to keep it from slamming into my rib cage repeatedly. Tori pulls me to a stop and turns me to face her. Her big round eyes are soft and sympathetic; her lips are turned up at the edges in a little hint of a smile. She looks like she's amazed or perplexed by something.

"You're in love with him," she says with a little bit of awe in her voice.

I swallow, my throat suddenly dry and tight. "I am. I'm in love him."

"When did that start?"

"It never stopped," I confess, and that dark cold ball of feelings in my gut—a mixture of panic, fear and desperation—is suddenly mixed with elation.

"I love him," I repeat quietly, and I know I sound scared. I am.

Tori hugs me.

"Don't tell *me*," she advises in a soft voice, patting my back as she breaks the hug. "Tell him."

"How? How do I get to him?"

I feel frantic. Panicked. Like I'm in the middle of something I can't control. Something I *need* to control. It's like when I was eight and my mother died. She was just gone, and it was the last thing in the world I wanted. I would have done anything and everything to change it, but I could do nothing but watch it happen.

Tori yanks on my arm, turning me toward a small set of doors next to one of the concession stands. "We can get to the VIP area through there. It's on the lower level so once we're down there, we just need to sweet-talk a security guard to get into the training area."

I nod and follow her toward the doors. Tori pulls our VIP passes out of her back pocket and flashes them at the guard. He opens the door. On the other side is a small marble-tiled area and an elevator. Tori punches the down button and we wait impatiently. I hear the final buzzer go off, signaling the end of the game.

He has to be okay. This can't be a serious injury. Players have lost part of their vision taking pucks to the face, and because he had his gloves to his face, I don't know where it hit him. He doesn't wear a damn visor so it could have hit his eye.

Once off the elevators, we have to show our passes to another security guard and then we charge down the hall toward the VIP room. There's a velvet rope just past the door to the room, sectioning off the VIP guest area from the locker rooms and training and medical facilities. There's yet another security guard standing there.

I walk right up to him and try my best to appear calm and professional. "Hello, sir. My name is Jessie Caplan. My colleague Tori and I are physiotherapists. We've been working with Garrison. Number forty-four. He was just injured so we're—"

"Pass," he barks gruffly, and then frowns when I show him my VIP pass. "This doesn't give you access to the training area, sweetheart."

I try not to get ruffled by his condescending tone. Behind us, I hear a group of people chatting as they wander by, heading to the VIP room. I look back to the security guard and take a deep breath. "I've known Jordan since I was eight. I'm here because he gave me tickets. I just want to make sure he's okay."

The security guard smirks. "First you're his therapist and now you're his childhood friend. Save your breath, honey. I've heard all the excuses you pretty little things can think of to try and see these jocks in the showers. You're not getting in."

Tori steps forward, her eyes shooting daggers at the guard, but before she can say anything someone calls my name. I glance behind guard and see Chance walking toward us. He'd emailed me a few times asking for me to call him, so we could talk about what he said the last time he was in town and punched Jordan, but I'd ignored him. In the messages he told me he was serious about wanting a second chance with me, even after what Jordan had said. I'd hoped to never run into him again but right now I couldn't be happier to see him.

"Hey, gorgeous!" He gives me his typical wide smile that Rose always told me looked more like a sneer. I never saw it before but I see it now.

"Hey!" I take a step toward him but the guard holds out his arm, blocking my path. I glance up at the scowling guard.

Chance doesn't even hesitate. He flashes his own pass to the guard. "These two are with me."

The guard hesitates for only a second before stepping out of the way.

As we slip by him, Chance wraps an arm around my shoulders. "You want to see the media room? I just finished my postgame interviews so I'm all yours."

He winks and I shrug out of his grasp. "Where are the medical rooms?"

He stops in the middle of the hall and frowns. "Please don't tell me you're looking for that putz, Jessica."

"Where is he, Chance?" I say, ignoring his comment. "Is he still getting stitched up? Did he have to go to the hospital? Is it serious?"

He rolls his ice blue eyes. "The bastard is the luckiest unlucky person I know. It was just a nick above his eyebrow. He'll be fine. Probably won't even miss a game."

The fact that Chance sounds disappointed that Jordan wasn't more gravely injured creates a wave of anger. I glare at him. "You're a dick, you know that?"

"Relax," Chance says, and tries to look innocent. "I'm just kidding around."

"Sure you are," I bark back sarcastically. "Now, where is he?"

"Haven't seen him. He refused to do interviews. Diva."

I ignore him and turn back to Tori. She looks around the hall and points to the sign that says "Training Room." "I'm going to try and find Mick, the trainer we worked with. See if he can find Jordan."

I nod but before I can follow her, Chance reaches out and takes my hand in his. His face is sincere and his eyes are pleading as he says, "Jessie, he's not the one for you. I was the one for you in high school and I'm the one for you now. Just give me a another shot."

Before he can say another word or I can tell him to fuck off, Tori calls out, "Jordan!"

I turn and see Jordan's big frame coming down the hall. As is the norm with hockey players before and after the game, he's wearing a suit. Well, most of one. He's got on charcoal gray pants and a crisp white shirt, but he's missing his tie and jacket.

His eyes land on Tori and then slide toward me. Chance and I standing together, my hand still in his. I know how this looks, and it causes a flood of panic to wash through my veins like a tsunami, yet all I can think is Jordan looks fucking gorgeous. Even with the angry red slice and dark, blood-crusted stitches just above his left eyebrow where the puck got him, he's the most beautiful man in the room. In the world.

"You're kidding me," he says, his eyes fixed to where Chance is still grasping my hand.

Chance smiles smugly and squeezes my hand tightly. "How's the face?"

Jordan ignores him and stares at me—right at me—with eyes full of contempt and pain.

"You're fucking kidding me," he repeats in a hiss.

"I'm only here to find you," I tell him, and yank my hand away from Chance.

"It's true." Tori backs me up. "She's looking for you."

Jordan looks at Tori, at Chance, and then back at me. His teammates Seb and Dix have wandered out into the hall. They're dressed in suits too. They both stop short at the scene in front of them.

"Whatever," he says, and turns to walk away. I take a step to follow but then he stops and turns back to face me, his blue eyes hard. "But since you're here I'll let you know I don't want your house."

He turns and storms toward the exit. Before his teammates can follow him, I push past them. He may be done with me, but I am *not* done with him. I'm not running away this time.

Chapter 34

Jordan

Jordan, wait!"

I hear her plea, but I ignore it and keep walking. She calls my name again and I just kind of lift my hand. I'm not sure if I'm waving good-bye or just blowing her off with a general gesture. I'm too angry to figure it out, but either way I'm not stopping.

I'm near the end of the hall, a few feet from the door that leads to the parking garage. I hear her feet pounding on the floor behind me and then feel her hand close around my forearm just above my wrist, tugging hard. If I wasn't slight woozy from the painkillers, she wouldn't have been able to move me. But in this state, she spins me around rather easily.

"Why don't you want the house?" she demands, not letting go of my arm.

"It was a stupid idea," I say harshly.

I pull my arm away from her and shove my hand deep into the pocket of my slacks. She's so petite, yet right now her indignation makes her seem imposing. There's a fire in her green eyes and her perfectly symmetrical, full lips are pouting just a little bit, like she's holding back a frown.

"The flowers were stupid too," I add. I run a frustrated hand through my hair, I'm sure sending it askew.

"I loved the flowers," she says, her eyes wide and pleading. "I told you that. Didn't you get my text?"

"Yeah. You think I'm adorable." I let out a short, hard burst of air through my nose and smirk petulantly. "I didn't do it to be adorable, Jessie. Puppies are adorable. Fuck adorable."

I hear footsteps shuffling and glance past her to see Seb, Chance, Dix and Tori have inched their way down the hall too. My eyes land on Chance, who is still smiling smugly. I can't hit him. I want to, but I can't.

"Chance again, Jessie?" I'm fighting to keep my voice from sounding as heartbroken as I feel. "What are you doing with him? You fucking hate me, but you forgive him? Seriously?"

"Chance?" She glances back over her shoulder then turns to me with stern green eyes. "I don't give a crap about Chance. I haven't given a crap about him since I was eighteen. I never had to forgive him, Jordan, because I just stopped caring about him instead."

"Nice!" I hear Seb chuff as he, Dix and Tori all start to laugh.

"Fuck you, Sebastian," Chance mutters. He storms past us toward the exit, not even looking at us as he goes.

"You can have her, Garrison," he hollers as he reaches the reception area. "I can do better."

I turn and take a step, but Jessie grabs my arm again and squeezes, stopping me. The door opens then closes behind Chance. My eyes fall back on Jessie. She doesn't look the least bit hurt by Chance's words. In fact, she doesn't even act like she heard them.

Her eyes are focused solely on me. They don't move, they don't waver, they don't blink.

"If you don't want my house, that's fine," she says in a soft voice that's dipped in disappointment. "I can sell it to someone else."

"It was never about the stupid house, Jessie! I didn't want to buy the house because I care about the damn house," I explain angrily, turning and walking to the wall. I want to punch it, but again, I can't. Instead, instead I turn and lean my back against it. I put a hand to my forehead and take a deep, shaking breath.

My fingertips graze the stitches in my head, and it stings. "Do you know how hard it would be to live in that place if it was just me there?" I'm almost yelling, but I don't really recognize my own voice. I thump the back of my head against the wall softly but repeatedly. My hands ball up and cover my eye sockets and I rub them roughly.

"Jordan, I don't understand," she says, sounding frustrated. "Is this because—"

"Do you know how many people I slept with since you ran away?" I ask hotly, and then go on before she can answer. "Because I don't. But not being able to remember all of them was one hell of a wake-up call."

She shakes her head and starts to form a protest. I know she doesn't want to hear this, but I don't care. She's going to fucking hear it. This may not be the grand romantic gesture Luc had in mind, but it's all I have now. My last move to play in this ridiculous dance we've been doing since she reappeared in my life.

"Do you know what I learned from the last six years? I learned that nothing can replace you. Nothing. I thought I was sleeping around because I wanted to avoid feeling something for someone, because you had destroyed me and I didn't want to be that vulnerable ever again. But I was kidding myself." I take a breath because my heart is pounding in my ears. Jessie is just staring at me, so I go on. "I was trying to find something to numb the pain. Because it never left. I never stopped missing you. I never stopped needing you. There was a constant ache in my chest for you. I tried to convince myself it was anger, but it was love. And no one could fix it. You're the only one who can fix it."

The hallway is deathly silent. Tori, Kelli, Dix and Seb look like statues. I'm not even sure they're breathing. Jessie doesn't look like she's breathing either. "I wanted to buy your stupid house because I thought maybe, if you ever did take me back, it could be ours. I could make it into the happy home you deserved to have growing up. I wanted it for you, Jessie, not for me. For us. Because no matter what I did to try to move on and get over you, I haven't been able to like you have."

All of a sudden she's pressing her lips to mine. I can't seem to fully grasp what's happening and when her tongue breaks my lips apart and slips into my mouth, my brain melts and I stop thinking. I just react. I kiss her back, rolling my tongue across hers. Her hands hold onto my face on either side as if she's scared I might pull away. Fat chance. My hands land on her hips, pulling her closer, right up against me, before sliding to her ass to lock her in that position.

I think I hear cheering or whistling—or maybe both. After minutes—so many minutes, I'm light-headed, my lips feel swollen and my pants feel tight. She pulls back just far enough so our lips can no longer touch. Her body is still pressed to mine. Her hands are still on my cheeks. Mine are still on her ass.

I keep my eyes closed.

"I'm sorry," she says. "Sorry I ever made you think I didn't love you."

Now I open my eyes. Her moss-green ones are brimming with tears, threatening to spill over, and it makes me ache.

I lift my hand and touch her cheek. Her hands slip from my face to my chest and rest there, palms flat against my hammering heart.

"I love you, Jordan," she tells me, quiet but confidant. "I've always loved you, even when I didn't want to love you. I know now, I always will love you." She smiles even though her eyes are wet. "I didn't run off to Arizona to hurt you. I did it because I was scared and I had trust issues. But if I could change my mind, if I could go back and do it over... I would have never left you, Jordy."

I hear cheers and squeals of delight from our audience. But Jessie is crying and that's all that really has my attention. I wipe a tear that trickles down her cheek with the pad of my thumb.

"I don't want to make you cry," I whisper tenderly. My lips brush the hair falling down by her ear. "I love you."

I kiss her again. It's soft, tender and light.

"I love you too." Jessie says, kissing me back. She reaches up and her fingers lightly trace the stitches in my head. "I'll love you even more when you start wearing a visor."

I smile.

"Let me take you home," she whispers, her hands tugging on the hem of my shirt.

"Yeah."

Chapter 35

Jessie

It takes everything in me not to pull the car over and rip his clothes off.

It doesn't help that he keeps touching me: his hand on my neck, his hand in my hair, his hand on my knee. His lips on my neck. It's almost impossible to follow his directions, but I manage to get us to his house. When I finally pull into his driveway, Jordan gets out of the car almost before I put it in park.

I glance up at the beautiful, massive two-story wood-and-stone house that sits on a long narrow piece of rocky land with the water behind it. This place easily costs a million bucks. I think of the simple Craftsman house he grew up in and can't help but compare it to this place. It's hard to believe the same boy who grew up in that humble house is the same man who owns this piece of modern art.

He opens my door and all but pulls me out. He bends down and his lips meet mine. His tongue slides over my lips, pushing urgently into my mouth. My tongue eagerly greets him. He pushes me against the now-closed driver's side door, and his whole body presses into mine. I'm so turned on I can barely stand it.

"God, I love this," he whispers into my mouth.

I capture his bottom lip lightly between my teeth and pull back, letting it slide slowly from my grasp.

"Take me inside," I beg him in a heated whisper. "Or we're doing it right here in front of your neighbors."

He laughs. It's deep and throaty and sexy. He pulls my coat off my shoulders so it's hanging from my elbows and moves his lips to my throat.

"I'm game if you are," he murmurs against my skin, sending an electric current down my spine.

I smile and decide to call his bluff.

I tug at his shirt, untucking it from his dress pants. My hands roam under the hem of his shirt and I run my fingertips over the tight, taut skin of his lower abdomen. I rock onto my toes and take his earlobe between my teeth. He sighs. Instead of moving my hands upward, I move them down, slipping my fingers into the waistband of his pants. The feeling of his treasure trail against the back of my fingers makes me grin. He shudders as my knuckles roll over the front of his underwear and his hardening erection inside them.

"Jessie," he breathes as I undo his belt.

His mouth covers mine again and his hands move down the front of my top, stopping to cup my breasts through the fabric. God, I wish we were naked. I lower his fly and slip my hand into his boxer briefs, sliding my fingers over and then around his thick shaft.

He makes an unintelligible sound. I thought he would back down and move things inside after we got this far. But my actions just seem to make him even more irrational. He grabs the back of my neck and kisses me breathless.

His free hand moves from my chest and, in one assertive tug, he opens the front of my jeans, effortlessly sliding his hand into them. He pushes roughly under the front of my lace thong and, before I can protest, he has two fingers inside me. Who am I kidding? I wasn't going to protest.

"Jordan. Fuck," I hiss into his mouth, my hand tightening around him and rubbing him in rhythm with his own strokes inside me.

He grunts and swears and pushes his hips into me. Our hands in each other's pants smash together. We're like crazy, horny teenagers.

"Inside" is all he says, and when he pulls his hands from between my legs I groan in complaint.

My hand falls free of his underwear and he grabs my arm and almost drags me up the winding front walk. As he unlocks the front door I stand behind him my arms wrapped around his waist, my head on his back. The door opens and he turns and pulls me inside, kicking it shut behind us. I drop my bag onto the wood floor and he almost rips my jacket from my body. He doesn't stop there. In one fast, decisive action he pushes my shirt up over my head and off my body. His head drops and he kisses the curve of my breast above my bra as his hands move behind me to unhook it. Suddenly I'm naked from the waist up and his hot, wet mouth is licking and sucking at my nipples. I grab onto his hair and sigh with desire. He cups my ass and picks me off the ground and starts up the stairs, my legs around his waist, his mouth still enjoying my breasts.

Once we're in his bedroom Jordan tosses me backward. I squeal as my back hits his king-size bed. It's like landing on a cloud. He stands at the foot of the bed, undoing only half the buttons on his dress shirt before pulling it over his head and pushing his pants off his hips and stepping out of them. My eyes land on the cut of muscle above his hip and follow the curve downward.

I crawl to the edge of the mattress and perch up on my knees. I kiss his bare stomach just below his belly button. He sighs. His hands slide over my back. I pull his underwear down his long, muscular legs. His cock is directly in front of me, hard and thick. I kiss it softly. Jordan shivers. I curl a hand around his base and my lips around his tip, and then slowly take him completely into my mouth.

"Jesus fucking Christ, Jessie," he moans in one long breath.

I close my eyes and enjoy the feel of him on my lips, the taste of him in my mouth. I roll my tongue all around him as I slide forward and back.

He's grunting in fast succession, his hands tangled in my hair, holding on for dear life. I love this. I love owning him like this, making him helpless, stealing all his rational thoughts. I have wanted to do this to him for a very, very long time. And I hope to keep doing this to him for the rest of my life. I feel his body tense. I know he might come but I don't stop. I move faster. His hands tighten in my hair and he pulls me off him.

Before I can object, he's pushing me back on the bed and he's climbing on top of me. His lips find mine briefly, his tongue sliding out to graze my lower lip before he moves to that spot—that sensitive, perfect spot under my ear where my jaw almost starts. His tongue runs over it teasingly. It makes me so fucking hot. He pulls away and I let out a soft groan of protest.

Jordan moves back on his knees and pulls my jeans off in one hard but deliberate tug that makes me flash back to Christmas. He looks down at my skimpy lace thong and runs his fingers over the fabric. His eyes are dark and lust-filled as I reach for him, trying to pull him back down on top of me. He seems way too far away. He resists and I frown.

"I want you closer."

"And I want to look at you," he whispers with a devious smile. "All of you. And I'm bigger, so I win."

He starts to pull the thong down my legs. Before I can get self-conscious about him staring down at my completely exposed body, he slides two fingers into me. My eyelids crash down as my lower back arches off the bed.

"You're so beautiful," he whispers as his fingers start slipping in and out of me in a gentle yet urgent rhythm.

I force myself to open my eyes. He's smiling down at me. He looks angelic. Perfect. And he's mine, I realize as a wave of euphoria builds in my belly and my heart. Jordan Garrison is finally mine.

His thumb moves to my clit, rolling over it gently at first and then more forcefully. My back arches again and I let out a whimper and a pant.

"Jordan," I pant. "Oh God…Jordan."

My orgasm rocks me, sucking away my air, snapping my eyes closed, curling my toes. My eyes are still closed and my limbs are still numb as he scoops me off the bed and holds me to his chest. My wobbly legs land on either side of his bare thighs.

Jordan kisses my lips, my jaw, my neck. My eyes flutter open and I rest my hands on his shoulders. Our lips meet. The kiss is long and slow and luxurious. I pull back and glance downward as I lower myself onto his cock.

Chapter 36

Jordan

I feel her wetness graze the tip of my dick and my lips freeze on her jaw. She lowers herself steadily and deliciously, nice and slow. She's so hot and wet and tight from her orgasm, and it's creating the most incredible sensation. My eyes close and my breath catches and then my mind goes blank. Her slow descent ends and I'm completely inside her.

She sighs and brushes her lips across mine, running her hands through my hair, her nails grazing my scalp and making me shiver.

"I love you so much," she whispers as she lifts herself almost completely off me and then slowly lowers back down.

"I love you too," I murmur. I have never meant anything more in my life.

As her body recovers from her orgasm and adjusts to me, her rhythm goes from slow and erratic to steady and frenetic. My arms tighten around her back. I drop my head to her shoulder and bite down lightly, sucking her sweet-tasting skin into my mouth, as I fight off the imminent release. It feels so good. I don't want it to end. I want to stay like this—holding her to me, my throbbing cock inside her, teetering on the edge—forever.

My balls tingle. Her hands grab the short tufts of my hair and tug. I push my hips up, filling her hard and fast.

"Jordy," she whispers, her words tickling my ear. "Come for me."

I let out a sound—a guttural, incoherent sound—and my balls pull up. My brain liquefies as my dick quivers and I release everything I have inside her. My body is suddenly useless. I have no strength left. I drop back onto the bed, taking her with me. Flat on my back, she cuddles her tiny naked body against me. Neither of us says anything. It's a contented, perfect silence that lulls me into a blissful sleep.

I'm awakened by the coldness of the sheets. I reach out for her, but there's nothing there. My eyes open. My bed is empty. What the fuck? I prop myself up on an elbow and survey the room. I'm definitely alone.

"Jessie!" I call out, knowing how needy it sounds. I don't give a fuck. There's no response, and my chest tightens painfully. Then the bathroom door opens and she comes out in nothing but a towel, her auburn hair wet and her skin pink from the hot water of her shower.

"You okay?" she asks, concerned.

"I thought you left," I admit, totally embarrassed.

"Really?" she questions with a soft smile on her perfect lips. "I hate to break it to you, but you can't get rid of me that easily. Not this time."

"Good," I say, and reach for her.

She moves closer so I can grab her hand and pull her back down on the bed beside me. I lean over her, pushing her wet hair off her neck and kissing her gently on the mouth. Her tongue slips out and runs over my bottom lip teasingly. She tastes like my cinnamon mouthwash.

"I didn't get to wake up beside you," I complain, quietly nuzzling her neck. "It's been over six fucking years and I still haven't woken up with you."

"Sorry. I didn't want to wake you," she says, running her fingers down my bare chest. "You look so pretty when you sleep."

"Pretty?" I make a face at her choice of word.

She laughs. "Sorry. You look *sexy* when you sleep. Hot. Manly."

Now I laugh. She kisses me quickly, but I lean in hungrily looking for more. She gives it to me, opening her mouth and deepening the kiss. My hand slides over the fuzzy blue towel and then starts to make its way under it, but she pushes me away and gets up off the bed.

"Jessssssie," I hiss in protest.

"I'm sorry, but you have to get to practice and I have to get home." She grins a little self-consciously. "Sunday is laundry day and if I don't do it, I'm going to work underwear-less tomorrow."

I watch her drop her towel and it makes my cock twitch under sheets.

"I like the idea of you underwear-less," I tell her with a smile.

She laughs. "While I stand over my male clients and rub their aches and pains away?"

"Okay, now I don't like it," I reply quickly.

"Besides, you leave soon, don't you?"

I glance at the clock. I have to be at the airport in less than two hours. I groan.

She leans over me again and kisses my forehead. "Don't worry. I promise to let you wake up with me soon."

She pulls on her clothes from last night, some of which she must have retrieved from the front hall.

"So, how attached are you to your apartment?" I ask casually as I sit up and push my pillow back against the headboard.

She stops what she's doing and turns to me. "It's a place to live."

I smile shyly. "*This* is a place to live. A big place. With lots of room for you and your stuff. And free laundry!"

She blinks and looks stunned. Not scared, which is a good sign, just stunned.

"You want me to move in here?" she says, clarifying. "Already?"

Quietly I say, "Let's be honest, you should have been here six years ago."

She blinks and then smiles. "Yeah, I should have."

"Basically, I want you around all the time. I don't want to lose another second," I confess, and twist my hands nervously in the sheet covering my waist. "So move in. Please."

"So much for your mom's old-fashioned values," she says, and I laugh.

"My mother would throw her old-fashioned values out the window if it meant she could see her favorite son happy with her favorite pseudo-daughter."

"She wants me with Cole?"

"You're such a smartass," I tell her but can't help laughing at her joke.

I push back the covers and get out of bed, walking toward her. I'm still as naked as I was last night, and my morning wood is flying high. But I don't care.

She giggles as I take her into a hug. "Does that thing ever go down?"

"Not with you around," I admit, and lightly kiss her favorite spot just under her earlobe.

She lets me hold her, wrapping her arms around my neck and nuzzling my shoulder.

Earnestly I say "I'm serious, Jessie. I want you to live with me. If you think it's too soon..."

"It's not too soon," she quickly replies. "Like you said, I should have been here years ago."

My heart skips. "So, you'll do it?"

She looks up and smiles her beautiful, perfect smile. "I'll give my notice to my landlord today."

I kiss her hard on the mouth, pushing my tongue through her lips. She tightens her grip on my neck and my hands cup her ass. I start to move her back toward the bed as one of her hands snakes between us and grazes the tip of my hard-on. Just when I've happily decided to skip practice, my cell phone starts to ring from the pocket of my jeans at the end of the bed.

I swear and march over and dig it out. I look at the call display and smirk.

"It's Dev."

Jessie laughs, walks over and takes the phone from my hand.

"Hi, Devin!" she sings into the phone. "Yeah, he's here. He's supposed to getting ready for practice but we got...distracted. How are you? How's Ashleigh? Conner? That's good. Tell them I said hi. Me? I'm good. I'm a little tired. Your brother is a freaking animal in bed. I don't know if I'm even going to be able to walk in a straight line today."

She laughs and I can actually hear Devin's groan from a foot away.

"Oh, relax. At least now you won't have to phone every Garrison or Caplan in North America to figure out what's going on with us," she says to him. "Anyway, talk soon. Here's Jordy."

She hands me the phone and I watch her bounce back into the bathroom. I smile so wide my face hurts.

"Hey, Dev," I say brightly.

"Dude, tell her to stop messing with me!"

"She's not. I totally am a freaking animal in bed."

"Shut up," my older brother groans. "Or I'm going to think twice before calling you from now on."

I laugh at his dramatics. "You're going to have to get over it. She'll probably answer my phone a lot more now since she's going to be living with me and everything."

There's an expected stunned pause and then I can actually hear the smile in my older brother's voice. "Jordan, I'm so happy for you."

"Yeah. Me too, Devin. Me too."

Epilogue

Jordan

Rosie!" Jessie calls as we unlock the front door and walk inside, dragging our bags with us.

"She's at work, remember?" I tell her, hauling our suitcases into the living room.

Jessie goes in the opposite direction, into the kitchen. She flips on the light and looks around. I come up behind her and survey the work myself.

Gone were all the flipping sunflowers. The torn beige linoleum floor is now a smooth gray slate. The appliances are no longer avocado green, they're gleaming stainless steel. The walls are a warm gray blue.

The sink had been replaced with a large white sink similar to the one in our house in Seattle. The cabinets are now white, and the uppers have old-fashioned leaded glass doors. The countertops are beautiful granite in the same shade as the floors, except for the piece just right of the sink, closest to the entryway.

That is still the original sparkly, off-white Formica. Jessie doesn't notice this yet, so I wait.

"You like it?" I ask hopefully.

"It's gorgeous!" Jessie beams. "You did good, Garrison."

"*We* did good," I correct her.

I wrap my arms around her waist from behind and kiss the side of her neck. She giggles and pulls away.

"You need to get over your aversion to playoff beards," I whisper in her ear, making a point of nuzzling my unruly facial hair against her cheek. "The whole point of playing hockey is to make it to playoffs every year, which means us having to grow one every year. It's good luck."

She chuckles again. "You look like an Amish person. And the playoffs are over now. You need to shave."

And then she notices it. She turns in my arms.

"Did they run out of granite?" she says, pointing to the section of Formica countertop. I gave the contractors explicit instructions not to touch it.

I glance at it now and a wave of nervous butterflies takes flight in my gut. Theoretically, I could do it right now. Right freaking now. But…I have a plan and I want to stick to it. So, I lie.

"I guess maybe they did." I shrug. "I'll call the contractor in the morning."

She nods. It's the first time I have lied to her since we got together, but I have a feeling she'll forgive me.

"In the meantime…" I wrap my hands around her narrow hips and push her backward toward the countertop we just discussed. When her perky butt gently connects to it, I lift her up and set her down on it.

She smiles at me. God, she is fucking beautiful. I smile down at her—on this counter once again. Just like seven years ago, almost to the day.

Just like last time, she's wearing a little sundress; only this one isn't pink and frilly, it's jersey material. The top of it kind of looks like a tank top. It's clingy until just under her breasts, where it gets looser and it remains that way until it stops just above her pretty little knees. It's olive green and it makes her eyes look a darker, deeper green than I've ever seen them.

"This brings back memories," she whispers as she grabs the front of my T-shirt and tugs me closer. I put my hands on her knees, parting her legs slowly and stepping between them.

Our lips connect and she reaches up to hold the sides of my furry face in her hands. The kiss is slow and sensual, and I close my eyes to drown in the feel of her. Her soft, full lips on mine, our tongues touching, and her warm breath tickling my cheek.

"I'm so glad you bought this place," she whispers against my ear.

"As soon as I knew you'd be living in it with me, it was a no-brainer," I tell her honestly. "That was exactly why I wanted it in the first place."

The sale had happened shortly after Jessie moved into my place in Seattle. Rose had finished her semester at college in Vermont in April, and I made a deal with her that she could live here all summer for free while she worked at Cole's bar if she oversaw the renovations while I was in the playoffs.

Our playoff run had ended last night in the Western Conference finals. It sucked. I know that rationally, considering our injury-plagued season, we had nothing to be ashamed of—we almost made it all the way to the finals. One series away from a chance to play for the Cup. But that also made it even harder—because we pushed through adversity and were so freaking close. Another Cup would have been fan-fucking-tastic.

But, as soon as we lost, I knew I had her to console me. And because of her, it was less painful than it had been in the past. That was when I decided to act on this idea—one that I'd been thinking of almost nonstop since Jessie moved in with me in late March.

Hell, if I was honest with myself, it was an idea I had been thinking about way longer than that.

The end of our playoff run, the last day of May, felt like the universe telling me to go for it.

So, I had insisted we come back to Silver Bay right away. Jessie spent most of the day at her work rearranging her schedule for the early time off. I spent it booking our plane tickets and shopping. I had Dix and his wife, Maxine, come along to help me. My good, but single, friends like Seb, Chooch, Alex and Avery wouldn't have been able to help with this purchase.

And now here we are. It's a little after ten and she's sitting in front of me on that old Formica countertop I refuse to get rid of.

"Should we call your parents and tell them we're home?"

I shake my head and grin devilishly. "No," I say softly, and my hands start sliding up under her dress.

"Your mom will be thrilled we're back early," she says, smiling, as my hands reach her upper thighs.

"Tell her later," I whisper, kissing the side of her neck.

My hands are gliding over the front of the black cotton boyshorts I saw her put on earlier. I hook my fingers under the front of them and she smiles.

"Shouldn't we go upstairs?" Her lips brush mine.

"Nope. It's my house now. I intend to have you naked in every room of it by the end of the summer."

"Could be tricky with Rose living here," she says, but she's smiling.

My fingers start pulling her underwear off her body as my tongue finds its way back into her mouth. Her hands move up the sides of my face, and she pulls the hat off my head and runs her hands over my hair, tugging it gently as our kiss deepens.

Her underwear is halfway down her thighs, the fabric pulled to its limits. I step out of the space between her legs, allowing her knees to inch closer together and my hands to pull the underwear completely off. She leans over the counter and watches them fall to the floor. Her eyes find mine and she cocks an eyebrow but says nothing. I grin at her as I push her knees apart again and step back in between them.

My hands move to her lower back and I pull her body to the edge of the countertop. Her bare pussy bumps against the front of my shorts and she lets out a bit of a gasp. I nuzzle her neck and suck her earlobe into my mouth. She squeals.

"Damn beard!" She laughs as it tickles her.

I move my hands to her thighs and start sliding upward again. Her dress comes with me. I kiss her lips, hard, hot and needy. She stops giggling.

"I think I know how to make you love playoff beards," I murmur against her mouth before I lower my head to kiss her collarbone, her bare shoulder and the fabric covering her breasts. I bend over and start kissing her thighs. Her dress is now bunched up around her waist. My eyes glance upward. She's bare and exposed, her slick folds inches from where my lips are sucking on her skin.

"Jordan," she says quietly.

She's nervous. I can tell. I've done this before to her, countless times now. Just not on the kitchen counter and not with the beard. She's says it's scratchy and tickles. She's refused this activity since I started the beard. But tonight she isn't getting a choice in the matter.

I put a hand on her torso and gently push her back. Her shoulders rest against the wall behind her and her elbows are back on the counter supporting her weight. I push the dress farther up her body, slide my hands around her lower back, under her ass, and I lift her to meet my mouth. My tongue delves right into her essence. I don't hesitate. I don't tease. Her entire body shudders almost violently. I close my eyes and revel in the taste of her, the feel of her, the warmth of her. My tongue moves upward…

"Fuck. Jordan."

I remove one of my hands from under her ass and bring it between her legs, slipping two fingers into her wet, warm center as my tongue continues to explore her. She whimpers. Loudly.

Her hand is behind my head, her fingers curled into my short hair. Her legs, now over my shoulders, tremble. She's close. I can tell.

"Jord…" Her release rips the rest of my name from her lips as she shakes and her thighs quiver.

I let her ride it out, my face pressed into her, my tongue still lapping eagerly. When she's done, I pull back. I can't wait. My cock is throbbing so hard in my shorts I think it might explode. I drop my shorts and underwear.

She's flushed and panting and beautiful. She reaches for me, her small hand wrapping around my neck while the other one grabs my shoulder. Her lips land on mine and I grab her hips, and as she hooks her legs behind my back, I push into her. She whimpers again. While one arm stays around my neck, the other reaches backward as she braces herself against the counter. She's so unbelievably tight. And wet. It's heaven. It's honestly fucking heaven.

I start to move in and out in a fast and frenzied rhythm. She's attacking me with her mouth, sucking on my neck, biting my collarbone, pulling my earlobe between her teeth.

"You're making me so crazy," she whispers in my ear.

I grunt and grin against her neck, pushing in deeper, harder. She reaches down and wraps her hand around my balls, rolling and tugging them until I feel a jolt of pleasure rush through me. Her lips find mine again and she sucks on my bottom lips greedily. I move one hand between us, my thumbing pressing down on her in just the right place...

"You're going to make me..." Her words get lost in a pant.

"That's the point," I say, panting in return.

She arches her back and gets wetter and tighter around me. So tight. It's too much.

"Jessie."

I erupt inside her, my knees barely able to keep me upright. My upper body curls onto hers, my head dropping into the crook of her neck as I struggle to catch a full breath.

"Happy anniversary," she whispers, running her fingertips down my back.

I pull back and catch her pretty eyes in shock.

"You thought I didn't remember?" she asks with a sly smile.

I glance at the clock on the gleaming new stove.

"It's not for another hour," I remind her.

She smiles. "Well, that sure as hell felt like a celebration."

I reluctantly slide out of her and pull her off the countertop.

She grabs her underwear off the floor and kisses my furry cheek.

I follow her out of the kitchen and grab our bags on the way up the stairs. The upstairs renovations haven't started yet, but I had the contractor get rid of all the furniture in the master. That meant we were relegated to Jessie's old bedroom again until the new master bath and the expanded closet was put in and the room could be furnished again with new furniture.

We drop our bags in there and then her cell phone starts to buzz. She pulls it out of her purse and smiles.

"Your mom," she tells me. "It's like she has ESP."

"It's the Bay, Jessie," I say, rolling my eyes in mock disgust. "Someone probably saw us at the airport so now the whole town knows we're back."

"Hi, Donna! No, you didn't wake us." Jessie grins deviously. "Actually we're back home. Yes! In Silver Bay. I know. Jordy really just wanted to get back. Are you free for brunch tomorrow?"

I head into the bathroom and start the shower. As the steam fills the room, I pull my electric razor out of my travel toiletry bag and start to shear off the beast on my face. Ten minutes later, I've got the regular razor out and I'm covered in shaving cream. I'm halfway back to my baby face when Jessie walks in, naked. I see her naked on a regular basis now—have for three months—but it still never ceases to take my breath away or make my dick throb.

"That was a long conversation," I say with a grin. "Were you explaining what you were doing in the kitchen and how you love playoff beards now?"

"Oh, yeah, totally. Your mom is impressed with your skills." She rolls her eyes and I make a grossed-out face. "Leah is at your parents' with Cole. I ended up talking to her about the wedding."

I swallow and nod. She doesn't seem to notice the nervous glint I know I must have in my eye.

"The wedding is almost two months away, but Leah is totally stressed out," she tells me as she pulls back the curtain and steps into the shower.

"I'm sure it'll be fine," I reply as calmly as possible. "Leah is just a perfectionist."

"Yeah. I think you're right." she says.

I finish shaving and get in with her.

Jessie says, "She should be having fun with the preparations, though."

"Well, you're here now," I say, kissing her shoulder. "You can help her out."

"Right." She takes her soapy washcloth and starts to run it over my chest.

We spend the next fifteen minutes bathing each other and kissing under the warm spray. I could easily take her here again—even so soon after the last time—but I have a plan. I can't veer off track or I'll lose my nerve and ruin everything.

We get out and I wrap her in a towel; she ties one around my waist. Back in her old bedroom, I quickly throw on a pair of workout shorts. As she busies herself pulling her pajamas from her suitcase, I slide something into my shorts pocket.

"I'm going to see if there is anything to eat," I lie, and head downstairs.

By the time I get to the kitchen, there are at least a thousand butterflies soaring inside me. I pull the small bright blue velvet box from Tiffany's out of my pocket and set it in the middle of the counter. I glance at the clock: 12:02 am.

I open the new fridge, which Rosie has stocked nicely. There's fruit and vegetables, bottled water, milk and what looks like left-over homemade lasagna. I think I may actually be hungry, but the butterflies make it impossible to tell. And then I hear her padding down the stairs.

Turning to lean against the fridge doors, I stand there clutching the water bottle in my hand so tightly I'm surprised I'm not crushing it.

"Hey!" she says as she enters the kitchen, her damp hair twisted up on top her of her head with an elastic. She's in a pair of sleep shorts and a heather gray tank top. "Is there anything to eat in there? I'm..."

Her eyes land on the slab of original Formica with the pretty blue box now sitting in the middle of it. She looks up at me. Her eyes are wide.

Finally, I can tell her. I fight to keep my voice even and under control. "I had them leave that piece of countertop on purpose. I just couldn't get rid of it."

She says nothing. Her gaze moves from me to the box and back to me.

"It's where it all started," I say, even though I know she knows.

Now her eyes move from me to the clock. "It's June first."

"It is." I smile at her.

She smiles back, but it's timid.

"Seven years ago today, you sat on that counter and I told you I loved you. And then you totally jumped my bones."

She bursts into laughter at that, and it makes me feel slightly less terrified.

"Remember a month or so ago when we decided this was our true anniversary?" I anxiously twist and untwist the bottle top in my hands. "You said, as far as you were concerned, today—June first—would go down in history as the day your life changed for the better forever. Well, I figured if it's going to change again—get even better—that it should change again today."

"Jordan," she says quietly her eyes back on the box. "What's that?"

I lift the water bottle to my lips and take a swig, my mouth suddenly very dry.

In a gravelly voice, I say, "Open it."

"An anniversary gift?" she says as she nervously tucks a wayward lock of damp hair behind her ear.

"Yeah, kind of. Not really," I reply, and grin awkwardly. "Open it."

As she reaches for the box, I notice her hand trembles ever so slightly. I realize suddenly she knows exactly what is in that box. Deep in her heart, she knows. The trembling hand is either excitement or trepidation. Maybe both. I guess I'm about to find out.

Epilogue 2

Jessie

It's too small to be a necklace.

That's all that keeps running through my brain. It's a ring box. It's a ring box from Tiffany's. *It's a freaking ring box from Tiffany's.* I will myself to calm down as I pick it up and bring it close to my chest.

"Open it," he repeats, and then he suddenly adds, "Wait!"

I wasn't about to open it, anyway, I'm too stunned. I watch as he pushes himself off the fridge that's been holding up his massive frame and walks over to me. He puts the water bottle he's been gripping down on the kitchen table, then stands in front of me. Nervously he runs a hand through his damp golden hair and then he shoves his hands in his pockets. And then he takes them out.

And then he reaches up and cups my face.

"I love you," he says, and his voice is thick.

I gaze at him. "I love you too."

"I've only ever loved you. This whole time. Since that night."

"I've only ever loved you too."

He leans down, kisses me soft and long, and then he pulls his lips from mine.

"Open it before I freak out," he urges, his cheeks turning red.

I hold my breath and open the box.

I'm a little scared it's what I think it is, and I'm a little scared it's *not* what I think it is. I'm generally, overwhelmingly terrified.

"OhmyGodJordan." It comes out in one fast, breathless word.

I know nothing about engagement rings. Nothing. I've never even thought about them. I mean, recently—since March—I had become fairly confident that one day I would get one—and from Jordan—but I had no idea when. I just knew we'd do it. But I didn't care what it looked like. All I cared about was what it meant—that he wanted me forever. Which is exactly how I wanted him—forever.

"I picked it because Maxine—you know, Dix's wife—told me the three diamonds meant past, present and future. And I thought that was cool and important to us, you know—our past, present and future. And I like the tiny diamonds on the band. But, if you don't like it, they said we could go back and pick another one," he assures me nervously. "I mean, that is, if you want a ring at all."

I glance up at him finally. The poor thing looks completely petrified. His face is pale and his light blue eyes are wide. He rakes his teeth over his bottom lip again and again, just like he used to do in math class when he was doing badly on a test. Well, he's not failing this time. But, before I can assure him, he starts talking again.

"I just know you're it, Jessie. I've known that forever," he stammers, his voice suddenly hoarse. "I know we've only been back together for three months, but those months have been the best of my life. You're the one. The only one I want to be with. The only one I've ever wanted to be with. This just feels..."

"Completely and utterly right?" I playfully finish his sentence, and he nods emphatically.

I can't see him anymore. I blink and suddenly my face is wet. I'm crying. That makes him panic more.

"It's okay if it's too soon. I'll wait. I won't be upset or anything. I can wait. As long as you...As long as you think you will say yes someday."

"Say yes to what?" I say softly, giving him a shaky smile. "You haven't asked me anything."

He cups my face in his giant hands again and tilts it so I'm looking right at him. He takes a deep breath. And then he stops.

"Do you want me on a knee? Like old-fashioned? 'Cuz I can totally do that if you want."

"No, it's okay."

"Are you sure? I know that's, like, traditional and everything."

"Just ask the damn question, Jordan."

"Are you going to say yes?" he says with that adorable, lopsided grin taking over his face now.

I laugh. "Put yourself out there, Garrison. Take a risk!"

He kisses me. It's slow and sweet. And then he pulls back, closing his eyes and then opening them again.

"Jessie, I love you. Will you marry me?"

"Yes."

"Yes?" He seems honestly stunned. It's adorable.

"Of course."

We stare at each other. His hands are on my face, my hands are on the open ring box. And then he grins. So big and bright and beautiful. And I know I am grinning too—and crying—but, mostly grinning.

He kisses me again, pulling me into his arms and swinging me around. I laugh. And then his hands take the box from me and he slips the beautiful platinum ring with three beautiful, sparkling princess-cut diamonds and the matching little ones around the band onto my finger.

"Holy crap, I am going to marry you," he breathes, and laughs.

"Yeah. You totally are." I giggle and I look up at him.

There he is. Everything I have ever wanted. And all he wants is me.

Please turn the page for a preview of the next book in Victoria Denault's Hometown Players series, *Making a Play*.

Available September 2015!

Prologue

Luc

Six years earlier

She's drunk. She thinks she's just tipsy but she's full-on, will-probably-puke, massive-hangover-guaranteed, drunk. I should be panicked, worried and—more than anything—unsupportive of her behavior but… she's just so damn cute.

I watch her as she concentrates really hard on the lines she's drawing in the sand. Her eyebrows are drawn together, her lips slightly parted and the tip of her tongue is sticking out ever so slightly as she uses her index finger to create a masterpiece. Well, a bunch of random crooked lines and uneven divots in the sand she's declared is my portrait.

I've been avoiding Rose lately, but when she called and left a message with slurred words, going on about my best friend Jordan breaking her sister's heart and ruining everything, I knew I had to come. She's fifteen, three years younger than me, and although my life has been far from perfect, hers was much rougher. And she was there for me when I needed someone, so I'll always be there for her. I've been avoiding her because I think she's developing a crush. I'm a born flirt.

I can't help it, it's like breathing air, so of course I've been doing it with Rose—but with Rose's ideals, it was playing with fire. Rose Caplan is sweet, smart and definitely beautiful, but she has all these fantastical ideas about love. She's a romantic and she dreams of an epic love story with a prince charming and a happily ever after. She deserves nothing less, but I'm not at all interested in that.

"Hrmpf," she makes this weird sound, like a sigh, a huff and a grunt all at once, and uses her palm to smooth away the sand drawing. "I can't do you justice."

I smirk and tilt my head so I'm in her sight line. She's sitting in the sand at my feet. Her back between my legs, against the log I'm sitting on. In front of us the bonfire, built by friends and high school classmates, is in the final stage before becoming nothing more than smoldering ash. The minimal light dances over her skin, making it sparkle. Her cheeks are flushed from what she says was only three beers and "maybe a wine cooler thingy."

"Justice?" I repeat and her near-black eyes catch mine.

"You're too pretty for a sand drawing," she says with a frown and a glare, like she's honestly mad at me. Rose has never called me pretty before and her confession makes me warm. If this were any other girl, I'd take advantage of the confession. I've never been one to turn down an opportunity for a bonfire make-out session. But… it's sweet, young and innocent Rose, and I just can't do that to her. Luckily she continues in a tirade without waiting for my response.

"Jordan's too stupid. Callie's too angry. Jessie's too stubborn. You're too pretty and I'm too lame. Everything is too. I hate too. Too is ruining my life."

She looks completely despondent, and totally sincere, so I feel bad when I can't keep the giant grin from overtaking my face. Her wide eyes get wider and that pouty, pink mouth—the one that is quickly maturing into something any man would have sex dreams about—drops into a perfect O. *She whispers, "Crap. I said that out loud."*

She tries to move away from me, but I reach out and gently cup the side of her face in the palm of my left hand. Now she's stuck twisted around between my legs, staring at me. "Rosie, your life is not ruined. Everything will be okay."

"You don't know that."

"I do know that because I will make it okay," I vow, my voice dropping an octave. "I will always have your back."

"Why?"

"Because you've always had mine."

She stares at me for another second as that sinks in. I know, even drunk, she knows why she's as close a confident as my best friend Jordan, and one of the few people I let completely in. She suddenly shifts her eyes back to the sand and slides away, so I can no longer touch her pretty face.

"But I want you to have more than my back," she mumbles in such a low, slurred voice I almost miss it. "No one wants more than my back. Because I'm too lame."

She starts to try to stand up but tips right back over and lands with a thud on her ass in the sand. I slip off the log and drop to my knees, reaching out the take her hands and keep her from falling all the way back and into the fire. I pull her close, sneaking the opportunity to sniff that amazing smell that is Rose Caplan. Some kind of soft, powdery-smelling perfume that screams innocence but makes my dick hard at the exact same time. I'm sure it's some generic kind of perfume, because Rosie doesn't have money for anything more than that, but on her, it's priceless.

I prop her up against the log again and lean in closely, taking another deep inhale of that perfect, dick-twitching scent. "Oh, Fleur, you're a drama queen when you drink."

Our eyes meet again. I force myself to move back to the log and sit behind her. If I look at that face a second longer I'm going to kiss her. Because she's pretty, and adorable, and I can. But I shouldn't, and with Rosie that matters. I have to remember, that matters. Once safely behind her, I put my hands on her shoulders and lean down, with my lips just behind her ear.

"You are not too lame. And all the other 'too' problems with Jessie, Jordan and whoever else will work out," I pause and tell her what I have been thinking for months...only I do it in French. "Votre vie sera belle parce que vous, Fleur, êtes belle. Et vous trouverez quelqu'un qui vous aimera pour ça."

She twists her head and blinks up at me. "Not fair. I don't understand."

I smirk and give her a small wink. "One day I'll translate it for you."

She turns back to the fire in front of her, staring at the flickering flames, and murmurs "I'm too scared to go for what I really want."

She tips her head back and looks up at me. This time, I don't know if I'm going to be able to stop myself from kissing her. I don't even think I want to stop. Maybe she'll be too drunk to remember. Maybe...

"Luc!" My best friend Jordan's deep voice fills the night air and causes Rose to snap her head away from me. "Have you seen Jessie?"

Rosie jumps to her feet and starts congratulating Jordan on being drafted into the NHL. Our moment disintegrates and I'm grateful. As much as I wanted her in that moment, it's for all the wrong reasons. I would break her heart and I refuse to do that to Rose.

About the Author

Victoria Denault loves long walks on the beach, cinnamon dolce lattes and writing angst-filled romance. She lives in LA but grew up in Montreal, which is why she is fluent in English, French and hockey.

Learn more at:

VictoriaDenault.com

Facebook.com/AuthorVictoriaDenault

Twitter: @BooksbyVictoria

www.ingramcontent.com/pod-product-compliance
Ingram Content Group UK Ltd.
Pitfield, Milton Keynes, MK11 3LW, UK
UKHW022259280225
455674UK00001B/94